WARRIORS

A WARRIOR'S CHOICE

WARRIORS

NOVELLA COLLECTIONS

WARRIORS

A WARRIOR'S CHOICE

INCLUDES
Daisy's Kin
Spotfur's Rebellion
Blackfoot's Reckoning

ERIN HUNTER

HARPER
An Imprint of HarperCollinsPublishers

Library of Congress Control Number: 2020945261
ISBN 978-0-06-285743-9

Typography by Hilary Zarycky
21 22 23 24 25   PC/BRR   10 9 8 7 6 5 4 3 2 1
❖
First Edition

CONTENTS

WARRIORS

DAISY'S KIN

Special thanks to Cherith Baldry

ALLEGIANCES

THUNDERCLAN

ACTING LEADER   **SQUIRRELFLIGHT**—dark ginger she-cat with green eyes and one white paw

ACTING DEPUTY   **LIONBLAZE**—golden tabby tom with amber eyes

MEDICINE CATS   **JAYFEATHER**—gray tabby tom with blind blue eyes

               ALDERHEART—dark ginger tom with amber eyes

WARRIORS   (toms and she-cats without kits)

               WHITEWING—white she-cat with green eyes

               BIRCHFALL—light brown tabby tom

               MOUSEWHISKER—gray-and-white tom
               APPRENTICE, BAYPAW (golden tabby tom)

               POPPYFROST—pale tortoiseshell-and-white she-cat

               BRISTLEFROST—pale gray she-cat

               LILYHEART—small, dark tabby she-cat with white patches and blue eyes
               APPRENTICE, FLAMEPAW (black tom)

               BUMBLESTRIPE—very pale gray tom with black stripes

               CHERRYFALL—ginger she-cat

               MOLEWHISKER—brown-and-cream tom

               CINDERHEART—gray tabby she-cat
               APPRENTICE, FINCHPAW (tortoiseshell she-cat)

               BLOSSOMFALL—tortoiseshell-and-white she-cat with petal-shaped white patches

IVYPOOL—silver-and-white tabby she-cat with dark blue eyes

EAGLEWING—ginger she-cat
APPRENTICE, MYRTLEPAW (pale brown she-cat)

DEWNOSE—gray-and-white tom

THRIFTEAR—dark gray she-cat

STORMCLOUD—gray tabby tom

HOLLYTUFT—black she-cat

FERNSONG—yellow tabby tom

HONEYFUR—white she-cat with yellow splotches

SPARKPELT—orange tabby she-cat

SORRELSTRIPE—dark brown she-cat

TWIGBRANCH—gray she-cat with green eyes

FINLEAP—brown tom

SHELLFUR—tortoiseshell tom

PLUMSTONE—black-and-ginger she-cat

LEAFSHADE—tortoiseshell she-cat

SPOTFUR—spotted tabby she-cat

QUEENS (she-cats expecting or nursing kits)

DAISY—cream long-furred cat from the horseplace

ELDERS (former warriors and queens, now retired)

CLOUDTAIL—long-haired white tom with blue eyes

BRIGHTHEART—white she-cat with ginger patches

BRACKENFUR—golden-brown tabby tom

SHADOWCLAN

LEADER   **TIGERSTAR**—dark brown tabby tom

DEPUTY   **CLOVERFOOT**—gray tabby she-cat

MEDICINE CATS   **PUDDLESHINE**—brown tom with white splotches

    SHADOWSIGHT—gray tabby tom

    MOTHWING—dappled golden she-cat

WARRIORS   **TAWNYPELT**—tortoiseshell she-cat with green eyes

    DOVEWING—pale gray she-cat with green eyes

    HARELIGHT—white tom

    ICEWING—white she-cat with blue eyes

    STONEWING—white tom

    SCORCHFUR—dark gray tom with slashed ears

    FLAXFOOT—brown tabby tom

    SPARROWTAIL—large brown tabby tom

    SNOWBIRD—pure white she-cat with green eyes

    YARROWLEAF—ginger she-cat with yellow eyes

    BERRYHEART—black-and-white she-cat

    GRASSHEART—pale brown tabby she-cat

    WHORLPELT—gray-and-white tom

    HOPWHISKER—calico she-cat

    BLAZEFIRE—white-and-ginger tom

    CINNAMONTAIL—brown tabby she-cat with white paws

FLOWERSTEM—silver she-cat

SNAKETOOTH—honey-colored tabby she-cat

SLATEFUR—sleek gray tom

POUNCESTEP—gray tabby she-cat

LIGHTLEAP—brown tabby she-cat

GULLSWOOP—white she-cat

SPIRECLAW—black-and-white tom

HOLLOWSPRING—black tom

SUNBEAM—brown-and-white tabby she-cat

ELDERS   **OAKFUR**—small brown tom

SKYCLAN

LEADER   **LEAFSTAR**—brown-and-cream tabby she-cat with amber eyes

DEPUTY   **HAWKWING**—dark gray tom with yellow eyes

MEDICINE CATS   **FRECKLEWISH**—mottled light brown tabby she-cat with spotted legs

FIDGETFLAKE—black-and-white tom

MEDIATOR   **TREE**—yellow tom with amber eyes

WARRIORS   **SPARROWPELT**—dark brown tabby tom

MACGYVER—black-and-white tom

DEWSPRING—sturdy gray tom

ROOTSPRING—yellow tom

NEEDLECLAW—black-and-white she-cat

PLUMWILLOW—dark gray she-cat

SAGENOSE—pale gray tom

KITESCRATCH—reddish-brown tom

HARRYBROOK—gray tom

CHERRYTAIL—fluffy tortoiseshell and white she-cat

CLOUDMIST—white she-cat with yellow eyes

BLOSSOMHEART—ginger-and-white she-cat

TURTLECRAWL—tortoiseshell she-cat

RABBITLEAP—brown tom
APPRENTICE, WRENPAW (golden tabby she-cat)

REEDCLAW—small pale tabby she-cat

MINTFUR—gray tabby she-cat with blue eyes

NETTLESPLASH—pale brown tom

TINYCLOUD—small white she-cat

PALESKY—black-and-white she-cat

VIOLETSHINE—black-and-white she-cat with yellow eyes

BELLALEAF—pale orange she-cat with green eyes

QUAILFEATHER—white tom with crow-black ears

PIGEONFOOT—gray-and-white she-cat

FRINGEWHISKER—white she-cat with brown splotches

GRAVELNOSE—tan tom

SUNNYPELT—ginger she-cat

QUEENS   **NECTARSONG**—brown she-cat

ELDERS   **FALLOWFERN**—pale brown she-cat who has lost her hearing

WINDCLAN

LEADER   **HARESTAR**—brown-and-white tom

DEPUTY   **CROWFEATHER**—dark gray tom

MEDICINE CAT   **KESTRELFLIGHT**—mottled gray tom with white splotches like kestrel feathers

WARRIORS   **NIGHTCLOUD**—black she-cat

BRINDLEWING—mottled brown she-cat
APPRENTICE, APPLEPAW (yellow tabby she-cat)

LEAFTAIL—dark tabby tom with amber eyes
APPRENTICE, WOODPAW (brown she-cat)

EMBERFOOT—gray tom with two dark paws

BREEZEPELT—black tom with amber eyes

HEATHERTAIL—light brown tabby she-cat with blue eyes

FEATHERPELT—gray tabby she-cat

CROUCHFOOT—ginger tom
APPRENTICE, SONGPAW (tortoiseshell she-cat)

LARKWING—pale brown tabby she-cat

SEDGEWHISKER—light brown tabby she-cat
APPRENTICE, FLUTTERPAW (brown-and-white tom)

SLIGHTFOOT—black tom with white flash on his chest

OATCLAW—pale brown tabby tom

HOOTWHISKER—dark gray tom
APPRENTICE, WHISTLEPAW (gray tabby she-cat)

FERNSTRIPE—gray tabby she-cat

ELDERS

WHISKERNOSE—light brown tom

GORSETAIL—very pale gray-and-white she-cat with blue eyes

RIVERCLAN

LEADER

MISTYSTAR—gray she-cat with blue eyes

DEPUTY

REEDWHISKER—black tom

MEDICINE CATS

WILLOWSHINE—gray tabby she-cat

WARRIORS

DUSKFUR—brown tabby she-cat

MINNOWTAIL—dark gray-and-white she-cat
APPRENTICE, SPLASHPAW (brown tabby tom)

MALLOWNOSE—light brown tabby tom

HAVENPELT—black-and-white she-cat

PODLIGHT—gray-and-white tom

SHIMMERPELT—silver she-cat

LIZARDTAIL—light brown tom
APPRENTICE, FOGPAW (gray-and-white she-cat)

SNEEZECLOUD—gray-and-white tom

BRACKENPELT—tortoiseshell she-cat

JAYCLAW—gray tom

OWLNOSE—brown tabby tom

GORSECLAW—white tom with gray ears

NIGHTSKY—dark gray she-cat with blue eyes

BREEZEHEART—brown-and-white she-cat

QUEENS   **CURLFEATHER**—pale brown she-cat (mother to Frostkit, a she-kit; Mistkit, a she-kit; and Graykit, a tom)

ELDERS   **MOSSPELT**—tortoiseshell-and-white she-cat

GREENLEAF
TWOLEGPLACE

TWOLEG NEST

TWOLEG PATH

TWOLEG PATH

CLEARING

SHADOWCLAN
CAMP

SMALL
THUNDERPATH

HALFBRIDGE

GREENLEAF
TWOLEGPLACE

HALFBRIDGE

CAT VIEW

ISLAND

STREAM

RIVERCLAN
CAMP

HORSEPLACE

HAREVIEW
CAMPSITE

SANCTUARY
COTTAGE

SADLER WOODS

LITTLEPINE
SAILING
CENTER

LITTLEPINE ROAD

TWOLEG VIL

LITTLEPINE
ISLAND

RIVER ALBA

WHITECHURCH ROAD

KNIGHT'S
COPSE

CHAPTER 1

Daisy crouched low in the soft bedding of the nursery, hardly aware of the trailing stem of moss that tickled her nose. She didn't have the energy to raise a paw to swipe it away, or to groom her long cream-colored fur, still stiff with mud from the rain a few days ago. The mouse that Cinderheart's apprentice, Finch-paw, had brought her first thing that morning lay untasted beside her.

She stared unseeing at the nursery wall. Instead of the neatly interlaced bramble tendrils, or the chinks where sunlight seeped in, her vision was overwhelmed by the memory of her kits, Rosepetal and Berrynose, lying in the center of the camp after the battle where they had died fighting for their Clan. She had licked them clean of blood and smoothed their fur and sat vigil, but now there was nothing more she could do for them.

There's nothing more I can do for any *cat in this Clan,* she thought. *Nothing at all.*

Life in ThunderClan had started to go wrong when Star-Clan had withdrawn from the living Clans, silent even to the medicine cats. The cruel, controlling behavior of their leader, Bramblestar, had made things even worse, until finally the Clan had discovered that he wasn't Bramblestar at all. A long-dead warrior, seeking revenge, had somehow managed to escape from StarClan's hunting grounds, and he had seized control of Bramblestar's body when the leader lost a life.

In the battle that followed the revelation, the impostor had been taken prisoner, and was now being held on ShadowClan territory while the leaders and medicine cats decided what to do with him. Squirrelflight had taken over as leader of ThunderClan, with Lionblaze as her deputy, while the whole Clan worried about whether the real Bramblestar, or StarClan itself, would ever return.

But Daisy's anxiety about her Clan was swamped by a smothering wave of grief for Rosepetal and Berrynose, and for her other lost kits, Toadstep and Hazeltail, who had died many moons before.

Do I belong here in the nursery now? she asked herself. *Here where kits are born and cared for? So many of my kits are gone forever.*

Not for the first time, Daisy wondered if she should have joined the number of her Clanmates who had asked Squirrelflight for permission to leave the Clan for a while. The day before, Flipclaw, Thornclaw, Flywhisker, and Snaptooth had all left so they could think things through in peace. Even more shocking to every cat, their former deputy, Graystripe, had accompanied them. No cat claimed to understand what was going through the elder's mind, or why he had made that choice.

If even a beloved, respected cat like Graystripe is wondering whether

ThunderClan is the place for him, Daisy thought, *is it really so crazy for me to question my place here?*

A shadow fell across the entrance to the nursery as Mouse-whisker pushed his way inside. He paused, then padded nervously up to Daisy across the layer of moss that covered the floor.

My last surviving kit . . .

Daisy blinked up at him, admiring his strong, muscular body and his thick, soft gray-and-white pelt. She felt a pang of relief that she still at least had Mousewhisker, but love and grief for the kits she had lost threatened to tear her apart. She missed them so terribly it felt like claws digging into her heart.

"You've been in here for days now," Mousewhisker mewed gently, seeming to sense the raging conflict within his mother. "Wouldn't you like to come out and help the Clan a little? Maybe going on a hunt or a patrol would make you feel better."

"I'm not sure. . . ." Daisy's voice croaked in her throat; they were the first words she had spoken in days. "I don't think I could manage it."

"I know." Mousewhisker bent over to nuzzle his mother's shoulder, his nose pressed deep into her fur. "But Rosepetal and Berrynose would want you to move on, to be the helpful Clanmate you've always prided yourself on being."

A swell of fury rose in Daisy's chest, but she forced it down. *Where did being a "helpful Clanmate" get me?* she asked herself bitterly. *I've lost all but one of my kits. Now Mousewhisker is my only surviving kin. . . .*

But Daisy knew that sooner or later she would have to leave the nursery and find a way to carry on. ThunderClan needed all its members to make an effort, especially in these difficult times. After taking a deep breath, she gave a tiny nod.

"Good." Mousewhisker gave a relieved purr as Daisy struggled to her paws and followed him out into the camp.

As she emerged, Daisy became aware of surprised glances coming her way, as if her Clanmates couldn't believe she was appearing at last. She tried to ignore them, concentrating instead on the life of the Clan: She saw Squirrelflight in the center of the stone hollow, her green gaze fixed on Lionblaze as he organized Bristlefrost, Cherryfall, and Stormcloud into a hunting patrol. As they headed out of camp, Daisy spotted Sparkpelt's kits, Flamepaw and Finchpaw, bounding eagerly up to their mentors.

"They're so strong and capable," she murmured to herself. "It won't be long before they have their warrior ceremony."

"It's partly because of you that they've grown up so well," Mousewhisker told her, touching his nose to her ear. "You took such good care of them when they were in the nursery."

Daisy's heart clenched as she remembered how she had helped Sparkpelt when she was struggling after kitting, licking the two little scraps of fur, one black and one tortoiseshell, until they could snuggle into their mother's fur and start feeding.

Now the two apprentices barely seemed to notice her. As their mentors led them out of camp, they strode eagerly behind, strong and capable.

I was needed then, but it feels so long ago, Daisy thought. *Will I ever have a purpose in ThunderClan again?*

Extending her claws, Daisy combed through the moss and bracken of her nest. It was the second time that day that she had rearranged her bedding, and she wished she could find a thorn, or a bit of holly leaf, just to prove to herself that she wasn't wasting her time. A half-moon had passed since Mouse-whisker had first lured her out of the nursery, and though she had taken part now and again in hunts and patrols, she knew that she would never be a real warrior.

"My job is looking after kits," she mewed. "My own, and all the kits of ThunderClan. So what am I supposed to do when there are no kits? Oh, StarClan, I'm so *bored!*"

It seemed like moons had passed since the Clans had learned that the cat they thought was Bramblestar was actually an impostor, but the leaders couldn't seem to decide what to do with him now that he was a prisoner on ShadowClan territory. Bristlefrost and Spotfur had left ThunderClan with Rootspring and Needleclaw from SkyClan on a quest to find the Sisters, in the hope that the group of she-cats could help them discover whether the real Bramblestar was still around in spirit form.

Daisy had only been on the fringe of the recent Clan meetings and Gatherings, and even she knew that there had been bitter quarrels among the leaders. But those were nothing compared to the bickering and sniping between Squirrel-flight and Lionblaze as they struggled to lead the Clan in

Bramblestar's absence. Even now she could hear sharp meows drifting in from outside the nursery, though she couldn't make out the words.

They're not the cats I thought I knew, Daisy reflected. *This isn't the Clan I thought I knew. Where will it all end?*

Letting out a long sigh, she padded out into the camp. Ivypool was leading a hunting patrol across to the fresh-kill pile, the jaws of all four cats laden with prey. Flamepaw and Finchpaw were dragging a big ball of soiled bedding away from the elders' den, while Squirrelflight was bounding up the tumbled rocks, leaving Lionblaze to turn away and head for the warriors' den. It should have been an ordinary, peaceful day in camp, but all Daisy could see was the underlying tension shrouding everything like a clinging fog. She knew that not every cat accepted Squirrelflight as the new leader, even though they were all hoping it would only be temporary.

But what other cat could take on the task right now? she asked herself. Squirrelflight was Firestar's kit in addition to being Bramblestar's mate. She'd been able to observe the last two leaders up close. Squirrelflight was a wonderful deputy, and Daisy often felt that she'd been born to fill the role. She loved ThunderClan. Daisy could see that keeping the Clan going gave her purpose.

I only wish I felt the same.

She was padding across to choose a piece of prey from the fresh-kill pile when a scuffling from the camp entrance made her turn back sharply. Mousewhisker burst into the camp with his apprentice, Baypaw, scurrying after him, and Sparkpelt bringing up the rear. Mousewhisker pelted across the camp until he stood underneath the Highledge, where Squirrelflight sat.

"Squirrelflight!" he called. "Smoky from the horseplace is outside. He says he wants to talk to Daisy."

Daisy stiffened in mingled curiosity and apprehension. She had once lived at the horseplace on the other side of the lake, and Smoky had been her mate, the father of her first litter. But Daisy had left with her kits because she had been afraid that the horseplace Twolegs would take them away. She'd made a home for all of them in ThunderClan. Since then, she had occasionally seen Smoky when she passed the horseplace on her way to Gatherings, but apart from one difficult visit just before the Great Storm, they hadn't had the chance to say much to each other. She couldn't imagine what reason Smoky would have to want to talk to her now.

Does Mousewhisker remember that Smoky is his father? she wondered. *He was old enough, when I last took him to the horseplace.*

Squirrelflight rose to her paws and arched her back in a long stretch. "Did he say what it's about?" she asked Mousewhisker.

The gray-and-white tom shook his head. "Just that he wanted to see Daisy."

Daisy padded up to stand beside her son and dipped her head respectfully to her Clan leader. "I'd like to talk to him, if it's okay with you," she meowed.

Squirrelflight hesitated, then gave a curt nod. "Mousewhisker, bring him in. But keep an eye on him."

Mousewhisker bounded across the clearing and disappeared into the thorn tunnel. Cats across camp gathered around as they heard the news, their eyes glinting with suspicion and their shoulder fur beginning to rise. Squirrelflight padded down the tumbled rocks to the floor of the camp and came to stand close to Daisy.

That isn't necessary, Daisy thought, though she didn't say the words out loud. *Smoky isn't dangerous. I don't need protecting.*

It felt like a quarter moon before Mousewhisker returned, leading Smoky into the stone hollow. Seeing the two toms together—both strong and muscular, both with fluffy gray-and-white pelts—Daisy thought that no cat could doubt that they were father and son. She noticed too that Mousewhisker was looking awkward, as if he wasn't sure how to behave toward the cat he scarcely knew, even though they were such close kin.

It's good that Smoky came to visit, Daisy thought. *Maybe he and Mousewhisker can get to know each other better. And it'll be nice to talk to him again.* But even as she formed that thought, another icy wave of grief washed over her, for the kits she had lost in the battle. *Berrynose was Smoky's son, too; oh, StarClan, I'll have to break the news to him!*

Then, as she took in the troubled expression on Smoky's face, Daisy realized that he wasn't just dropping in for a pleasant chat. Whatever had brought him to the ThunderClan camp, it was serious.

CHAPTER 2

As soon as Smoky spotted Daisy, he darted across the camp toward her, so swiftly that Squirrelflight stepped forward, ready to intercept him, while several of her Clanmates edged closer.

Reaching Daisy's side, Smoky pressed himself against her and gave her ear an affectionate lick. "I'm so glad to see you!" he purred.

Daisy was aware of her Clanmates relaxing as she returned Smoky's greeting by touching her nose to his shoulder. She could taste the fear-scent on him and see the anxiety in his eyes.

"What is all this about?" Squirrelflight asked.

Smoky gathered himself, faced the Clan leader, and gave her a respectful dip of his head. "I came to ask Daisy for help," he replied. "My mate, Coriander, has started kitting, back at the horseplace, and she's having so much trouble! I'm really worried about her, and Daisy once told me that in the Clans there are cats who can help with problems like that." With a pleading glance at Daisy, he added, "I know I'm not part of your Clan, but I'd be so grateful if you could spare one of those cats, just for a little while."

Daisy stared back evenly, taking in Smoky's request. She and Coriander hadn't had the best of first meetings. It had stung Daisy that Smoky had seemed to have so easily replaced his previous denmate, Floss—a cat she had cared about deeply. Still, the news of a kitting queen who needed help sent a tingle of purpose from the tips of her ears to the bottom of her pads. *I might not be much help with the Clan's problems right now—but I know exactly what to do to help Coriander, and I could never refuse a cat who needs me. It's me Smoky really wants—or me as well as a medicine cat.*

She shook out her pelt, ready to leave at once. She knew she owed Smoky all the help she could give, after she had taken his first litter away from him, when she left the horseplace to return to the Clans. *The least I can do is guide his new litter safely into the world.*

Seeing Smoky so worried for his unborn kits gave her a twinge of regret, though, that he, and not she, was going to be a parent again. She didn't feel jealous of Coriander, exactly, but the memory of her own kits when they were tiny and new made her heart ache. *It's all right,* she told herself. *I can still help these kits, even if I'm not their mother. I help other queens' kits all the time!* Although, after all the recent trouble in ThunderClan, she wondered whether this was the right time for her to leave.

Smoky's pleading gaze was still fixed on her. "Coriander is in so much pain," he went on. "She's trying so hard, but the kits won't come. Please—we need help, as soon as you can!"

The desperation in Smoky's voice, and the way he was working his claws in the earth of the camp floor, made up Daisy's mind for her. "I'd like to go," she mewed, turning to

Squirrelflight with a deferential dip of her head. "And we can spare a medicine cat, can't we?"

Squirrelflight hesitated for a moment, blinking thoughtfully, then nodded. "I could never refuse a queen in need of help," she responded. "And even though the kits won't be Clanborn, new life is needed around here, after the death and destruction we've all faced lately. You may go, Daisy. I'll send Alderheart with you, and a couple of warriors in case you run into trouble."

"Thank you, Squirrelflight!" Daisy exclaimed, warm anticipation rushing through her. At the horseplace, she could make herself useful. And perhaps there could be an opportunity for Mousewhisker, as well. . . . "Could Mousewhisker be one of the warriors you send with us?"

"Of course," Squirrelflight replied, while Mousewhisker gave Smoky a sidelong look filled with embarrassment, as if he wasn't looking forward to spending time with a father who was almost a stranger to him. Daisy hoped the awkwardness between them would fade soon. Mousewhisker deserved to know his father.

"And maybe Sorrelstripe?" Daisy suggested. "We'll need an extra set of paws to help Coriander, and Sorrelstripe birthed a litter not that long ago. She's experienced in raising kits, and she'll be gentle."

"Yes, she can go too," the Clan leader agreed. "Mousewhisker, go and find her, and I'll fetch Alderheart."

Mousewhisker darted off so quickly that Daisy wondered whether he was eager to escape the strangeness of trying to interact with Smoky. As Squirrelflight padded toward the medicine cats' den, Daisy and Smoky were left facing each other.

"That tom is our son, isn't he?" Smoky asked, angling his ears after the departing Mousewhisker. "He's grown so much since he came to the horseplace."

"Yes, that's Mousewhisker," Daisy replied proudly. "He's become a strong warrior! And he was such a comfort to me when . . ." Her voice choked on the last words, and she couldn't go on.

Smoky glanced from side to side, as if he was looking for some cat. Daisy knew, with a sinking sense of dread, exactly which cats he was hoping to find: their other two kits, Hazeltail and Berrynose. Panic clawed at her heart as she wondered how she would break it to him that both of them had died—especially since she had seen him after they'd lost Hazeltail, and had not told him then.

I just couldn't bring myself to, that day, she thought, not for the first time. *It shocked me, the way he said Coriander had "replaced" Floss. . . . The words wouldn't come.*

She was having a similar feeling—like words were dying in her mouth—now that she had to give him the awful news.

But Smoky seemed to understand without words. Daisy saw a flash of pain in his eyes, and his head drooped with grief. She realized that he knew exactly what had happened to his other kits.

"There . . . there was a battle . . . ," she began, still struggling to explain, but once again the words wouldn't come.

Smoky straightened up and shook his head as if he was getting rid of a troublesome fly. "You can tell me some other time," he meowed. "Now we have to go. Coriander can't wait . . . these kits are coming whether we're ready or not!"

As soon as Alderheart joined them, a leaf wrap of herbs in his jaws, and Mousewhisker returned with Sorrelstripe, the group set out toward the horseplace.

"We're on WindClan territory now," Sorrelstripe murmured as they splashed through the stream that marked the border. "We should be on the lookout for a patrol."

"WindClan shouldn't give us any trouble, seeing that we're with Alderheart," Daisy pointed out, shaking drops of water from each of her paws in turn. "Besides, we'll stay close to the lake, and we won't be taking prey."

Even while she was speaking, she wondered whether what she said was entirely true. They were traveling with a cat from outside the Clans, and with so much tension between the Clans after the recent battles, Daisy wouldn't be surprised to meet with hostility from WindClan warriors.

Thinking of the battles, and how Berrynose had died, reminded Daisy that sooner or later Smoky would want the full story of what had happened to their other kits. Her gaze rested on Mousewhisker, who had taken the lead with Smoky; they were padding along side by side in silence, as if neither cat really knew how to talk to the other.

Daisy stifled a sigh. *Please relax and get to know each other,* she thought. *You're both such strong, clever cats.*

They had covered about half the distance through Wind-Clan territory when Daisy spotted cats outlined against the sky at the top of the moorland ridge. One of them let out a yowl, and the patrol bounded down to intercept the Thunder-Clan cats at the edge of the lake. Daisy and the others drew to a halt and waited for them.

As the WindClan cats approached, Daisy recognized Hootwhisker in the lead, with Crouchfoot and their appren-tices, Whistlepaw and Songpaw. She was briefly worried that they meant to attack, only to puff out her breath in relief as Hootwhisker called to them in a friendly voice.

"Greetings, ThunderClan! What brings your paws this way?"

They must have seen Alderheart. That would reassure them that the ThunderClan cats meant no harm.

But Daisy's relief was short-lived. As Hootwhisker and the rest of his patrol halted on the lakeshore, the dark gray tom's gaze fell on Smoky, and his whiskers began to bristle in sus-picion.

"What's a rogue doing here?" he demanded.

Before Smoky could respond, Mousewhisker stepped pro-tectively in front of his father. "Are you blind, or have the bees swarmed in your brain?" he retorted. "This isn't a rogue; he's Smoky from the horseplace. You must have seen him often enough on your way to Gatherings. He came to ThunderClan to ask for a medicine cat's help, that's all."

Daisy's heart clenched and she felt a heavy weight in her belly as she watched her last surviving son squaring up to cats from another Clan. She couldn't help but imagine Mouse-whisker falling in battle, blood gushing from many wounds until he collapsed in death, gone forever. *I can't bear it—I can't!* Hardly knowing what she meant to do, she stepped in front of Mousewhisker, determined to protect her kit.

But only a couple of heartbeats passed before Alderheart moved up to the head of the group and laid his leaf wrap down on a nearby flat stone. "A cat needs help, and I'm going to help," he explained calmly. "We pose no threat to WindClan."

For a moment Hootwhisker remained rigid, still staring at Smoky, who faced him without flinching. Then Crouchfoot poked his Clanmate in the side with one paw. "Stupid fur-ball!" the ginger tom meowed.

To Daisy's relief, Hootwhisker relaxed, ducking his head with embarrassment. "Sorry," he muttered. "We're all on edge these days. I'm sure you understand."

Every cat murmured agreement. "Yes, it's been a terrible time for the Clans," Sorrelstripe meowed.

Daisy noticed that Smoky's gaze was flicking from one cat to another as he followed the argument. She wondered whether he was asking himself if the Clans saw "terrible times" often, and if two of his kits had met their deaths because of them. She had no idea how she would ever explain to him everything that had happened since the grim leaf-bare just past, when even the Moonpool had iced over.

"Good-bye, then," Hootwhisker mewed, gathering the WindClan patrol together with a sweep of his tail. "May Star-Clan light your path."

"And yours," Alderheart responded, picking up his leaf wrap from where he had left it.

The WindClan cats headed along the lakeshore in the direction of the ThunderClan border, while Mousewhisker took the lead again on the way to the horseplace. Smoky followed him, casting a glance back over his shoulder at Daisy, as if he wanted to talk to her, but Daisy pretended that she hadn't noticed.

The sun hung low in the sky by the time Daisy could see the horseplace looming up in front of them. Mousewhisker picked up the pace, heading for the barn behind the shiny mesh fence.

"No, not that way!" Smoky called out to him. Catching up with Mousewhisker, who had paused and turned back, he explained, "Coriander and I had to make another den for ourselves."

"Why?" Sorrelstripe asked.

"Things have changed at the horseplace," Smoky began. "We—"

Smoky broke off as a terrible yowl of pain rose from a hollow a little way up the moorland slope that edged WindClan territory. The sound made Daisy feel as though every drop of blood in her body had turned to ice.

Her foreboding increased as she saw the look on Alderheart's face, a look that said, *That doesn't sound good.*

CHAPTER 3

❧

Smoky raced up the hill and plunged into the hollow under the shelter of an overhanging stunted thorn. Daisy and the rest of the ThunderClan cats followed, pausing at the edge to look down into the dip. The grass that lined the sides was sparse and muddy, but Daisy reflected that the den had probably provided reasonably good shelter during that last, terrible leaf-bare.

At one side of the den, in a nest between two of the thorn-tree roots, Coriander's long tortoiseshell body lay stretched out in a nest of moss and bracken, her flanks heaving as she struggled to birth her kits. Her amber eyes were glazed with pain.

Smoky was already crouched beside her, gently licking her ears in an attempt to comfort her, and reassuring her that he had brought help. Alderheart skidded down into the hollow to join them, with Daisy and Sorrelstripe hard on his paws. Mousewhisker hung back, looking uncomfortable.

"Stay up there!" Daisy called out to him. "Keep watch. There might be predators."

Mousewhisker nodded, clearly relieved to make himself

useful in a way that didn't involve caring for the laboring she-cat. But Daisy hadn't just told him that to keep him busy; there was a reek of blood in the air that could easily attract a fox or a badger, and Daisy could see it pooling around Coriander and smudging her white belly fur like the prints of scarlet paws.

"You can relax now," Alderheart meowed to the tortoise-shell she-cat. "Everything's going to be fine."

His words sounded confident, though Daisy, who knew him well, could hear the tension in his voice. He spread out the contents of his leaf wrap, snagged a juniper berry on one claw, and held it out to Coriander. "Eat this," he told her. "It will give you strength."

"I can't!" Coriander wailed.

"I can help," Daisy said. She took the berry from Alderheart and quickly dropped it into Coriander's gaping jaws, before she could argue. "It's okay, Coriander—we're here to help," she promised as she massaged the queen's throat. Soon she felt Coriander swallow the berry. Smoky gave her a grateful nod.

Daisy moved herself near Coriander's hindquarters, where she could stroke the she-cat's fur and keep an eye on the progress of her labor. Her anxiety grew as she realized that in spite of the blood and Coriander's obvious straining, nothing much seemed to be happening. *That isn't good!*

"You're doing well," she reassured the young tortoise-shell, wanting to keep her calm. Calm queens reserved more strength for pushing later. "It won't be long now, and then think how happy you'll be to see your kits."

"It'll be so great!" Smoky agreed; Daisy could tell that he had to force an excited purr into his voice when clearly he knew that something was seriously wrong. "We'll have to think of names for them, and we'll show them how to play with moss balls, and how to catch mice . . . Coriander, it's all going to be wonderful!"

Listening to her former mate talking so excitedly, watching him as he tried to soothe Coriander, Daisy once more felt a stab of guilt at how she had taken their kits away so many seasons ago. Until their deaths, she had never regretted raising them as warriors. *But if I'd stayed here with Smoky, would I have been spared the grief of outliving four of my kits? Could I have been happy with Smoky if I'd never known life in a Clan?*

Coriander didn't respond to her mate's encouragement. She was thrashing her head from side to side. "I can't do this!" she choked out.

"You can," Daisy told her firmly. "Every queen says that, but every cat in the world got here this way." *Except the ones who didn't make it,* she added silently to herself.

Sorrelstripe had dashed away for a moment, and now she returned, dragging a stick. Daisy nodded at her gratefully, then pushed the stick toward Coriander's head. "Bite down on this when the pain gets bad," she instructed her. "I had one when I was kitting, and it really helped."

"Some water would help, too." Alderheart looked up from where he was running his paws over Coriander's belly. "Could you fetch some, Sorrelstripe? There are pools in the marshes."

"Keep a lookout for RiverClan patrols," Daisy warned

Sorrelstripe, as the dark brown warrior headed out of the hollow again. "They won't appreciate unexpected visitors on their territory."

"Like I care," Sorrelstripe retorted. "If they try to stop me helping a kitting she-cat in trouble, I'll claw their ears off!" She vanished with a flick of her tail.

"Smoky . . . Smoky . . ." Daisy's attention was dragged back to Coriander as the she-cat struggled to raise her head, reaching out one paw to her mate. "Smoky, you have to promise me . . . don't let the Nofurs take our kits."

Daisy suppressed a shudder at the memory of how Floss's kits had been taken from her by the Twolegs at the horseplace. That was why Daisy had left with her own kits and found refuge with ThunderClan.

"Coriander, don't upset yourself." Smoky's voice was shaking as he stroked Coriander's shoulder, urging her to lie down again in her mossy nest. Nodding vigorously, he added, "I promise. Our kits will grow up as true cats, not the pets of the Nofurs."

Daisy wasn't sure that was the best idea. While it broke her heart, she had to admit that Coriander seemed to be doing poorly. Daisy had assisted in enough deliveries to know that they didn't always end happily. Coriander might not survive her kitting. And if Coriander died, her kits' chance of surviving without a mother was slim. At least with the Twolegs, the kits would be safe and cared for.

But I can't say that to Smoky and Coriander. Not now.

Daisy's heart ached more and more as she listened to Smoky,

who was telling Coriander about everything they would do when the kits were born. "Greenleaf is coming, and we can romp around with them on the grass," he meowed. "And at night we'll all curl up together in our cozy nest."

That's not going to happen, and Smoky knows it, Daisy realized from the tremble in his voice. *Coriander knows it too.*

Then Daisy saw that Coriander had turned her head and was gazing straight into her eyes. "That means that my kits won't grow up in the Clans, either," she rasped.

"I'll never take them there," Smoky meowed before Daisy had a chance to respond. "I promise, the kits belong here, with you and me."

Another massive ripple passed across Coriander's belly, and she let out a shriek of pain before sinking her teeth into the stick Sorrelstripe had brought. Daisy stroked her back as the pain ebbed.

"With you," Coriander corrected in a gasp, when she could speak again.

"Don't talk like that," Smoky implored, turning in an anxious circle. "Please, Coriander, you have to be strong. I need you. Our kits need you."

Coriander shook her head. A calm had come over her, as if she'd suddenly made peace with her fate. "I know I won't survive this," she murmured. "But that's okay, because I'm bringing new life into the world. As long as you promise that you'll raise our kits the way I've asked you, I'll be at peace."

Daisy was reminded of what Squirrelflight had said when she'd left: *New life is needed around here, after the death and destruction we've all faced lately*. Perhaps Coriander felt this, too. Daisy made a silent promise to protect the life Smoky and Coriander had created to the best of her ability.

"No! You'll be here, too," Smoky protested. "We'll raise our kits together. Alderheart, you have to do something!"

The ThunderClan medicine cat had been chewing up a scrap of chervil root, and now he offered it to Coriander spread out on a dock leaf. "Lap this up," he told the tortoise-shell-and-white she-cat. "It should help your kits to come."

But Coriander turned her head away. All her attention was fixed on Smoky. "I need to know you can do this without me," she insisted through gritted teeth. "You can't let me die not knowing whether my kits will be okay. You have to promise."

"But you're not going to—" Smoky began helplessly, then broke off. Daisy could hardly bear to watch or listen as he leaned closer to Coriander and touched noses with her. "I promise," he whispered.

Coriander let out a long sigh. Daisy nudged the leaf toward her, and at last she lapped up the root. The ripples across her belly were coming stronger and faster now, and she bit down hard on the stick when the pain throbbed through her. Sorrel-stripe returned, her jaws full of dripping moss, and in a brief respite Coriander lapped eagerly at the water.

Come on . . . come on . . . Daisy was desperate to safely deliver these kits. It felt like the least she could do. But Coriander was struggling, and she could tell the queen was growing weaker. Daisy felt as though the ordeal had continued for season upon season, when at last Alderheart exclaimed, "They're coming!"

The words had hardly left his mouth when a small, squirming bundle plopped out onto the moss of the nest. Daisy felt relief course through her. *One kit!*

"Our kit!" Smoky exclaimed, his voice shaking with wonder. "Oh, Coriander . . . well done! We have our first kit!"

While he was speaking, a second bundle followed the first, its tiny paws batting the air. Daisy felt overcome with emotion as Alderheart looked over the tiny scraps of fur. *They made it!*

"They're wonderful!" Smoky breathed out. "Alderheart, is that all?"

The medicine cat ran an expert paw over Coriander's belly. "One more to come," he mewed.

One more? Daisy looked back at the exhausted queen, hoping it would come quickly. A massive spasm shook Coriander, her body convulsing over and over again until the third kit appeared. This one was smaller than its littermates, and lay still and silent on the moss. Smoky looked on, his eyes wide with mute appeal, while Alderheart bent and gave the tiny creature a long sniff. Daisy realized she was holding her breath. *Please be all right!* But finally he shook his head, and clawed a pawful of moss over the dead kit so that Coriander wouldn't see.

Smoky closed his eyes for a moment; Daisy's heart almost broke at the sight of his struggle. Smoky hadn't been there for her own kitting; she'd been so worried about getting the kits away from the Nofurs that she'd hidden from him, too. Now he was watching new kits come into the world, but he also had to watch one leave. And she still wasn't sure what would happen to Coriander. Smoky let out a shuddering sigh and turned to his weakened mate.

"Look at our kits," he urged her, joy piercing through his grief and fear. "Coriander, we have kits. . . ."

But Coriander didn't respond. Her eyes were closed and her chest no longer rose and fell.

Daisy stared at her. *No!* She'd known it was possible, but still, the reality of Coriander's death hit her like a fallen branch. She could barely breathe, she felt so devastated, so useless. Even outside ThunderClan, it seemed, she couldn't do what she was meant to. *I came to save her,* she thought miserably. *I'm meant to protect queens and kits, but now these kits are motherless.*

Her heart broke for Smoky. Her former mate stretched out a shaking paw and stroked Coriander's shoulder fur. "Coriander, look. . . . Please . . . look. . . ."

"She's dead," Daisy whispered. "Oh, Smoky, I'm so sorry."

CHAPTER 4
✣

For a long time Smoky sat beside his dead mate, gazing silently down at her. As Alderheart put away the rest of the herbs and moss around them, Daisy showed Sorrelstripe how to help her clean up the two surviving kits, licking their fur the wrong way to stimulate them and warm them up.

Daisy began roughly licking the kit, encouraged by its warmth and strong heartbeat. Soon the two tiny scraps were clean and dry enough that she could see them clearly: a dark gray tom and a tortoiseshell-and-white she-cat, almost exactly like her mother. They were so lovely it made her heart ache. *Such perfect little kits, orphaned before they could even open their eyes!*

Eventually Alderheart nodded at Daisy. "These kits need to eat right away if they're to survive," he told her. "They can't nurse from their mother, so we'll have to find another way to feed them. How are you at hunting?"

"I can hold my own. But surely they can't eat prey yet," Daisy meowed. "They're so young!"

"I can make it small enough for them to digest," Alderheart assured her. "It's what we did for Twigbranch and Violetshine, when Needletail and I found them alone just after they were born. They'll need to nurse eventually, if they're going to make it," he continued with a doubtful shake of his head, "but some prey will keep them going for now."

His words had roused Smoky from his grief over his lost mate; he rose and padded over to where the kits were lying. Their shrill mewling was growing louder and more demanding with every heartbeat that passed.

"I know where to find prey," he meowed, giving the kits a long look, as if he was afraid to leave them. Then he turned and raced up the side of the hollow. "Come on!" he yowled. "Follow me!"

It was strange but sweet, hunting with her former mate and their grown kit. Daisy hadn't had much experience hunting—back in ThunderClan, the warriors took care of that, and Daisy ate with the queens and kits. But as a loner at the horseplace, she'd learned how to scent birds and mice, and she was adequate at stalking and pouncing. With Mousewhisker's help, she trapped a mouse and bit hard on its neck to kill it. The fresh blood that filled her mouth was satisfying. She remembered what she'd told Alderheart: *I can hold my own.* It was nice to remind herself that it was true.

By the time Daisy, Smoky, and Mousewhisker returned from the hunt, carrying a couple of mice and a blackbird, they found Sorrelstripe on watch. Alderheart remained in the hollow with the kits, curled around them to keep them warm. To Daisy's relief the two little creatures were still squirming around, their hungry wailing even more desperate.

As soon as the hunting patrol dropped their prey in front of Alderheart, he seized one of the mice and began to chew it up into a pulp. Then he dabbed one paw into the mushed-up prey and held it out to the tiny gray tom. Daisy did the same for the little tortoiseshell.

At first the kits thrashed their heads from side to side, avoiding their outstretched paws. *They don't understand,* Daisy thought anxiously. *They don't know this is food.*

"Eat, little ones," she mewed encouragingly. "It's good."

Both tiny pink mouths were wide open as the kits let out their shrill squealing. Daisy gently wiped some of the mouse pulp onto the tortoiseshell she-cat's lips, and instinctively the kit swiped at it with her tongue to get it off. A heartbeat later she craned her neck forward to take another lick from Daisy's paw.

"She's getting the idea," Alderheart commented, with a nod of approval at Daisy. He tried the same method with the little tom, and soon both kits were sucking ravenously at the mouse pulp.

All the while Smoky was watching with a keen and desperate gaze. Daisy could see that he was enthralled by the tiny kits, but at the same time terrified that Alderheart's improvised way of feeding them wouldn't work. Mousewhisker was watching too, deep sympathy in his eyes, as if he was also concerned for these tiny scraps who were his kin.

But gradually the kits settled; their frightened mewling

changed to satisfied purrs, and they curled up together in the soft moss. Once they were quiet, Alderheart looked up at the older cats.

"Smoky, you're going to have to face a difficult decision," he meowed, his tone grave. "In spite of what Coriander wanted, letting the Twolegs know that you have kits might be their only chance of survival."

As he gazed at the kits Smoky's eyes widened into a horrified stare. For a moment Daisy thought he would give in, but then he shook his head emphatically.

"No way am I giving up my kits to the Nofurs," he insisted. Turning to Daisy, he continued, "Surely you remember how they gave away Floss's kits? That's why you left the horseplace—to prevent them from getting our kits, too."

"But, Smoky—" Daisy tried to interrupt.

"If the Nofurs find out about the kits, they'll take them away," Smoky swept on, "and I'll never see them again. Do you really want to put me through that *again*?"

"No, of course not," Daisy choked out around a hard lump in her throat. "But—"

Before Daisy could continue, Alderheart spoke, his tone sympathetic but firm. "If you don't get help from the Twolegs, your kits might not make it at all. Surely it's better to give them a chance at some kind of life, rather than watch them die before they can live?"

"Please listen to Alderheart," Daisy begged Smoky, as the tiny tortoiseshell let out a sleepy mew. Daisy couldn't mask her sympathy as she looked at the small, hungry kit, who looked so much like her mother.

"No." There was the beginning of a snarl in Smoky's voice. "I'm keeping the promise I made to Coriander. That's final."

Daisy exchanged a glance with Alderheart. Somehow they had to change Smoky's mind. "I know what the pain is like, of seeing my kits die," she meowed, trying a different argument. "Believe me, Smoky, that's not something you want to go through, if you can avoid it."

Smoky glared at her. "But knowing my kits are alive, and never being able to see them—I know what *that's* like, very well. I'm not going to go through that again, if I can help it. Thanks to the decisions *you* made in the past, I don't know how to handle the grief of losing a kit. I've found out just today that I already lost two, even though you never actually told me, and I don't know how to mourn them in the way a father should, because I *never knew them*."

An aching regret overcame Daisy, like a vast paw grabbing hold and squeezing the breath out of her. She dropped her gaze, unable to meet Smoky's reproachful look, though she was aware of Mousewhisker crouching with his ears laid back. It couldn't have been easy to hear so much confusion and grief from the father he'd never had a chance to know.

"I'm going to obey Coriander's last wish," Smoky repeated. "The Nofurs will *never* take my kits from me."

Daisy felt as though the strained silence would go on forever. Finally Alderheart let out a heavy sigh.

"I want you to be clear about this, Smoky," he began. "Just because I'm a medicine cat doesn't mean I can guarantee that your kits will survive. I'll do what I can, of course I will. But it would help if somehow we could find a nursing queen, and I don't know how quickly we can do that."

Smoky blinked thoughtfully. "There's a kittypet called Coco," he mewed, "living over there in the Twolegplace." He angled his ears in the direction of the Twoleg dens on the far side of RiverClan territory. "I think she had kits recently."

"How recently?" Daisy asked.

"I'm not sure," Smoky admitted. "I've been so focused on Coriander this last half moon. . . ."

Daisy felt fear gathering in her belly, as if she were looking up at a dark sky about to unleash its storm. *If only there were a nursing queen in ThunderClan,* she thought helplessly. *Then the kits would be sure to survive.*

But the most recent additions to ThunderClan, Sorrelstripe's and Sparkpelt's kits, were all apprentices now—far too old for their mothers to be any help. Sorrelstripe was here because she had experience with kitting and raising kits, not because she still had milk to give the newborns.

I wish StarClan were still watching over us. Maybe then I'd have some idea about what to do.

The sun had started to go down, casting shadows into the hollow, though the hillside above was stained scarlet; it reminded Daisy too vividly of Coriander's blood.

"It's too late to go looking for Coco now," Alderheart meowed. "Twolegs normally shut their kittypets inside their dens when it gets dark. Smoky, can you lead another hunt—bring some prey for us as well as for the kits? We'll spend the night here."

Smoky murmured agreement, though he looked reluctant to leave his kits.

"Let's all go," Mousewhisker suggested. "Except for you, of course, Alderheart. That way it will be faster."

Daisy too was unhappy about leaving the kits, though she knew that no cat would take better care of them than Alderheart. But she didn't argue, bringing up the rear as the other cats headed out of the hollow.

Mousewhisker took the lead, padding cautiously along the lakeshore to the edge of RiverClan territory. Daisy was even more unhappy about taking prey from another Clan. *But this is an emergency,* she told herself, wondering whether Mistystar would see it that way if they were spotted by a RiverClan patrol.

To her relief, there was fresh RiverClan scent at the border, suggesting that a patrol had recently passed by. There was unlikely to be another one until dawn. But Daisy's fur still prickled with apprehension, and she volunteered to stay by the border to keep watch during the other cats' swift and silent hunt. She tried not to think about how impractical it was to rely on hunting to feed two tiny newborn kits, especially on another Clan's territory.

When Smoky came back, he was triumphantly carrying a vole. "Look at this!" he mewed around the mouthful of fur. "It will be perfect for the kits!"

Daisy wasn't convinced. *They won't thrive on fresh-kill, no matter how much we bring back—not like they would if they could nurse from their mother.*

Sorrelstripe and Mousewhisker returned a moment later, also carrying prey, and Smoky led the way back to their make-shift camp. Slipping through the twilight, Daisy became more and more certain that they would have to make a tough deci-sion. She tried to think of a way to keep the kits alive while still honoring Coriander's wishes, but she couldn't.

Somehow I'll have to persuade Smoky to give up these kits, even though that will break his heart all over again. Oh, Smoky, you really don't deserve that!

As they approached the camp, Daisy expected to hear the sound of hungry wailing from the kits, but all was silent.

Oh, StarClan! Surely the kits can't be dead already?

Smoky clearly shared her fears. Racing ahead, he came to a halt at the top of the hollow, staring down with the fur rising on his neck and shoulders. Daisy and the others caught up to him a couple of heartbeats later.

She had expected to see Alderheart crouched beside the bodies of Smoky's kits. But what she saw sent shock thrilling through her from ears to tail-tip. There was no sign of the medicine cat or the kits. The hollow was empty.

CHAPTER 5

♣

Smoky dropped the vole he was carrying and spun around to face the Clan cats. "My kits are gone!" he snarled. "Has Alderheart taken them to the Nofurs, even though he promised he wouldn't?"

"No!" Daisy protested. "He would never do that."

"Then where is he?" Smoky challenged her with a furious glare. "Where are my kits?"

Daisy shook her head helplessly. "I've no idea what happened," she confessed, "or where Alderheart could be. But I know he wouldn't take the kits."

Would he? she asked herself. *If it was the only way to save their lives? No . . . even if he wanted to, there's no way he could carry both kits by himself.*

Smoky flopped to the ground and threw his head back to let out a despairing wail. "The Nofurs must have come here, then! I've lost my kits again . . . I have no kits!"

Daisy was dimly aware of Mousewhisker tensing a little, as if wounded by his father's words. Part of her wanted to run her tail over Mousewhisker's back to comfort him. *It's not you;*

49

he never knew you. But there was no time right now to think about that.

Raising her head, Daisy tasted the air, trying to distinguish the various scents. It was difficult to identify any scent over the lingering reek of Coriander's blood. Finally, her nose twitched as she made out the scent she had been searching for.

"Can you smell that?" she asked the others. "It's Alderheart. . . ."

With Daisy in the lead, the cats followed the scent away from the makeshift den and around the edge of the horseplace territory. Daisy jumped, startled, as one of the horses loomed up out of the dusk and gazed at them over the fence, blowing out a long breath through its nostrils.

A few fox-lengths up the hill a tree grew with low, overhanging branches, and as they drew closer, Daisy spotted Alderheart's head poking out of a hollow at the foot.

"Over here!" he called.

The cats raced up the slope to join him; Smoky pushed past him into the hollow tree and exclaimed. "They're here! They're okay!"

"Thank StarClan you found us," Alderheart meowed, emerging into the open. "I had to move the kits away because there was a hawk circling above."

His words made Daisy realize with even sharper anxiety how bad the situation was. The kits were weak and would grow weaker without a queen who would let them nurse, which meant they would grow more vulnerable, too, to hawks or any other predators that might spot them or pick up their scent.

Over Alderheart's shoulder, Daisy could see Smoky crouched over the kits, who lay in a nest of dried leaves. They were squirming around, their tiny mouths stretching wide as they mewled for food. Smoky's eyes shone with love for them.

I have to make him understand how serious the problem is.

Turning to Sorrelstripe and Mousewhisker, Daisy instructed them to go fetch the prey they had abandoned by the den. Then she called Smoky to come out of the hollow tree. Reluctantly the gray-and-white tom padded out to her side, with a last adoring glance at his kits.

"What is it?" he asked.

"In the Clans," Daisy began, "when a cat dies, the whole Clan sits vigil for them and remembers their life. I thought you might like to sit vigil for Coriander."

Smoky's eyes widened a little, and for a moment he hesitated. Then he nodded. "I would like that."

"Good idea," Alderheart mewed approvingly. "Sorrelstripe and Mousewhisker can keep watch here, and I'll feed the kits."

Daisy led the way back to the hollow below the thorn tree, where Coriander's body still lay. She and Smoky cleaned and smoothed her fur, then sat beside her as the darkness deepened and one by one the stars appeared.

Even if StarClan were still connected to us, Coriander would never go there, Daisy thought, *but we can still honor her life, and treat her body with respect.* "You must have loved her very much," she meowed to Smoky.

The gray-and-white tom dipped his head. "More than I can say," he murmured. "She was so beautiful. And she wanted kits so much. She would have made a wonderful mother."

His words gave Daisy the opening to say what she really wanted to say, the reason she had arranged things so that she could talk alone with Smoky.

"If Coriander were here now," she began hesitantly, "do you think she would do whatever it took to take care of the kits?"

"Of course," Smoky retorted instantly.

"Then, right now, that means giving the kits to the Twolegs," Daisy told him. Smoky opened his jaws to protest, but she continued before he could get the words out. "Smoky, you have to understand how bad things are. Feeding the kits with prey won't work for long. They need milk, and the Twolegs have that. Surely Coriander would prefer that to letting them die?"

Smoky reached out a paw to stroke Coriander's fur. There was a hopeless, lost look in his eyes, but when he didn't immediately reject her advice, Daisy realized that he must be considering it. She knew how difficult it was for him, when clearly he loved the kits so much.

"I see the sense in what you say," he admitted at last. "But I want to do everything I can to honor Coriander's dying wish. She was my mate, and I loved her, and I owe her that."

Daisy's chest was roiling with mixed emotions as she listened to Smoky's words. *I wonder what might have been, if I'd stayed here with him,* she asked herself. Her guilt reawakened when she realized what a good father Smoky would have made, and how she had deprived him of the joy of watching their kits grow.

"We'll do all we can, until we can do no more," she

promised him, desperate to comfort him and offer him a way out of his dilemma. "Tomorrow, we'll do our best to find a nursing queen."

The sky was filled with the milky light of dawn when the Clan cats returned to the hollow, Sorrelstripe and Alderheart each carrying a kit. Smoky sprang to his paws as soon as he saw them and hurried over to nuzzle his kits anxiously. Daisy couldn't help noticing how limp and fragile they looked, even more than when they were born the day before.

Beckoning Mousewhisker over to her, she mewed, "We'll have to go to the Twolegplace to find this kittypet Smoky told us about. But before that, I want you to go with Smoky and help him to bury Coriander."

"Do I have to?" Mousewhisker asked.

Daisy met his reluctant gaze with a stony glare. "Yes, you do."

If that doesn't make them start acting like father and son, she thought as she watched the two toms bearing Coriander's body out of the makeshift camp, *nothing will.*

While they were away, Daisy and Sorrelstripe hunted, bringing back enough prey to keep Alderheart and the kits fed while they journeyed to the Twolegplace.

"We'll have to persuade Coco to come back here with us," Daisy mused. "If we take the kits with us, Coco's Twolegs will be bound to notice them."

"Better for them not to be dragged around," Alderheart agreed, pausing as he chewed up a piece of a mouse to feed the kits. "I'll take good care of them here."

As soon as Smoky and Mousewhisker returned, the four cats set out for the Twolegplace. Daisy stayed alert, her fur prickling with apprehension, as they crossed through River-Clan territory, careful to stay within three tail-lengths of the lake. The sun had risen, glittering on the surface of the water, and the breeze carried the strong scent of RiverClan.

You were complaining about being bored, Daisy thought to herself, remembering how aimless her life had seemed in Thunder-Clan. *Well, you're not bored now!* But she still hoped they wouldn't meet a patrol.

"Smoky, do you know where to find Coco's Twoleg den?" Sorrelstripe asked as they reached the outskirts of the Two-legplace.

Smoky looked uncertain. "It's been a while since I hung out here," he replied. "I was too busy taking care of Coriander. But I think I can find Coco, and if not, we can always look for other kittypets to ask."

It would be nice to see Minty again, Daisy thought, remembering the little black-and-white she-cat who had found refuge with ThunderClan during the Great Storm. *I know she would help us.*

At first, as they traveled deeper into the Twolegplace, Smoky led the way confidently. Daisy noticed how Mouse-whisker padded along at his shoulder, listening to his every word. When a dog began barking ferociously from the other side of a fence, Mousewhisker obeyed Smoky's instruction to drop back and keep a lookout at the rear; Smoky picked up the pace until they were racing along, past den after den, and the barking died away behind them.

At the next corner they halted, panting. "Are there many dogs in this Twolegplace?" Daisy asked, trying to conceal how nervous the encounter had made her feel.

"More than you want to know about," Smoky told her. "But most of them are kept tied up in the dens or the gardens. If we stay alert, there's nothing to worry about."

Daisy wasn't sure she believed his reassurances. "We need to find Coco as quickly as we can," she meowed.

"Yes . . ." For the first time Smoky seemed unsure of where to go next. "We'd better cross this Thunderpath," he decided at last.

The Thunderpath was narrow, separating two rows of Twoleg dens, and at this early hour no monsters seemed to be stirring. But Smoky still hesitated at the edge for a long time before giving the signal to cross; Daisy could see Mousewhisker's tail-tip twitching impatiently, but he still waited for his father.

I was right, Daisy thought gratefully. *They are getting along better. And Mousewhisker is starting to show respect for Smoky.*

On the far side of the Thunderpath, Smoky gestured with his tail toward a gap in the fence of the nearest Twoleg garden. "I think this is it," he announced. Then, raising his voice, he called, "Coco!"

There was no response. After a few heartbeats, Smoky approached the gap, which was blocked by a barrier of shiny strips interlaced like bramble tendrils. Peering through, Daisy could see a stretch of smooth grass leading up to the Twoleg den, but no sign of a cat. However, she could pick up cat-scent:

the weird kittypet smell, mingled with traces of Twolegs.

"Follow me," Smoky mewed, beginning to wriggle underneath the barrier.

Daisy exchanged a doubtful glance with Sorrelstripe, and Mousewhisker was the first to obey his father. Sorrelstripe followed, and Daisy brought up the rear, keeping an anxious eye out for any wandering dogs.

As she pushed her way under the barrier, feeling the hard tendrils scrape along her back, Daisy heard Smoky calling out for Coco again. At the same moment, a small flap at the bottom of the den door flicked open, and a cat emerged into the garden.

Daisy hardly had time to feel relief that they had found the cat they were seeking before she realized that this was a tom: long-legged and strongly built, but looking soft in the way of all kittypets, with a fluffy ginger pelt.

"What do you want?" he yowled, stalking up to Smoky and standing in front of him, his tail bushed out until it looked twice its size. "Get out of here, right now, or I'll . . . I'll claw your fur off!"

"I'd like to see you try," Smoky retorted.

Mousewhisker and Sorrelstripe padded up to his side; Daisy straightened up and shook out her pelt before bounding over to join them. *We could* shred *this poor mouse-brain,* she thought, *but we shouldn't do that. We haven't come here to fight.*

"We aren't looking for trouble," she mewed softly to the young kittypet. "What's your name?"

The ginger cat glared at her suspiciously for a moment,

before replying, "I'm called Tom-Tom."

That's the weirdest name I've ever heard! Daisy thought. *It's hardly a name at all. It's like if my name were She-cat-She-cat!*

"We're not here to take your territory," Smoky meowed brusquely. "We're just hoping to find a cat called Coco. I think she lives around here."

Tom-Tom let his shoulder fur lie flat. Tilting his head, he seemed to lose himself deep in thought, though Daisy was pretty sure he was only trying to show off.

"Yes . . . ," he replied at last. "A cat called Coco did live here, a couple of dens in that direction." He angled his ears along the line of dens. "But her housefolk sent her away when she had kits."

Smoky's muscles went tense at Tom-Tom's words. "See?" he hissed bitterly. "You can't ever trust Nofurs."

Daisy stepped in front of her former mate, dipping her head politely to Tom-Tom. "Thank you for your help," she mewed. *Though it's not like it got us anywhere.*

Tom-Tom licked one forepaw and drew it over his ear, looking smugly pleased with himself. "Anytime," he responded. "But don't even think about coming back. I'll claw your ears off if you try to take my territory."

"Really?" Mousewhisker murmured. "I'm terrified!"

"So you should be!" Tom-Tom snapped. "There might be four of you, but I'm super tough. Every cat around here says so."

For a moment, Daisy was worried that her companions might ask Tom-Tom to prove it. "Come on," she meowed.

"We don't want any trouble with this cat. You can see how extraordinarily tough he is," she added, watching Tom-Tom as he sprang onto his hind paws to bat at a butterfly. "And we haven't got time to hang around here. We need to get back and see to the kits."

Smoky let out a low growl, but he bowed his head in agreement. Still, as they walked away, Daisy saw him glaring at the "super-tough" kittypet.

"You'll have to show me your terrifying fighting moves another time," he muttered.

Sunhigh was still some way off when Daisy and the others returned to the camp beside the horseplace. Daisy felt a sick apprehension like a stone in her belly as she wondered what might have happened while they had been away. But when she padded down into the hollow, she found Alderheart bending over the two kits, persuading them to lick up the thrush he had chewed into pulp for them.

He glanced up as Daisy, Smoky, and the other Clan cats came to join him. "Well?" he asked.

Smoky shook his head. "It didn't go well," he replied, his voice rough with emotion. "Coco doesn't live there anymore."

Alderheart's shoulders sagged. Daisy could tell from the growing concern in his eyes that they were running out of time to save the kits.

"I'll go hunt," Smoky continued, seeming to brace himself. "There's so much prey around here, I'm sure the kits will be well fed."

He bounded up the slope and disappeared. Mousewhisker and Sorrelstripe followed him.

Alderheart watched them go, shaking his head slightly. "Smoky is trying to convince us that the kits will be fine," he murmured. "But he can't even convince himself."

"I think he's still trying to prove there's no need to take them to the Clans, or to the Twolegs," Daisy pointed out.

"Yes, I'm sure you're right."

"Is there any hope for them if we don't?" Daisy asked, her heart pounding as she waited for the medicine cat's answer.

Alderheart hesitated before replying. "I'm very concerned," he confessed at last. "The kits are sleeping a lot, and they're hard to rouse. That's not normal."

"But they are feeding?" Daisy asked, dabbing her paw into the thrush pulp and offering it to the little tortoiseshell. The kit sniffed at it, then turned her head away.

"More than once, I've had to make sure they don't choke on the food," Alderheart told her. "They're too young and weak to swallow easily. They'll need proper nursing soon." He paused again, blinking thoughtfully. "I'm not sure, but I think there might be new kits in SkyClan."

Daisy's eyes widened in surprise. "That's a long way from here."

Alderheart nodded. "True, but at this point, it might be these kits' best chance of survival."

He had hardly finished speaking when Smoky reappeared at the top of the hollow, a shrew dangling from his jaws. "There!" he exclaimed, dropping it beside the kits' nest. "That should keep them going for a while."

Daisy felt her heart break to hear the bravado in his voice as he tried to reassure himself that his kits would live. "Smoky," she meowed, "I want a word with you. Come walk with me."

Smoky darted a suspicious glance at her, but made no objection when Daisy led the way out of the hollow once again and headed toward the lake.

"You're doing a great job for the kits," Daisy began. "But—"

"We need to stop calling them 'the kits,'" Smoky interrupted. "I should name them."

Daisy hesitated, not knowing how to respond.

"What's the matter?" Smoky asked, beginning to sound irritated.

He still reads me pretty well, even though it's been seasons since we were together, Daisy thought. "Nothing, except—" she began.

"Except you obviously think I shouldn't name them!" Smoky halted, glaring at Daisy. "Why not?"

"Okay, you're right," Daisy admitted. "I think maybe you should take a little more time. . . ."

Smoky drew his lips back in a snarl. "You would only say that if you were planning to take the kits away!"

"No, I'm only thinking of you," Daisy protested, refusing to let her former mate's hostility scare her. "I want nothing more than to see the kits stay with you. But if something happens, and we have to give the kits to the Twolegs to keep them alive, it might hurt you worse if you've named them."

Her reasoning seemed to enrage Smoky even more. "So you are still thinking about giving my kits to the Twolegs!" he snapped. "You've taken three of my kits away already. I finally have another chance to be a father—you can't take that away from me now. These two aren't even yours!"

Guilt surged over Daisy once more. Everything she did seemed to reawaken his sense of loss. But as a mother of kits, she could only think of what was best for the vulnerable newborns.

"Smoky, I don't want to take the kits away from you," she meowed. "But their lives are at stake." She paused, then continued when Smoky made no response. "Alderheart told me he thinks there's a nursing queen in SkyClan. I think we should take the kits there, and ask Leafstar for help. It could be their only chance."

"I made a promise to Coriander," Smoky growled. "I won't betray her the way you betrayed me!"

While he was speaking, Daisy realized that Mousewhisker had approached them unseen, from the direction of the makeshift camp. He looked startled and uneasy as he glanced from Smoky to Daisy and back again.

He's never seen his parents arguing like this, Daisy thought. *It must feel very odd.*

"I . . . er . . . I came to ask if you want any prey?" Mousewhisker stammered, giving his chest fur an embarrassed lick.

"Thank you, we'd like that," Daisy responded, with a glance at Smoky to warn him not to snap at their son.

Mousewhisker still looked very concerned as all three cats headed back toward the camp, though his eyes shone with pride as he presented a plump vole to his father. Smoky grunted thanks. "I'm not hungry," he mewed, "but I'll chew some up for the kits to eat later. They'll enjoy that."

"Smoky," Alderheart began, his voice gentle but firm, "giving the kits fresh-kill is because this is an emergency, and it's all we have. They need to nurse. I'm a medicine cat, and I won't argue about this. We need to take them to SkyClan right away. I promise you, that won't mean you have to stay there and raise your kits in the Clans, but you won't have kits to raise at all if you don't make the choice now."

Smoky looked up at the young medicine cat. Daisy could see how the stress of deciding was tearing him apart, and she stretched out her tail to touch him briefly on the shoulder.

"All right," Smoky agreed at last, with a heavy sigh. "We'll go to SkyClan."

Daisy's pelt tingled all over with relief, though now she worried about the long journey to reach the SkyClan camp.

The kits are weak and struggling even when they're resting. How will the journey to SkyClan affect them? Oh, StarClan, I just hope they survive. . . .

CHAPTER 6

Alderheart rose to his paws. "Smoky, you have to eat," he meowed. "It's a long way to SkyClan, and you'll need the energy."

Smoky rapidly gulped down the rest of the vole and padded over to where his two kits lay. He picked up the little tortoiseshell by the scruff; the tiny she-cat waved her paws feebly and let out a faint squeak. Daisy exchanged a glance with Alderheart; neither of them spoke, but Daisy knew they were both worried to see the kit so weak.

Mousewhisker finished off his blackbird and swiped his tongue around his jaws before joining Smoky to pick up the second kit. Instantly Smoky stepped forward to intercept him, giving him a fierce glare.

"Don't be a mouse-brain, Smoky," Daisy scolded him. "You can't possibly carry both kits all that way by yourself. Remember, you called us here for a reason—you don't have to do this alone."

"I only want to help my kin," Mousewhisker added, dipping his head respectfully to his father.

Smoky hesitated for a moment longer, then took a pace back, giving a grunt of assent. Mousewhisker picked up the gray tom-kit, and Alderheart led the way down to the lake.

As soon as they reached it, Daisy spotted a small group of cats in the distance, picking their way along the shoreline. "A WindClan patrol," she sighed. "That's all we need!"

As the cats drew closer, Daisy could make out the skinny black figure of Breezepelt in the lead, with Woodsong and Appleshine following him closely. She tensed, alert for trouble.

Breezepelt used to be a pain in the tail, she reflected, *though I have to admit, in the last few seasons he seems to have grown up at last. Even so, it doesn't take much to make him as angry as a fox in a fit.*

The black warrior was bristling with hostility as he padded up to Daisy and the others. "What are you doing on our territory?" he demanded, narrowing his eyes in a suspicious glare.

Alderheart stepped forward to face him with a polite dip of his head. "Nothing for you to worry about," he replied. "These kits have lost their mother, and they might not survive unless we can find a nursing queen."

Breezepelt glanced past Alderheart, and his unfriendly expression softened. "Sorry, Alderheart," he mewed. "I didn't see them there."

"Poor little things!" Woodsong pressed forward to sniff the little gray tom. "I wish I had milk! I'd feed them if I could."

"So would I," Appleshine added, her eyes wide with sympathy.

Breezepelt's shoulder fur was lying flat again. His suspicion seemed to be replaced by concern. "Is there anything we can do to help?" he asked.

"Not unless you have a nursing queen in WindClan," Daisy responded.

The WindClan warrior shook his head. "I'm sorry, we don't."

"Then just let us pass," Alderheart meowed with an impatient twitch of his whiskers. "We think there might be a she-cat in SkyClan who can help."

"I hope you're right." Breezepelt stepped back and urged Smoky and the ThunderClan cats along the shoreline with a swish of his tail. As Daisy passed him, he stretched out one paw to halt her. "Maybe I'm wrong, but those kits look like they won't even survive the journey to SkyClan," he murmured, his voice soft so that the other cats couldn't hear.

"That's what worries me," Daisy confessed. The kits' weakness was obvious now, as they hung limply from Smoky's and Mousewhisker's jaws like pieces of fresh-kill. "We've been feeding them pulped prey, but they're only getting weaker. We may not be able to save them, but we can try."

"Then I wish you good luck," Breezepelt responded.

As she hurried to catch up with the others, Daisy wondered once again whether it was getting too late to find some Twolegs to take care of the kits. With every paw step they were getting farther away from the Twoleg dens, so they wouldn't have the choice for much longer. *Have I made the right decision?* she asked herself. *Have I valued Smoky's feelings over the kits' survival?*

The cool water was soothing on Daisy's sore paws as she waded through the stream that marked the WindClan border with ThunderClan. "Maybe we shouldn't go straight to Sky-Clan," she meowed to Alderheart as they watched Smoky and Mousewhisker crossing, holding the kits high above the water so they wouldn't get splashed. "What do you say of going to our camp first, for a rest?"

Alderheart nodded. "I was thinking the same thing. I want to consult Jayfeather; traveling herbs might give the kits a bit of extra strength, and I know we have some in the herb store."

Daisy felt renewed optimism as they turned away from the lake and headed inland toward the ThunderClan camp. She felt as though the very worst couldn't happen now that she was back on her home territory . . . even though she knew there was no reason to feel that way.

When Daisy followed Alderheart through the thorn tunnel, the camp seemed almost deserted. Most cats, she guessed, would be out hunting or on patrol. Bristlefrost and Cherryfall were sharing a piece of prey beside the fresh-kill pile, while at the opposite side of the hollow the elders were sunning themselves on a flat rock near the camp wall.

As soon as they entered the camp, Alderheart bounded over to the medicine cats' den and disappeared behind the bramble screen. Alerted by the movement, Bristlefrost sprang to her paws and dashed across to stand underneath the Highledge.

"Squirrelflight!" she yowled. "Daisy and Mousewhisker are back!"

Squirrelflight emerged from her den onto the Highledge, followed closely by Lionblaze. Both cats leaped swiftly down the tumbled rocks and joined Jayfeather as he appeared from his den.

Daisy advanced to meet them alongside Smoky and Mousewhisker, each carrying a kit. Jayfeather's blind blue eyes widened as they approached, and he gave each kit a deep sniff.

"What in the name of StarClan are you *thinking?*" he snarled. "These kits are dying! They should be with their mother."

Daisy noticed Smoky's fur beginning to bristle with outrage. She stretched out her tail to lay it reassuringly on her former mate's shoulder, reflecting that he wasn't used to Jayfeather's abrasive tone. ThunderClan cats knew that he meant well, despite his brutal honesty.

Though I wish he'd kept the harsh truth about the kits to himself.

But seeing Squirrelflight and Lionblaze standing alert but calm beside the medicine cat, their past bickering apparently forgotten, Daisy felt a surge of strength and certainty she hadn't known for some time.

"Their mother is dead, Jayfeather," she meowed calmly. "We're doing the best we can."

"Your best might not be good enough," Jayfeather retorted. "Bring them into the den and let me examine them."

Smoky seemed reluctant to obey. "Who does he think he is?" he grumbled around his mouthful of fur.

"The best medicine cat in all the Clans," Daisy told him, giving him a shove in the direction of the den. "If you want your kits to survive, then move!"

Slowly, Smoky followed Jayfeather to his den, with

Mousewhisker and Daisy flanking him. Sorrelstripe padded up to Squirrelflight and began to report what had happened.

Inside the medicine cats' den, Alderheart was arranging moss to make a nest for the kits. Smoky and Mousewhisker gently set them down there. Their paws twitched a little as they settled into the soft bedding, but after that they didn't move, and Daisy could see that they were hardly breathing. A pang of guilt shook her. *What if I've killed them, by agreeing to take them to the Clans, when what they need is help from Twolegs? I know more about kits than Smoky; I should have insisted. . . .*

Trying not to let herself despair, Daisy let out a long, anxious sigh. *Oh, Jayfeather, you have to do something!*

"Okay, you can all leave now," Jayfeather announced. "Alderheart and I need space to work."

"I'm not leaving my kits!" Smoky protested, his fur starting to bush up again.

Daisy rested her tail on his shoulder. "You must," she mewed gently. "They'll be fine with Jayfeather."

Smoky opened his jaws to argue, then closed them again. His shoulders sagged. "Okay," he muttered.

Daisy urged him out past the bramble screen. Mousewhisker followed. "You two go and rest," he meowed. "I'll wait out here and bring you news as soon as there is any."

"Thanks, Mousewhisker," Daisy responded.

As she and Smoky padded away, Daisy could hear Jayfeather issuing orders. "Alderheart, fetch me traveling herbs from the store. Make sure you pick out the freshest ones."

Daisy guided Smoky into the nursery and showed him

where he could curl up, in her own nest. *This feels seriously strange,* she thought. *Almost as if Smoky had come to ThunderClan with me when I left the horseplace.* She stifled a small sigh. *Everything would have been different then.*

"How long will this take?" Smoky asked anxiously.

"We'll carry on to SkyClan soon," she mewed gently.

Smoky nodded, giving her a long look, and somehow Daisy knew what he was going to say before he spoke. "I know you're afraid the kits won't survive this journey," he began. "But there's something about them that convinces me they can make it. They're strong, like their mother." His voice shaking, he added, "Oh, I miss her so much!"

Daisy's belly lurched with the sympathy she felt for him, and she tried hard to ignore her twinge of regret that he had surely missed the kits they had together. He had lost Floss's kits, too, when the Twolegs took them. They were probably still alive somewhere, but Smoky would never see them again.

Daisy could understand why he wanted so desperately to keep these kits, but she was still worried they could die because of his stubbornness. *If they do, it will be my fault too,* she thought, with a renewed pang of guilt. *Oh, poor Smoky!*

From the nursery entrance, Daisy could see Mousewhisker waiting patiently outside the medicine cats' den. Silently she resolved that whatever happened, Smoky would have a relationship with one of his kits.

After what felt like an excruciating wait, but was probably only moments, Jayfeather poked his head out from behind the bramble screen and said something to Mousewhisker. The gray-and-white tom rose to his paws and padded across to the nursery.

Shaking her pelt, Daisy went out to meet him, with Smoky hard on her paws. She realized that Squirrelflight had waited, too, and came over to join them, her green gaze full of concern.

"What's happening?" Smoky asked, his voice hoarse with anxiety. "Are my kits okay?"

Mousewhisker nodded. "Jayfeather says they're strong enough for you to take them to SkyClan, if that's still what you want to do."

Squirrelflight let out a sigh. "What choice do they have?"

Crossing the camp, Daisy, Smoky, and Mousewhisker entered the medicine cats' den once more. There was a tang of fresh herbs in the air, and Daisy saw smears of green pulp on the kits' lips.

"They took quite a lot of the traveling herbs," Alderheart told them. "That should keep them going until we get them to SkyClan."

Smoky, gazing down at the tiny, limp bodies, didn't seem convinced. "I wonder if there's anything else we can do," he meowed. "I'm not sure they'll make it to SkyClan. Maybe you were right . . . about the Twolegs."

Daisy cast a worried glance at him. *Is he changing his mind?* she wondered. "It's too late for that now," she pointed out briskly. "We're closer to SkyClan now than to any Twoleg dens. And we think there might be a new litter just born in their camp."

"Which means, there's a queen who might be able to nurse these kits, and save them," Jayfeather added, from where he sat in his nest licking herb pulp off his paws. "And I'm sure Leafstar will allow her warriors to help, however they can. Getting the kits to SkyClan is the best chance they'll have. So get a move on—the sooner you're out from under my paws, the sooner you'll get there."

Smoky hesitated for a heartbeat more, then straightened up, looking resolved. "You're right, Jayfeather," he meowed. "Let's go."

Daisy nodded and followed. *Oh, StarClan, guide our paws, and help these kits,* she prayed, even though she wasn't sure her prayer would do any good. StarClan had been silent for so long.

Sorrelstripe had returned to her warrior duties, but Alderheart and Mousewhisker accompanied Daisy and Smoky as they left the ThunderClan camp. Squirrelflight followed them through the thorn tunnel and into the forest. "May StarClan light your path!" she called after them as they padded off through the trees.

Daisy kept a close eye on the kits, alert for any signs of distress, as they dangled from Smoky's and Mousewhisker's jaws. Her heart felt close to breaking at the sight of the determined look on Mousewhisker's face. It was clear he was doing all he could to help his tiny kin.

As they crossed a clearing near the ThunderClan border, Daisy's thoughts were interrupted by a shadow sweeping over her. Looking up, she spotted a hawk circling above them.

Smoky let out a yowl of alarm, instinctively curling up and tucking the kit close against his chest to shield her from the hawk's view. Mousewhisker set his kit down gently and stood protectively over him, arching his back and snarling in defiance at the fierce bird.

"Take cover!" Alderheart yowled.

The sight of the helpless kits sent a surge of fierce determination through Daisy, even though the hawk's flapping wings and gnarled talons chilled her as if every drop of her blood had frozen. The hawk swooped down on her; she caught a glimpse of its small, malignant eyes as she put all her strength into a slash of her claws.

For a moment the bird was driven back, but it wheeled and swooped again. This time it aimed over Daisy's head, flying straight for the toms, who were still crouched over the kits, trying to protect them. As its shadow fell across her again, Daisy leaped into the air, and she managed to snag one foreclaw into the hawk's foot.

The hawk let out a harsh cry, flapping its wings as it changed course and struggled to gain height. But Daisy's claw was stuck, and she weighed the hawk down, even though her hind legs were almost lifting off the ground. Her heart pounding with terror, she tried her best to sink her weight into her hindquarters, so the bird couldn't fly off with her.

But, oh, StarClan, it's so strong. . . .

The hawk's wings were flapping around Daisy's head, battering at her, and she felt her strength ebbing. Dimly she could hear her Clanmates and Smoky calling out to her.

"Protect the kits!" she called back weakly. "Get them to SkyClan, whatever happens!"

Then Daisy felt paws grasping at her hind legs, holding her down. Her grip gave way and the bird lifted up toward the sky with another harsh screech, almost drowned out by the defiant yowling of cats. She collapsed to the ground, shaking all over with a mixture of terror and relief. At the same time, her heart clenched with fear for the newborns. *If Smoky and Mouse-whisker are helping me, who is protecting the kits?*

Then, as Daisy dared to look up, she saw that it wasn't her companions who were driving back the hawk. Instead, three large, muscular she-cats were hurling themselves upward, snarling and lashing out at the fierce bird with extended claws.

Daisy blinked at them in bewilderment. *Who are they? Where did they spring from?* She tasted the air, vaguely aware that she should recognize their scent. But it took several heartbeats before she remembered where she had smelled it before.

It's the Sisters!

CHAPTER 7

Daisy watched, stunned, as the three she-cats drove the hawk away, leaping and yowling at it until it flapped its strong wings and took to the air, then vanished above the treetops. Then the Sisters turned back and padded over to where Daisy still lay on the ground, regarding her and the other cats with faint, almost bemused curiosity. Daisy was grateful that they showed no sign of hostility.

"My name is Snow. Are you hurt?" the one who seemed to be their leader asked.

Daisy stared at the leader's white pelt with its flecks of gray. "No, I'm fine," she replied, scrambling to her paws. "Thank you so much!"

"And the kits?" Snow asked.

"They're okay, too," Smoky told her. "The hawk didn't touch them."

"You smell of ThunderClan," Snow continued, purring warmly. "What is your name?"

"Daisy. I usually stay in the nursery and help with the kits." Snow nodded. "That is important work. I'm not surprised to see that you have distressed kits in need. I was pretty sure I scented them when we patrolled close to ThunderClan's camp."

"You could tell from that distance that kits were in trouble?" Daisy asked, amazed.

Snow nodded. "Yes, and that hawk isn't your only problem, is it?" Snow asked. "Why are you trekking through the forest with newborn ThunderClan kits? Why aren't they with their mother?"

"Their mother is dead," Smoky replied. "And they *aren't* Clan cats."

"We have to find a nursing queen," Alderheart replied. "We think there might be one in SkyClan."

"Yes, we scented their newborns too, on our patrols," Snow meowed. "But the Clans are unpredictable, as you know. Our Sister Sunshine has kitted recently. If you come to our camp, I'm sure she'd be happy to help you."

"Really? Oh, thank you!" Daisy exchanged a glance with Smoky, and saw her own joy and relief reflected in his eyes. Then she remembered that the Sisters never settled in one place. In fact, the Clans were not thrilled to have them nearby. *What will happen if they want to move on?* "Are you going to be here long?" she asked nervously.

"For a while," Snow responded. "We're staying near the lake for a moon or two. I don't believe you came to the ceremony we led to find Bramblestar, did you?"

Daisy shook her head. "I was away from camp at the time.

I heard about it when I returned, but . . . I can't say I fully understood."

Snow nodded seriously. "I am sorry for your grief. These seem like tragic times for your Clans. We were disturbed by the angry spirits we observed during the ceremony, and we felt it best to settle nearby. In the meantime, we'll be happy to help these poor orphaned kits."

"I'm really grateful to you," Smoky mewed, taking a pace forward. "But they're not orphans. They're *my* kits. And I don't intend to give them up."

Snow nodded, looking faintly surprised, but did not question Smoky further. Gesturing with her tail for the toms to gather up the kits again, she led the way into the trees.

Daisy brought up the rear, drawing in huge breaths of relief that she and her friends had found help where she never would have thought to expect it. *The Sisters,* she mused, following Snow and the others through the trees. *I still have so much to learn about you, but I'm so glad you're here.*

The Sisters had made their camp in a hollow just beyond the ThunderClan border. A stream trickled out from between two boulders, and there were gorse and elder bushes to provide shelter. Daisy didn't think she would want to live there permanently, but for the time being it made a comfortable camp, and she was thankful for the security and the Sisters' orderly way of life, especially when Smoky's kits needed so much care.

Sunshine, a plump cream she-cat, had welcomed the two tiny creatures warmly, purring as they burrowed into the curve of her belly beside her own two kits. After they had stayed a few days with the Sisters, Daisy began to believe that they would survive. At last their eyes had opened, the deep blue of newborn kits, and Smoky had hardly been able to contain his joy.

"They're looking much stronger, aren't they?" Daisy asked Alderheart as he ducked beneath a low-hanging gorse branch into Sunshine's den. The medicine cat had returned to ThunderClan, but he visited the kits every two or three days.

Alderheart gave the kits a good sniff. Sunshine's own kits were a few days older, but he had taken all four into his care, and Daisy realized that Sunshine welcomed the advice of a trained Clan medicine cat. And she wasn't the only one. *The Sisters might turn their noses up at our way of life in the Clans,* Daisy thought, *but they've no problem consulting Alderheart if they get sick.*

"They're doing fine," Alderheart replied to Daisy. "Sunshine, you're doing an excellent job."

"Thank you," Sunshine purred.

Crouched beside Sunshine, Smoky was gazing adoringly at his kits. He raised his head, fixing his look on Daisy. "I want to ask you something," he mewed. "Do you think the kits are strong enough now for me to name them?"

"I do," Daisy replied. "You heard what Alderheart said."

Smoky gazed at the kits for a long time, deep in thought. "I'll name the tom Coriander, after his mother," he decided.

"And I'll name the she-kit . . . Daisy, because if it weren't for you, she wouldn't be here."

Daisy felt overwhelmed. "I'm honored, but I don't deserve it," she meowed. "Alderheart is the one who treated them, and found a way to feed them. Mousewhisker and Sorrelstripe hunted for food with me."

"But you were the one who attacked the hawk," Smoky reminded her. "You were so brave! And it was because of you that Squirrelflight let you and Alderheart come with me in the first place."

Daisy bowed her head, deeply humbled. For a moment she almost felt like a mother to the two kits; that was the way she used to feel in ThunderClan, toward the kits she helped raise, but she hadn't felt it for quite a while.

What would my life be now if I'd stayed with Smoky all those moons ago? she asked herself once more. *If we'd stayed as a family with Berry, Mouse, and Hazel, as we called them back then . . .*

Clearly Smoky had noticed the way she was looking at the kits. "They're wonderful, aren't they?" he purred.

"They're perfect," Daisy agreed. "I'm really happy for you." Without really thinking, she added, "Finally you have the family you always deserved."

Smoky's expression darkened. "I would have had that a long time ago, if you hadn't taken our kits away," he told her, his voice harder. "And maybe . . ."

Daisy drew in a gasping breath, asking herself what Smoky would say next, though she already knew the answer. *He's going to blame me for their deaths, because I took them to ThunderClan. And maybe he's not wrong. . . .*

But Smoky didn't say the words, just settled down beside his kits, his head turned away from Daisy. Feeling she had been dismissed, Daisy rose to her paws and slipped out of the den.

CHAPTER 8
❧

Daisy and Smoky sat side by side in the shade of an elder bush, watching the kits play outside Sunshine's den. Almost a moon had passed since they had come to stay with the Sisters. Alderheart and Mousewhisker had long ago returned to ThunderClan to help deal with the problems their Clanmates still faced. Daisy hadn't been ready to go with them then. Though Alderheart had been deliberately vague about the news from ThunderClan, Daisy knew that the impostor who had taken Bramblestar's place had escaped the Clans' custody. Worse, Squirrelflight was missing, and every cat was worried about her. Daisy had no idea what was going in in the Clan now . . . or what she would find when she returned. She hadn't believed that things could get worse for ThunderClan when she'd left, but it seemed they had.

Coriander and Little Daisy were able to eat fresh-kill now, and were growing strong and healthy, with bright eyes and shining pelts. Just now they were padding around, pawing at everything, their eyes wide and curious. Their helpless squeaks had given way to strong, loud meows.

They'd make excellent apprentices, when they're old enough, Daisy thought. *But I wouldn't dare say that to Smoky. He's speaking to me again now, but he'd claw my ears off if I suggested that any more of his kits might go live within a Clan!*

Daisy was roused from her thoughts by the appearance of Snow, who padded over to join her and Smoky, and sat beside them, her tail wrapped around her forepaws.

"I think the kits are strong enough now," the Sisters' leader meowed.

Daisy didn't need to ask what she meant. She knew that the Sisters would not normally have hosted guests for this long. Some of them had grown fond of Daisy, Smoky, and the kits, even though they could not have been happy to have a full-grown tom staying in their camp. It was time for Daisy and Smoky to take the kits home.

But where is home?

"They aren't fully weaned yet," Daisy mewed hesitantly.

"They'll be fine," Snow reassured her.

Daisy didn't want to seem ungrateful for the Sisters' help by asking for more, when they had already done so much. And it was true that the kits had grown faster than she'd expected, nourished by Sunshine's abundant milk. *Another half-moon would be nice,* she thought, *but they're strong enough to survive now.*

"You're right," she told Snow. "We'll be ready when you tell us to leave." She couldn't manage to suppress a sigh.

Snow blinked sympathetically, clearly understanding Daisy's indecision. "I know things are strange for you, and the Clans, right now," she began. "I won't force you to make a decision right away. But it will need to be soon."

Smoky was padding beside his kits, telling them the names of the plants that edged the clearing, and nudging them back onto their paws when they tumbled over in their eagerness to explore. He hadn't heard what Snow said, and for the time being, Daisy didn't want to tell him. She needed a little space to think things out.

But by the time darkness fell, Daisy was no nearer deciding what was best to do. She realized that she couldn't keep Snow's message from Smoky any longer, so she padded across to Smoky's makeshift nest under a gorse bush, where he slept with the kits. She herself had made a nest in the shelter of a rock at the far side of the Sisters' camp, needing to make clear to every cat that she was not part of Smoky's family.

Smoky had curled himself around the sleeping kits, and he looked up drowsily as Daisy approached. "Is something the matter?" he asked.

"No, but Snow spoke to me today," Daisy replied, sitting beside him. "She says it's time for us to leave."

Smoky nodded, unsurprised. "I knew this day would come," he mewed. "I suppose you will go back to ThunderClan."

For a moment Daisy couldn't reply. She had assumed that, too, and was startled to find her feelings tugging her in another direction.

"Or will you?" Smoky was swift to seize on her hesitation. "I can see you haven't made up your mind."

"You're imagining things," Daisy responded. Part of her was pleased that he knew her so well, though she couldn't stifle a prickle of irritation too. "Of course I'm going back to

ThunderClan. More important, where are *you* going? Where are you going to take the kits? You can't go back to the horse-place with them."

"I've been thinking about that," Smoky told her. "And I've decided that maybe I can."

Daisy sat up straighter, her fur bristling with shock. "But you promised Coriander—"

"I promised her not to let Nofurs take the kits," Smoky interrupted. "But listen—all the time I've lived at the horse-place, the Nofurs have kept two or three cats there, to catch mice in the barn. Now they don't have any cats at all, so I reckon they must be missing them. And they've always seemed to *really* like kits. So I think there's a good chance that they'll let us all stay there together."

Daisy gave her shoulder fur a couple of thoughtful licks. "It's a risk," she mewed at last.

"I know," Smoky sighed. "But we can't live as loners, not with all the foxes and badgers around—and hawks," he added, reminding Daisy of the fearsome encounter in the forest. "And I would break my word to Coriander if I took the kits to live in a Clan. So the horseplace it is. Of course, the kits would be safer if there were some cat around who wasn't afraid to battle a hawk."

"You don't mean—" Daisy began, startled.

"Come with us," Smoky interrupted, his voice suddenly urgent. "I know it won't be the same as living in a Clan, but we could be a family."

"Oh, I couldn't . . . ," Daisy murmured, but even as she

spoke, she found she was beginning to doubt herself. *Maybe I could.*

It would mean changing everything about her life. Even if ThunderClan was going through difficult times, it had been her home for the most important years of her life, and there were many cats she loved there. She still had Mousewhisker to think of. The thought of not going back to the Thunder-Clan nursery felt wrong in so many ways. And yet . . . as Daisy returned to her own nest to settle down for the night, Smoky's words echoed in her mind. *I have a choice,* she thought. *Bramble-star is gone; Squirrelflight is missing; who knows whether StarClan will make contact ever again?* It was not the same ThunderClan that she had joined so many moons ago. And while it pained her to think it, still she had to wonder: *Would it be so bad if I joined Smoky in the horseplace?*

Saying good-bye to the Sisters, Daisy and Smoky set out the next morning with Little Daisy and Coriander. Daisy was escorting them to the horseplace, just to make sure that Smoky and the kits got there safely.

She couldn't help thinking how different this journey was from the one just over a moon before. Then the kits had had to be carried, hanging limply on the brink of death; now they were sturdy and very much alive, bouncing vigorously from one new and enticing scent to the next, filling the forest with their excited squeals.

They reminded Daisy so strongly of her own kits at that age that her heart filled with love and the need to protect them. *How can I even think about leaving them?*

To her relief, they didn't meet either ThunderClan or WindClan patrols on their way back to the horseplace. When they reached the fence that surrounded it, Smoky paused.

"Daisy, would you stay with us, at least for a while?" he meowed. "Just until the kits are a little older and more experienced. Then they won't be so upset when you go back to your Clan."

Daisy took a couple of heartbeats to think. She guessed that Smoky was hoping that once she settled down at the horseplace she would eventually decide to stay. *And I have to admit, I am considering it. . . .*

"For a while," she replied at last.

Smoky wriggled under the fence, gesturing for Daisy and the kits to follow him. Instead of heading for the barn, he turned toward the Twolegs' den. A monster was crouched outside it; Daisy's nose twitched with distaste as she picked up its acrid scent. She'd once lived among these monsters, but now she eyed it nervously, ready to skirt around it in a wide circle. Meanwhile, Smoky strolled nonchalantly up to it.

"It's asleep," he pointed out. "You and the kits hide here, behind it, and wait for me."

Daisy kept the kits close to her with a sweep of her tail while she crouched uneasily beside one of the monster's huge black paws. Meanwhile Smoky padded up to the entrance to the Twoleg den and let out a loud yowl.

Every muscle in her body tense, Daisy watched as the door opened and a male Twoleg emerged. He looked down at Smoky with an annoyed expression that suddenly changed to one of relief. Bending down, he scooped up Smoky in his forelegs and held him close. Daisy was surprised that Smoky let him do it, even pushing his face into the Twoleg's shoulder.

But I can tell that's a totally fake purr!

As soon as the Twoleg put Smoky down again, Smoky glanced over his shoulder and yowled to Daisy, "Bring the kits!"

Daisy rose to her paws and nudged the kits forward. At first Coriander and Little Daisy hung back, their eyes wide and nervous.

"Come on," Daisy urged them, giving each of them another gentle prod. "It'll be fine." *Please, StarClan,* she added to herself, *let that be the truth.*

Both kits were shaking with terror as they padded forward to where their father was waiting for them. A female Twoleg had joined the male at the entrance to the den; both of them let out astonished noises when they saw the kits. They crouched down, reaching out with their forepaws; Daisy braced herself to attack if they showed any signs of grabbing them and taking them inside their den. But the Twolegs seemed content to stroke Smoky and the kits, making happy, welcoming sounds.

They'd be purring, if they knew how!

Daisy relaxed, breathing a huge sigh of relief. It looked as if everything was going to be okay.

In the next few days Daisy could feel that she, Smoky, and the kits were settling down as a family. The Twolegs often came to visit the kits in the barn and play with them, but they never took them away. Instead they brought them food and bowls of milk, and round, brightly colored objects that made tinkling sounds when the kits batted them across the floor of the barn. The ThunderClan part of Daisy recoiled at the thought of being fed by Twolegs, but she knew that these Twolegs would make sure the kits were healthy and strong, just as they always cared for their horses. As long as they didn't take the kits away—which they seemed to have no intention of doing—they could only help Smoky and his new family.

Watching the kits as they wrestled together playfully, Daisy tried to imagine herself as a permanent part of that family. She had always been fond of Smoky, and she adored Coriander and Little Daisy. She felt that they needed her, which would give her life the purpose she felt she had lost in ThunderClan.

Going back to living so close to the Twoleg world, surrounded by their strange possessions and stinky scents, would be a big change from living in the forest. She tried to imagine never waking in the nursery again, never padding out to share fresh-kill with her Clanmates under a tree. She tried to imagine never helping a frightened queen with her kitting again. Never licking the kit clean or trying to warm a weak or ailing kit with her rough tongue. Never pushing a newborn kit toward a queen to nurse, or seeing the glazed happiness in the eyes of a new mother.

But that hasn't been my life in ThunderClan lately anyway, Daisy reminded herself. She'd been struggling with such a sense of uselessness before she left. *And when I did leave . . . I still lost*

Coriander. She shuddered. The last kitting she'd attended wasn't one she wanted to relive.

Still . . . am I ready to give up on them—on my Clan—forever?

A paw step behind her made her turn to see Smoky slipping into the barn through one of the gaps in the door. A vole was dangling from his jaws.

"I think the kits will enjoy this," he mewed. "I don't want them to always eat Nofur food."

The kits . . . our *kits.* Even though they weren't really hers, Daisy could help raise Little Daisy and Coriander. And while she didn't know what she'd face upon returning to Thunder-Clan, she knew what it was to raise a kit. She'd watch them grow and change. She'd fall in love with each new version of each kit, as they grew from helpless to awkward to assured. And she would adore the full-grown cats they would some-day become, just as she adored Mousewhisker. Just as she'd adored each of her kits. "Come along, kits!" Daisy called. "See what your father has brought for you!"

When they were all crouched together, sharing the vole, Daisy felt a warm sense of happiness spreading inside her. *This is perfect,* she thought, letting out a contented purr. *This is what I want . . . isn't it?*

Smoky raised his head to look at her; she saw hope in his eyes. *He wants me to stay.*

And as she bit into the vole, listening to the kits chatter happily, her memories of ThunderClan seemed to fade.

I think I want to stay.

* * *

Daisy slipped through the thorn tunnel into the Thunder-Clan camp. Darkness had fallen; a pale, eerie light lay across the stone hollow, though when she looked up she couldn't see the moon or stars.

Spotting her son Mousewhisker beside the fresh-kill pile with Sorrelstripe and Lilyheart, Daisy padded over to join them, calling out a greeting. Warmth filled her from ears to tail-tip as she realized how good it was to be home.

But none of the cats she spoke to seemed to hear her; instead, they carried on their own conversation.

"Did you see the squirrel Bristlefrost brought back?" Mousewhisker asked. "It was almost big enough to feed the whole Clan!"

"She's a great hunter," Lilyheart agreed.

"Hey, mouse-brain!" Daisy prodded Mousewhisker in the side. "It's me! I'm back!"

But Mousewhisker still didn't respond, as if he hadn't heard her voice or felt her prodding paw.

Annoyance began to prick Daisy like a horde of ants crawling through her pelt. *If this is their idea of a joke, I don't think it's very funny!*

Before she could speak again, paw steps sounded behind her, and Ivypool appeared, carrying a vole, which she let drop on the fresh-kill pile. Whitewing and Bumblestripe, the rest of the hunting patrol, followed her and deposited their own prey.

"Whitewing," Daisy began, knowing that the gentle she-cat wouldn't play a trick on her, "what's going on? No cat will speak to me."

But Whitewing's gaze slid across her as if she weren't there. Without a word she padded off toward the warriors' den.

Thoroughly frightened now, Daisy glanced around her. The walls of the stone hollow shimmered in the strange light and seemed to lean inward, as if they were going to collapse and bury her under a mountain of rock.

Throwing back her head, Daisy let out a terrified yowl . . . and woke in her nest in the barn at the horseplace.

Daisy raised her head, glancing across to the nest which Smoky shared with his kits. She was afraid that her cry had disturbed them. Smoky shifted a little, drawing the kits closer to him, and Coriander let out a drowsy squeak, but as Daisy watched, they settled back into deeper sleep.

Shuddering, Daisy remembered her dream and wondered what it could mean. She had been feeling so happy and content here with Smoky and the kits, but now she wasn't sure what she wanted. Could the dream be telling her that her Clan needed her, and she should go back? Or was the way every cat ignored her a sign that she didn't belong there anymore?

Daisy knew StarClan was still silent. Even if they weren't, she wasn't a medicine cat, so this was just a dream, not a prophecy. Still, she felt that her heart was trying to tell her something.

But what? she asked herself. *I'm so confused!*

CHAPTER 9

"Come and look!" Little Daisy dashed into the barn and skidded to a halt beside Daisy and Smoky, who were sharing a mouse in a shaft of sunlight that streamed from one of the gaps high in the wall. "There are cats coming!"

"Lots of cats!" Coriander added, bounding up to stand panting beside his sister.

"Lots?" Daisy echoed, wondering whether one of the Clan leaders had called an emergency Gathering. "How many?"

"Well . . ." Coriander scuffled his paws in the straw on the barn floor. "Three."

That sounds like a Clan patrol, Daisy thought. "Let's go see," she meowed, hearing the kits scampering after her. In the distance, Daisy spotted three cats picking their way along the shore of the lake, heading toward the horseplace through WindClan territory. As they drew closer, she recognized Mousewhisker in the lead, followed by Sparkpelt and Sorrelstripe. She felt a warm pulse of happiness to see her son and her friends, followed almost at once by a prickle of apprehension in her pads.

What do they want?

It had been a moon since Alderheart and Mousewhisker

had left the Sisters' camp, and that was the last time Daisy had seen a Clan cat. A moment later, Mousewhisker let out a loud yowl, and the three ThunderClan cats picked up the pace until they were racing along the shore. They slid underneath the horseplace fence and came bounding up to the barn.

The kits came to meet them and frisked around them as they approached.

"Greetings!" Little Daisy squealed excitedly.

"My name's Coriander," her brother announced. "What's yours?"

Sorrelstripe whisked her tail affectionately over the kits' ears. "My, you've grown!" she purred.

But most of the ThunderClan cats' attention was fixed on Daisy.

"Thank StarClan you're okay!" Mousewhisker exclaimed to his mother. "When the Sisters moved on, we expected that you would come back to us."

"When you didn't, we were worried that a fox might have gotten you," Sorrelstripe added. "Why didn't you come?"

At her Clanmates' concern, Daisy felt as if a claw were piercing her heart: half pain and half rejoicing, chasing away the ominous images of her dream the night before. She was uncertain how to respond, glancing from the ThunderClan cats to the barn where Smoky stood. She could see from the look in Smoky's eyes that he wanted her to stay here with him.

Meanwhile the kits' excitement had faded to bewilderment. Daisy could hardly bear to look at them, especially when Little Daisy piped up, "You're not going to leave us, are you?"

Mousewhisker too was looking bewildered. Daisy couldn't meet his gaze. "I'm . . . well, I'm needed here," she mumbled.

"You're needed in ThunderClan," Sparkpelt retorted. "It's really difficult now. So much has changed, but we still need you."

"But I—" Daisy began to protest.

"You can't leave ThunderClan!" Mousewhisker gasped, his eyes wide with horror. "A lot *has* happened, and it's not all bad. For one thing, Spotfur has had kits while you've been away."

"Spotfur!" Daisy responded, amazed. "I didn't know she was expecting kits."

"Nor did any cat," Mousewhisker told her. "Not even Spotfur, for a while."

"It's really sad," Sparkpelt added, "because her mate, Stemleaf, is dead. She'll need lots of help!"

For a few heartbeats Daisy felt as if she were standing in the middle of a storm; emotion tugged at her like a blustering wind. Joy that ThunderClan had new kits vied with her sympathy for Spotfur, struggling to raise her litter without a mate. Yet stronger than either was her feeling of confidence that she could help Spotfur with those kits. She didn't know what would happen with StarClan, whether Squirrelflight would be safe, whether the real Bramblestar would ever come back to ThunderClan. She didn't know whether she could keep Mousewhisker with her forever, or whether she risked losing him, too, to fighting or illness or bad luck.

But she knew she could help Spotfur with those kits.

With sudden clarity, she remembered the strength and

support Squirrelflight and Lionblaze had shown when she'd arrived in ThunderClan's camp with the ailing Little Daisy and Coriander more than a moon ago. Every cat in the camp had pulled together to try to save the kits, just as they would pull together to help Spotfur. And regardless of what else was going on, that was what a Clan was, at its heart, wasn't it? A group of cats working together, to help one another.

But the happiness she felt remembering her love for her Clan lasted for only a couple of heartbeats. As Smoky came out of the barn, drawing up alongside her, she felt a stab of grief as she realized she was feeling the pull of home—a pull away from Coriander and Little Daisy. She couldn't ignore it. Smoky would always protect his kits, and he had the Twolegs to help him. But the Clans had been clawing so desperately at survival for so long; so many Clanmates had been lost in the battle to preserve their way of life.

My Clan does need me. Can I really turn my back on them now?

Smoky nodded at their kit. "Hello, Mousewhisker."

Mousewhisker nodded back. "Smoky. I hope your kits are well?"

Smoky paused next to Daisy. "They're strong and healthy. I'll always be thankful to your Clan for helping them the night we found the Sisters."

Mousewhisker flicked an ear, seeming uncomfortable. "Oh, well, of course."

"You can come visit them anytime," Smoky went on. "Even though we don't live together, we're still kin, aren't we?"

Mousewhisker stared at him. He looked surprised.

"There's probably a lot you could teach them," Smoky meowed. "Such a bright, strong tom."

Daisy looked back at her former mate, overcome. She hadn't expected him to reach a paw out to his kit this way. And yet she could see in Mousewhisker's eyes how much it meant to him.

"That would be nice," Mousewhisker agreed. He shook his head as if to clear it. "One day." He turned back to Daisy. "I'm sorry to pressure you," he went on, "but we need you at home. Are you really going to give up ThunderClan and stay here?"

Daisy didn't know how to answer him. Thoughts of ThunderClan swirled in her head, but she knew she owed Smoky an explanation. "I'll think about it," she sighed.

"Don't think for too long," Sparkpelt mewed, stepping forward to touch noses with her. "We miss you, Daisy."

Bidding the ThunderClan cats farewell, Daisy stood outside the barn, watching them as they headed down the slope and along the lakeshore toward their territory. She felt her paws urging her to follow them, but at the same time they were tugging her back into the barn.

That night, Daisy couldn't sleep. She remembered over and over her conversation with the ThunderClan cats. They wanted her back, that was clear, and Spotfur needed her to help raise her kits. But that would mean leaving Coriander and Little Daisy, when she already loved them as if they were her own.

I don't know what to do!

Every scrap of straw in her nest seemed to be poking through her pelt. Daisy thrashed around in a vain effort to get comfortable. Finally she realized that Smoky had risen to his paws and padded over to her.

"It shook you, didn't it?" he asked. "Your Clanmates' visit."

Daisy gazed up at him, his gray-and-white fur glimmering in the dim light of the barn. At first she didn't want to reply, but she knew that Smoky wouldn't give up until she had explained.

"It's true . . . I'm feeling a pull to go back to them," she confessed at last. "I'm a Clan cat, and always will be."

Smoky looked down at her, sad resignation in his eyes. "I don't like it," he admitted. "But Clan cats are weirdly loyal! I wish you would stay with me and the kits," he added with a sigh, "but I won't try to stop you, if you want to go."

Daisy nodded, expecting to feel relief that Smoky wasn't going to hate her for her decision. But relief didn't come. Instead, an odd sense of grief crept over her. Until now she had been so focused on how she would feel about leaving the kits, she had never stopped to think about what it would be like to leave Smoky. Though they were no longer mates, she did care about him. He had become her closest friend.

"What if you and the kits came with me?" she suggested, the words popping out of her mouth before she could stop them.

Smoky stared at her for a long, long moment. "What are you saying?" he demanded, an edge of anger in his voice. "Do you expect me to go against Coriander's last wish? I know that she didn't want her kits raised in a Clan!"

"Of course I remember," Daisy replied. "But Coriander couldn't have known what would happen after she died. If she had known that there was a Clan out there, willing to take the kits on as Clanmates, to look after them—"

She broke off at Smoky's look of sad resignation. He turned and padded away, halting a few paw steps away from her. "I hoped you would stay," he meowed. "But I think we both know you belong with the Clans. If you really want to leave, I won't stop you—but if you do, it will be without me and the kits."

A soft mewling cry followed Smoky's last words. Glancing over to their nest, Daisy saw that both kits had woken up and were looking at Daisy and Smoky with bleary, sleepy eyes full of bewilderment.

Daisy rose to her paws and padded over to them. "Go back to sleep," she murmured, bending over to give their ears a loving lick.

"We can't," Coriander responded, blinking up at her unhappily.

"Are you fighting? We know something's wrong," Little Daisy added.

Regret surged through Daisy. "I have to go home to ThunderClan," she told them.

Both kits stared at her in disbelief, then broke out into anguished wailing. "No! No!"

Daisy tried to say something reassuring, but the words wouldn't come. She had grown to love these two kits so much, feeling almost as if they were a second chance for her and Smoky.

In the end it was Smoky who answered. "Daisy has to go back to her Clan now. It's where her true home is. Right, Daisy?"

Daisy could barely look at him, barely force herself to nod. Even though Smoky was right, this parting was hurting her so much that she could hardly bear it. She felt as though a fox were in her belly, tearing her apart from inside.

The kits grew quiet again. Their eyes were full of sorrow, but Daisy could see that they were struggling to understand. They pressed themselves against her, and the warmth of their small bodies against hers made Daisy want to break out into hopeless wailing.

"Promise you'll visit us," Little Daisy mewed.

"Of course I will." Daisy's voice was shaking. "If it's okay with your father."

"I'd like that very much," Smoky purred. "And bring Mousewhisker."

Daisy gently led the kits back to their nest and whispered stories about the fun she, Smoky, Mousewhisker, and they would have when they visited next. Soon the kits' eyes began to droop, and not long after, they were fast asleep. When she was able to sneak away, she settled down beside Smoky in the straw, talking quietly so as not to wake them again.

"Smoky," Daisy began, "are you really okay with me leaving you again?"

There was a glint of amusement in Smoky's eyes. "I'd

rather you stayed, but I understand your Clan is calling to you. That's always been so important to you. Besides," he added, "it's different this time. I realize we don't actually love each other anymore. Unless . . . ?" He tilted his head, waiting for Daisy's response.

"No," Daisy told him. "I care for you, and I always will. I've loved being a family with you. I think you're a wonderful friend—and a wonderful father—but I'm not in love with you anymore."

"Yes, those feelings are gone," Smoky agreed. "We'll always have a bond, because of what we've been through together, and because of Mousewhisker, but we've both moved on. We both have other concerns now."

Daisy was relieved by Smoky's firm tones and the certainty in his eyes. *He really will be all right.* "Mousewhisker and I will visit soon," she promised. "I'm sure he'd like to know his father, as well as his new kin."

Smoky nodded happily. "I'd be delighted to get to know him better," he purred.

The two former mates settled down together in the straw. *I'm sure I won't have any bad dreams tonight,* Daisy thought as she drifted into sleep.

Daisy bent down to touch noses with each of the small kits in turn. "Good-bye, Coriander. Good-bye, Little Daisy," she mewed. "I promise I'll come visit you, and so will your brother."

"Our brother?" Coriander gasped.

"We have a brother?" Little Daisy asked, equally astonished.

"Yes, you've met him," Daisy explained. "The big gray-and-white tom who was here yesterday. He'll come to see you again. That's something to look forward to, isn't it?"

"Yes," Coriander responded, blinking unhappily. "But it would be better if you stayed with us."

"I can't do that." Daisy bent down again to nuzzle both kits. Her heart felt as if it would burst with love, and she realized that if she stayed with them much longer she might not have the courage to leave. "But I'll be thinking about you—always."

Beckoning with her tail to Smoky, Daisy padded out of the barn, trying to close her ears to the kits' sad farewells.

Outside, clouds were racing across the sky, driven by a stiff wind that flattened Daisy's fur to her sides and made her eyes water. The surface of the lake was whipped into choppy, white-topped waves.

Daisy turned to Smoky, who had followed her out. "Are you going to be okay, raising the kits by yourself?" she asked.

"I'm sure I will," Smoky replied. "And if ever I need help, I'll come to find you in ThunderClan again, just as I did when the kits were being born."

"I'm so glad you did," Daisy told him, warm pleasure spreading through her at the thought that he had relied on her in a time of need.

Smoky ducked his head shyly. "You're often the first cat I think of."

Purring affectionately, Daisy nuzzled his shoulder, while

Smoky rubbed his muzzle against her. "Good-bye, Smoky," she murmured.

"Good-bye, Daisy. Come see us soon."

As Daisy left the horseplace and headed down to the lake, she didn't look back, though she could picture Smoky standing outside the barn, watching her dwindle into the distance. It was hard, putting one paw in front of another, letting them lead her away from a place where she was so deeply loved.

I'm going home, she thought firmly. She was determined to convince herself that she was making the right decision, but as she drew nearer and nearer to ThunderClan territory, she wasn't sure she had succeeded.

As soon as Daisy padded through the thorn tunnel into the camp, she spotted Mousewhisker, bounding toward her from the warriors' den.

"Daisy!" he exclaimed. "You came back! I was afraid you wouldn't."

He pressed himself close to her, nuzzling deep into her fur, as if he were still a kit. Joy burst within Daisy's chest; she was so grateful that she still had him, and so moved to discover how important she was to him. She realized how much he had held back when he'd visited her the day before, wanting her to be free to make her own decision.

"Of course I came back, you silly furball," Daisy purred lovingly. "But I had to promise you would go to see your kin at the horseplace. The kits were so excited to find out they have a brother."

Mousewhisker's tail curled up happily. "Of course I'll go!"

"Daisy! Welcome back!" another voice called from across the camp.

Daisy looked up to see Sparkpelt racing toward her, along with Hollytuft, Blossomfall, and Fernsong. Several others followed them, mostly cats Daisy had helped raise as if they were her own. They crowded around her, pressing against her until it was all she could do to stay on her paws.

"Oof! Get off, you great lumps!" she gasped. "Give me space to breathe!"

Then she saw Alderheart wriggle his way to the front of the crowd. "Daisy, you must come see Spotfur," he meowed. "She's had her kits, and they're so beautiful! But she could use you, Daisy. We all give her as much help as we can, but she needs an experienced she-cat to be with her all the time."

Daisy's heart swelled joyfully. That was all she wanted, to know that somewhere a cat needed her. Her Clan needed her. "Of course, Alderheart. Right away," she responded, heading for the nursery.

This is where I belong, she thought. She knew she'd made the right decision. *ThunderClan will always be my home.*

WARRIORS

SPOTFUR'S
REBELLION

Special thanks to Clarissa Hutton

ALLEGIANCES

THUNDERCLAN

LEADER   **BRAMBLESTAR**—dark brown tabby tom with amber eyes

DEPUTY   **SQUIRRELFLIGHT**—dark ginger she-cat with green eyes and one white paw

MEDICINE CATS   **LEAFPOOL**—light brown tabby she-cat with amber eyes, white paws and chest

                  JAYFEATHER—gray tabby tom with blind blue eyes

                  ALDERHEART—dark ginger tom with amber eyes

WARRIORS   (toms and she-cats without kits)

                  BRACKENFUR—golden-brown tabby tom

                  CLOUDTAIL—long-haired white tom with blue eyes

                  BRIGHTHEART—white she-cat with ginger patches

                  THORNCLAW—golden-brown tabby tom

                  WHITEWING—white she-cat with green eyes

                  BIRCHFALL—light brown tabby tom

                  BERRYNOSE—cream-colored tom with a stump for a tail

                  MOUSEWHISKER—gray-and-white tom

                  POPPYFROST—pale tortoiseshell-and-white she-cat

                  LIONBLAZE—golden tabby tom with amber eyes

ROSEPETAL—dark cream she-cat

BRIARLIGHT—dark brown she-cat, paralyzed in her hindquarters

LILYHEART—small, dark tabby she-cat with white patches and blue eyes

BUMBLESTRIPE—very pale gray tom with black stripes

CHERRYFALL—ginger she-cat

MOLEWHISKER—brown-and-cream tom

AMBERMOON—pale ginger she-cat

DEWNOSE—gray-and-white tom

STORMCLOUD—gray tabby tom

HOLLYTUFT—black she-cat

FERNSONG—yellow tabby tom

SORRELSTRIPE—dark brown she-cat

LEAFSHADE—tortoiseshell she-cat

LARKSONG—black tom

HONEYFUR—white she-cat with yellow splotches

SPARKPELT—orange tabby she-cat

QUEENS (she-cats expecting or nursing kits)

DAISY—cream long-furred cat from the horseplace

CINDERHEART—gray tabby she-cat (mother to Snapkit, a golden tabby tom-kit; Spotkit, a spotted tabby she-kit; and Flykit, a striped tabby she-kit)

BLOSSOMFALL—tortoiseshell-and-white she-cat with petal-shaped white patches

(mother to Stemkit, a white-and-orange tom-kit; Eaglekit, a ginger she-kit; Plumkit, a black-and-ginger she-kit; and Shellkit, a tortoiseshell tom-kit)

IVYPOOL—silver-and-white tabby she-cat with dark blue eyes

ELDERS (former warriors and queens, now retired)

GRAYSTRIPE—long-haired gray tom

MILLIE—striped silver tabby she-cat with blue eyes

SKYCLAN

LEADER **LEAFSTAR**—brown-and-cream tabby she-cat with amber eyes

DEPUTY **HAWKWING**—dark gray tom with yellow eyes

MEDICINE CATS **FRECKLEWISH**—mottled light brown tabby she-cat with spotted legs

APPRENTICE, FIDGETPAW (black-and-white tom)

PUDDLESHINE—brown tom with white splotches

WARRIORS **SPARROWPELT**—dark brown tabby tom

APPRENTICE, NECTARPAW (brown she-cat)

MACGYVER—black-and-white tom

APPRENTICE, DEWPAW (sturdy gray tom)

PLUMWILLOW—dark gray she-cat

SAGENOSE—pale gray tom

APPRENTICE, GRAVELPAW (tan tom)

HARRYBROOK—gray tom

APPRENTICE, FRINGEPAW (white she-cat with brown splotches)

BLOSSOMHEART—ginger-and-white she-cat
APPRENTICE, FINPAW (brown tom)

SANDYNOSE—stocky light brown tom with ginger legs
APPRENTICE, TWIGPAW (gray she-cat with green eyes)

RABBITLEAP—brown tom
APPRENTICE, PALEPAW (black-and-white she-cat)

BELLALEAF—pale orange she-cat with green eyes
APPRENTICE, REEDPAW (small pale tabby she-cat)

ROWANCLAW—ginger tom

TAWNYPELT—tortoiseshell she-cat with green eyes
APPRENTICE, SNAKEPAW (honey-colored tabby she-cat)

JUNIPERCLAW—black tom
APPRENTICE, WHORLPAW (gray-and-white tom)

STRIKESTONE—brown tabby tom

STONEWING—white tom

GRASSHEART—pale brown tabby she-cat

SCORCHFUR—dark gray tom with slashed ears
APPRENTICE, FLOWERPAW (silver she-cat)

VIOLETSHINE—black-and-white she-cat with yellow eyes

MINTFUR—gray tabby she-cat with blue eyes

NETTLESPLASH—pale brown tom

QUEENS   **TINYCLOUD**—small white she-cat (mother to Quailkit, a tom with crow-black ears; Pigeonkit, a gray-and-white she-kit; and Sunnykit, a ginger she-kit)

SNOWBIRD—pure white she-cat with green eyes (mother to Gullkit, a white she-kit; Conekit, a white-and-gray tom; and Frondkit, a gray tabby she-kit)

ELDERS   **FALLOWFERN**—pale brown she-cat who has lost her hearing

OAKFUR—small brown tom

RATSCAR—scarred, skinny dark brown tom

WINDCLAN

LEADER   **HARESTAR**—brown-and-white tom

DEPUTY   **CROWFEATHER**—dark gray tom

MEDICINE CAT   **KESTRELFLIGHT**—mottled gray tom with white splotches like kestrel feathers

WARRIORS   **NIGHTCLOUD**—black she-cat
APPRENTICE, BRINDLEPAW (mottled brown she-cat)

GORSETAIL—very pale gray-and-white she-cat with blue eyes

LEAFTAIL—dark tabby tom with amber eyes

EMBERFOOT—gray tom with two dark paws
APPRENTICE, SMOKEPAW (gray she-cat)

BREEZEPELT—black tom with amber eyes

LARKWING—pale brown tabby she-cat

SEDGEWHISKER—light brown tabby she-cat

SLIGHTFOOT—black tom with white flash on his chest

OATCLAW—pale brown tabby tom

FEATHERPELT—gray tabby she-cat

HOOTWHISKER—dark gray tom

HEATHERTAIL—light brown tabby she-cat with blue eyes

FERNSTRIPE—gray tabby she-cat

ELDERS **WHITETAIL**—small white she-cat

RIVERCLAN

LEADER **MISTYSTAR**—gray she-cat with blue eyes

DEPUTY **REEDWHISKER**—black tom

MEDICINE CATS **MOTHWING**—dappled golden she-cat
WILLOWSHINE—gray tabby she-cat

WARRIORS **MINTFUR**—light gray tabby tom
APPRENTICE, SOFTPAW (gray she-cat)

DUSKFUR—brown tabby she-cat
APPRENTICE, DAPPLEPAW (gray-and-white tom)

MINNOWTAIL—dark gray-and-white she-cat
APPRENTICE, BREEZEPAW (brown-and-white she-cat)

MALLOWNOSE—light brown tabby tom
APPRENTICE, HAREPAW (white tom)

CURLFEATHER—pale brown she-cat

PODLIGHT—gray-and-white tom

HERONWING—dark gray-and-black tom

SHIMMERPELT—silver she-cat
APPRENTICE, NIGHTPAW (dark gray she-cat with blue eyes)

LIZARDTAIL—light brown tom

HAVENPELT—black-and-white she-cat

SNEEZECLOUD—gray-and-white tom

BRACKENPELT—tortoiseshell she-cat
APPRENTICE, GORSEPAW (white tom with gray ears)

JAYCLAW—gray tom

OWLNOSE—brown tabby tom

LAKEHEART—gray tabby she-cat

ICEWING—white she-cat with blue eyes

ELDERS   **MOSSPELT**—tortoiseshell-and-white she-cat

GREENLEAF
TWOLEGPLACE

TWOLEG NEST

TWOLEG PATH

TWOLEG PATH

CLEARING

SHADOWCLAN
CAMP

SKYCLAN
CAMP

HALFBRIDGE

SMALL
THUNDERPATH

GREENLEAF
TWOLEGPLACE

HALFBRIDGE

CAT VIEW

ISLAND

STREAM

RIVERCLAN
CAMP

HORSEPLACE

MOONPOOL

ABANDONED
TWOLEG NEST

OLD THUNDERPATH

THUNDERCLAN
CAMP

ANCIENT OAK

LAKE

WINDCLAN
CAMP

BROKEN
HALFBRIDGE

TWOLEGPLACE

THUNDERPATH

KEY
To The
CLANS

THUNDERCLAN

RIVERCLAN

SHADOWCLAN

WINDCLAN

SKYCLAN

STARCLAN

NORTH

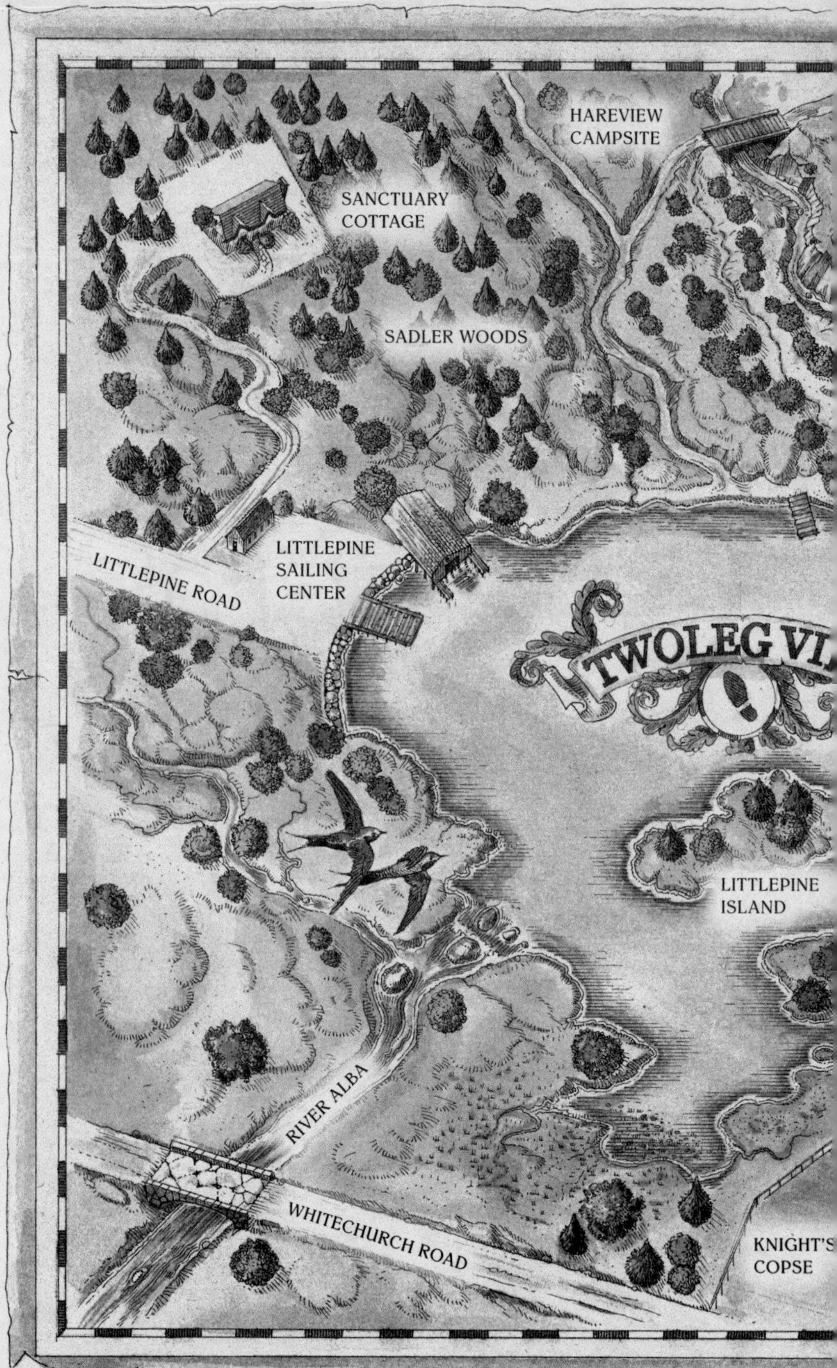
HAREVIEW
CAMPSITE
SANCTUARY
COTTAGE
SADLER WOODS
LITTLEPINE
SAILING
CENTER
LITTLEPINE ROAD
TWOLEG VI
LITTLEPINE
ISLAND
RIVER ALBA
WHITECHURCH ROAD
KNIGHT'S
COPSE

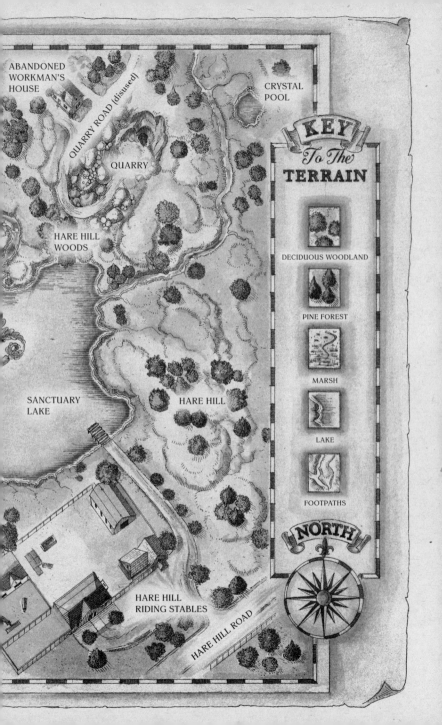

CHAPTER 1

❧

"Take a deep breath," Leafshade meowed "What can you smell?"

Spotpaw opened her mouth, letting air roll over her tongue as she tried to pick out the different scents. "The stream," she answered confidently, flexing her gray-and-white spotted paws at the edge of the water as she glanced down at its surface. "Marsh grasses. Vole. Rabbit." She breathed in again, wrinkling her nose at the earthy smell of another Clan. "And WindClan. Is it true they sleep outside on the grass instead of in dens?"

"Right now, we're just talking about Clan borders," Leafshade meowed patiently. "That was good scenting, Spotpaw. This stream is part of our border with WindClan. Can you tell where exactly they've set their border markers?"

Spotpaw sniffed the air again. "I'm not sure." The other Clan's scent was everywhere, but she couldn't pick out specific spots where it had been left. It just drifted to her from across the water. She glanced out of the corner of her eye at Stempaw and his mentor, Rosepetal. The older apprentice flicked his tail at her in encouragement.

"The borders are even more important when they're hard

to pick out," Leafshade told her. "Confusion over whose territory is whose can lead to conflict. We don't want to get too close."

Rosepetal scented the air, too. "It doesn't seem like WindClan has marked their borders since it rained," she commented to Leafshade. "It might be too hard for Spotpaw and Stempaw to scent it now."

Leafshade and Rosepetal both sniffed thoughtfully, then turned to each other to begin a low-voiced discussion. Spotpaw shifted her paws impatiently and fluffed her thick fur. Leafshade *always* took a long time to consider anything suggested to her. Why couldn't they just get moving?

Spotpaw inched closer to the stream. The earth was muddy beneath her paws, and she glanced at Stempaw again. The white-and-orange apprentice was looking away, toward their mentors, and Spotpaw felt a sharp rush of longing. *Pay attention to me.* Stempaw was a few moons older than Spotpaw and her littermates; as a kit she'd watched enviously as he and the other apprentices learned to fight and hunt and patrol, following their mentors in and out of camp on important tasks while she was stuck in the nursery.

And now, finally, *she* was an apprentice, too. She wanted Stempaw to notice her. She wanted him to want to be her friend.

"Stempaw," she whispered. "Hey, Stempaw. How close do you think I can get to WindClan territory?"

Stempaw cocked his head, his green eyes narrowing. "What do you mean?"

Spotpaw inched farther forward. Her toes were touching the stream now, their fur getting damp and cold. "Well," she meowed, "if we can't scent where WindClan's border markers are, then we don't know exactly where the border is, right?"

"Right," Stempaw agreed.

"If they don't keep their border markers fresh, it's not *our* fault if we cross them. Maybe they've moved the border since the last time one of our patrols came through." Spotpaw lifted her paw and stretched, reaching all the way across the narrow stream. Her toes just brushed the opposite bank. "Maybe the border's over here now."

"Spotpaw!" Leafshade hissed, and Spotpaw jerked her paw back to the ThunderClan side of the stream. Her mentor was glaring at her, tortoiseshell fur puffing in outrage. "This isn't a joke," she mewed sharply. "With all the trouble between Sky-Clan and ShadowClan over territory, the last thing we need is a ThunderClan apprentice trying to start fights with Wind-Clan."

"I'm not trying to start a fight!" Spotpaw yowled. She was just playing a little!

"You're not?" Leafshade's gaze was cold. "In that case, you clearly aren't thinking at all. You need to show some respect, and you need to take the other Clans seriously. I'm not teaching you these things for my own pleasure, you know. It was apprentices not following the code that led to ShadowClan falling apart, and *that* led to Darktail taking over."

Spotpaw cringed, feeling small beneath her fur. She'd been too young to know everything that happened when the dangerous rogue Darktail had taken over ShadowClan, but she knew that cats had died, and had heard stories of frightened warriors fleeing from him and hiding with ThunderClan. She didn't want to be responsible for anything like that ever happening again.

But . . . .wait. Darktail had taken over an entire Clan because *apprentices hadn't listened to their mentors well enough?*

Spotpaw's pelt prickled with indignation. That was *very* hard to believe.

Rosepetal interrupted before she could argue. "Don't be too tough on her," the cream-furred she-cat purred. "These apprentices don't know what life was like before Darktail came. They're too young. How could they possibly understand how things are supposed to be?"

Spotpaw stiffened, more indignant than ever. All right, she had been misbehaving. She should have resisted the urge to play around when her mentor was trying to teach her something important. And she should have taken the border with WindClan more seriously.

But it wasn't that she didn't *know* any better. She'd rather get into trouble than be treated like an ignorant kit! "I know—" she began, but Leafshade spoke over her.

"You're right," she told Rosepetal. "We're going to have to teach them *everything*." Still solemn with disapproval, she turned away from the border. "Come on."

Spotpaw glanced at Stempaw, who was watching her, his eyes bright with curiosity. Pricking up her ears, she imitated Leafshade's unimpressed look, then rolled her eyes. "Come on, Stempaw," she meowed, trying to sound just as disapproving as her mentor. "We're going to have to learn *everything.*"

Stempaw gave a muffled *mrrow* of laughter, and Spotpaw's paws felt lighter as she walked past him. Stempaw thought she was funny!

Back at camp, Spotpaw took a couple of mice to the elders sunning themselves outside their den.

Millie sniffed at one of them doubtfully. "Is this fresh?" she asked. "I don't want crow-food that's been sitting around all day."

Next to her, Graystripe's tail twitched. "We saw Twigbranch carrying these into camp a little while ago when she brought in her patrol." He put out a paw and drew the other mouse closer. "Thanks, Spotpaw, my stomach's been growling like a badger."

Millie snorted. "Don't let him fool you. Flypaw brought him a vole earlier. He's not hungry; he's just greedy." Graystripe batted at his mate playfully as Spotpaw purred with laughter.

As both elders settled down to their meal, Spotpaw took a sparrow of her own and went to eat outside the apprentices' den. Its bones crunched satisfyingly between her teeth. After they'd left the WindClan border, Rosepetal and Leafshade had led them around the edges of ThunderClan's whole territory, scenting all the different border markings, and she was *starving.*

Stempaw sat down next to her and she pushed the sparrow

toward him. "Have some," she offered.

"Thanks." Stempaw took a bite, watching her out of the corner of his eye. He swallowed, then meowed, "I thought it was brave of you to get so close to WindClan's territory."

"*Really?*" Spotpaw asked, thrilled. "Leafshade acted like one apprentice putting a toe over the border would lead to a battle."

She glanced around the camp, checking that none of their Clanmates were in earshot. Outside the medicine den, Jayfeather was basking in a sunny spot, and Spotpaw eyed him suspiciously, knowing how sharp the medicine cat's hearing was. Lowering her voice, she murmured, "I knew where the border markers were the whole time. I was just *pretending*."

Stempaw's eyes went wide. "You're so rebellious!" he meowed, purring with laughter. "Don't you worry about getting in trouble?"

"Does it really matter?" Spotpaw asked airily. "The older warriors act so serious all the time. They need to have some fun." Her pelt was tingling with excited pride. *Stempaw thinks I'm brave and rebellious!*

Stempaw looked around the clearing thoughtfully. Spotpaw followed his gaze. Graystripe and Millie had gone back into the elders' den. Squirrelflight and Bramblestar were having a conversation on the other side of the fresh-kill pile, while Alderheart was laying out fresh herbs to dry behind the medicine den. Birchfall was leading a hunting patrol out of camp, their tails high. The camp was busy but calm, each cat going about his or her duties.

"I think you're right," he told her, "Maybe it's because of all that trouble with Darktail and ShadowClan that Leafshade mentioned earlier. The warriors worry too much about bad things starting to happen again."

Spotpaw shivered, suddenly chilled by the idea of their peaceful clearing being invaded. Cats had *died* when Darktail had ruled ShadowClan. She steeled herself, imagining sinking her claws into an enemy. "They're right that we'd need to fight if another cat like Darktail came to the lake," she meowed. "But we'd be ready. We wouldn't get fooled by an evil rogue like ShadowClan did. *I* wouldn't."

Stempaw snorted. "I'm not sure you'd be much of a challenge for a big evil rogue. At least not while you're still an apprentice."

"I'm brave!" Spotpaw puffed up her fur, trying to look bigger. "Look at what I did today. I went right up to the WindClan border, even when Leafshade told me not to. I was *born* brave!"

"What a mouse-brain!" The sharp voice came from behind them, and both apprentices turned quickly. Shellpaw, one of Stempaw's littermates, was standing with his mentor, Bumblestripe, staring at Spotpaw. "You can't fight rogues," Shellpaw told her dismissively. "You're too little. You've been an apprentice for, like, two sunrises." Next to him, Bumblestripe looked down at them with disapproval, his eyes narrowed.

Spotpaw ignored him and bared her teeth at Shellpaw. "I'm already tougher than you." She didn't like Shellpaw anywhere near as much as she liked Stempaw. When she and her littermates were still in the nursery, he'd always lorded over them how much more important apprentices were than kits. And now that she was an apprentice too, he *still* thought he was better than her.

"Tough isn't the point," Bumblestripe reprimanded her. "No good apprentice would purposefully disobey their mentor. ThunderClan needs strong, honorable warriors, not rebels." He flicked his tail dismissively. "Come on, Shellpaw."

Tail slashing, he stalked toward the camp entrance, Shellpaw beside him.

Spotpaw watched them go, her whiskers twitching with indignation. *I am a strong, honorable warrior apprentice!*

But couldn't she have a little fun, too? As Bumblestripe and Shellpaw left camp, Spotpaw began to feel light with excitement again: She'd had an idea.

"Let's follow them," she whispered to Stempaw.

He looked puzzled. "What for?"

"Don't you want to know what the other apprentices are learning?" she asked. "What if Bumblestripe is teaching Shellpaw something we don't know?"

Stempaw hesitated. "I don't think we should be spying on our Clanmates," he meowed.

"It's not spying," Spotpaw told him. Was it? Not really. *It's just an adventure.* "We should learn everything we can, right? We won't get in trouble for wanting to learn."

"I guess not." Stempaw's green eyes began to shine with excitement. "I bet we can be sneaky enough that Bumblestripe never catches us watching them. Rosepetal's taught me a lot about stalking prey."

As they got to their paws, they checked to make sure their mentors weren't watching. Rosepetal and Leafshade were chatting with Poppyfrost and Cherryfall on the other side of the clearing. Quietly, Spotpaw headed for the camp entrance, Stempaw behind her. As she passed through the thorn tunnel, Spotpaw felt a thrill of excitement. Now that she was an apprentice, she could leave camp whenever she wanted to!

By the time they got out of camp, there was no sign of Bumblestripe and Shellpaw.

"Can you pick up their scent?" Stempaw meowed, sniffing.

Spotpaw tasted the air, then the ground, the familiar scents of the forest and her Clanmates flooding her nose. "They went this way."

They padded silently under oaks and alders, sticking to the shadows as much as possible. Spotpaw could hear the tiny scrabblings of mice beneath some bracken as they passed, but she ignored them: They were on a mission tracking Bumblestripe and Shellpaw, not a hunting patrol.

The scent trail led toward a mossy clearing where apprentices often trained, and as they got closer to the clearing, Spotpaw could hear Bumblestripe's voice. She stopped, laying her tail across Stempaw's back. "Listen."

"Pull your paws back so they're right under your shoulders," Bumblestripe was saying. "You'll leap higher that way."

"Like this?" Shellpaw asked.

Spotpaw edged forward to peer around a birch tree.

Bumblestripe was tapping the back of Shellpaw's leg so that the apprentice would slide his left front paw forward. "Much better," he meowed.

Spotpaw slunk forward another mouse-length, craning her neck to get a better look at Shellpaw's hunting crouch. A leaf crackled under her paw and she froze, but neither Bumblestripe nor Shellpaw looked up, too absorbed in the lesson.

"After all Bumblestripe's fussing at *us* about being strong warriors, he isn't even paying attention to what's around him," she whispered to Stempaw behind her.

"I'm glad he's not," Stempaw whispered back.

Spotpaw lashed her tail. Bumblestripe *should* be paying attention! "He's so focused on teaching Shellpaw that a badger could sneak up on him and he wouldn't even hear it coming," she murmured.

"I know! *He's* the one who needs to work on being a better warrior," Stempaw agreed.

Spotpaw padded quietly forward another tail-length. "I'm going to teach him a lesson," she decided. "It'll be good for him."

"What?" Stempaw hissed. "Spotpaw, come back!"

But she was already slinking forward, trying to remember everything Leafshade had taught her in her first lesson on stalking prey. She stayed low to the ground, her belly fur just brushing the grass, and placed each paw carefully, silently, her leg muscles taut and ready to spring. *I hope Stempaw is watching.* She really wanted him to notice how bold she was, and how skilled, even though she hadn't been an apprentice nearly as long as he had.

Bumblestripe didn't turn.

I'll jump on his back, but I'll make sure my claws stay sheathed, Spotpaw thought. *That'll teach him to keep his ears pricked.*

Bumblestripe was going to be *so* embarrassed that an apprentice had snuck up on him. Spotpaw took a deep breath, her chest tight with excitement, and began to run.

Just as she launched into her best spring, Bumblestripe whipped around, a blur of pale gray fur. Before Spotpaw knew what was happening, he'd snatched her from the air and slammed her to the ground, knocking her breathless. Spotpaw gasped, her eyes clouding with panic, unable to speak. Bumblestripe seemed huge above her, teeth bared, unsheathed claws sharp and deadly over her throat.

"Wait!" she wheezed. "It's me! I was only *playing.*"

CHAPTER 2

♣

"I've never seen an apprentice behave this way. You should be ashamed." Bumblestripe glared down at Spotpaw as she marched along beside him, too scared to talk back. Bumblestripe, his claws out and his yellow eyes glaring, had looked like he was going to *kill* her. She'd never seen the usually calm tom like that. If she had, she wouldn't have dared to attack him, even in play.

"She was only—" Stempaw tried to speak up, but Bumblestripe cut him off.

"And *you* should have stopped her. You should set a good example for the new apprentices, not encourage their mouse-brained ideas."

It wasn't Stempaw's fault. Spotpaw's stomach felt heavy with guilt: He *had* tried to stop her. What must he think of her, now that her idea had gotten him in trouble? But she stayed silent as Bumblestripe ushered them both through the thorn tunnel, Shellpaw close behind.

"Mouse-brains," Shellpaw whispered.

When they came into camp, it felt like every cat's eyes were on them. Spotpaw was miserably conscious of how they looked, marched along like prisoners with Bumblestripe glowering at them both.

"Looks like the 'paws are in trouble," Cloudtail purred, sounding amused. Spotpaw hunched her shoulders and licked quickly at her chest, hot and embarrassed beneath her fur.

"What's going on?" Leafshade hurried over to them, Rosepetal behind her. "Spotpaw, what have you been up to?"

"I didn't mean to make him mad," Spotpaw muttered, staring down at her paws.

"She and Stempaw came to spy on Shellpaw's training; then Spotpaw attacked me," Bumblestripe told Leafshade bluntly. Several of the cats in the clearing gasped.

"*Attacked* you?" asked Cherryfall.

"I was only playing!" Spotpaw yowled, for what seemed like the hundredth time. Why was every cat taking this so seriously?

"We really didn't mean any harm," Stempaw meowed, his head bowed. "We wanted to see what Shellpaw was learning, and then . . . we got carried away."

He means I got carried away. Spotpaw looked gratefully at Stempaw out of the corner of her eye. *But he's still standing up for me.*

Bumblestripe spoke up again, his whiskers quivering with rage. "What kind of mentors are you?" he snarled, turning on Leafshade and Rosepetal. "The other apprentices don't act this way."

Spotpaw stifled a gasp. She hadn't meant for any cat to get mad at Leafshade! "We snuck out of camp," she confessed, feeling desperate. "It's not Leafshade's or Rosepetal's fault."

"Spotpaw, be quiet," Leafshade cut in sharply. She nodded to Bumblestripe. "We'll make sure it doesn't happen again."

"It had better not," Bumblestripe growled. He padded away, his tail still twitching angrily, and Shellpaw hurried after him.

Leafshade and Rosepetal led their apprentices to the edge of the clearing. "I'm very disappointed in you both," Leafshade mewed, glaring at them.

"No matter what your intentions were, this is completely unacceptable behavior," Rosepetal added sternly.

Spotpaw bristled and opened her mouth to protest. Even though things had gone terribly wrong, they hadn't done anything *that* bad. No cat had gotten hurt. And Stempaw really didn't deserve to be in trouble.

"The only thing coming out of your mouth right now should be an apology," Leafshade warned, looking even angrier.

Spotpaw hunched her shoulders. Why wouldn't any cat listen to her? "Sorry," she muttered.

"I'm sorry too," Stempaw added, and he sounded a lot more sincere than Spotpaw felt.

"As punishment," Leafshade began, "you two—"

Rosepetal cleared her throat. "I think they should be punished separately," she meowed. "Clearly, they're bad influences on each other." She turned to Stempaw, who was staring at her with appalled green eyes. "Stempaw, I want you to spend the next half-moon running errands for the medicine cats. Looking for herbs, gathering cobwebs . . . whatever they need. I'll talk to Leafpool and the others about it."

Spotpaw wrinkled her nose. Jayfeather was so bossy—she was glad she wouldn't have to spend a half-moon following his orders. At least not alone. It would have been fun with Stempaw.

"Spotpaw, you're going to be responsible for keeping Bramblestar's den tidy for the next moon," Leafshade told her briskly. "You can make him a clean nest every day and bring him fresh-kill. I'll let him know."

That didn't sound *so* bad, even if she was being punished for twice as long as Stempaw. It had been her idea, after all. Stempaw nudged her. "At least we'll still be training together," he murmured.

"Oh, I don't think so," Rosepetal meowed. "I think you'll both learn better separately."

"That's not fair!" Spotpaw protested. *I'll barely get to spend any time with Stempaw!*

"We'll be good," Stempaw added, looking up at his mentor beseechingly, but Rosepetal only curled her tail around her paws.

"You can start being good right now," she told him. "Go ask Alderheart if he'd like you to change the moss in his nest."

Leafshade looked over at the entrance to Bramblestar's den, where the Clan leader was deep in conversation with Lionblaze and Squirrelflight, and clearly decided that it wasn't a good time to interrupt him. "Spotpaw, go to the apprentices' den and think about what you've done," she mewed wearily.

The fur along Spotpaw's shoulders bristled as she headed

for the den. She'd been so excited to move out of the nursery and in with the other apprentices, but now the empty cave felt damp and lonely. The others were out learning hunting techniques or exploring the territory, and she was all alone.

She crawled into her nest at the edge of the den and shifted around. The moss beneath her felt lumpy and dry. "It's not fair," she muttered. *Bumblestripe was just embarrassed that I could sneak up on him. He should be! What kind of warrior doesn't hear an apprentice coming?*

Now she was in trouble. She was being punished for an entire *moon*. And she and Stempaw wouldn't get to train together anymore. Spotpaw dropped her head onto her paws, anger and sadness all mixed up inside her.

"Spotpaw?"

Her mother and father were peering in through the den entrance.

"We heard what happened," Cinderheart mewed gently as she and Lionblaze came into the den.

Spotpaw sat up in her nest. "Bumblestripe wasn't paying attention," she told them, her words tumbling over each other in her eagerness to get them out. "If I could sneak up on him, any cat could. A ShadowClan cat, or a rogue, or even a badger! *He* should be the one in trouble."

Lionblaze sat down in the nest beside Spotpaw's with a sigh. "I'm disappointed in you," he told her, his amber eyes fixed on hers. "I thought you were smarter than this."

Spotpaw's mouth fell open. After a moment of silence, she growled, "It's Bumblestripe who wasn't smart. He should have been watching to see if any cat was coming." The silence stretched on, and it was hard to look at either of her parents. She shifted her paws uncomfortably in the moss that lined her nest. "Shouldn't he have?" she asked at last.

Cinderheart pressed her warm tabby pelt against Spotpaw's side. "Maybe," she agreed. "You're right that it's important to stay alert." Then she added, "But it's more important to be loyal to your Clan."

"I *am* loyal," Spotpaw meowed, outraged.

"Interrupting Shellpaw's lesson wasn't loyal," Lionblaze told her. "An apprentice's training is important for the whole Clan. If Shellpaw doesn't learn what he needs to, Thunder-Clan will suffer. Isn't that true?"

Spotpaw wanted to argue. *Shellpaw's getting plenty of training. One interruption isn't going to make a difference!* But her father was looking at her so sternly that she only dipped her head. "I guess."

"Bumblestripe is a fully trained warrior," Cinderheart added. "He's an excellent fighter. You're a brand-new appren-tice. What if he had hurt you before he realized who you were? That's half the reason he was so angry. He was imagining what *could* have happened."

"I can take care of myself," Spotpaw protested. Even to her own ears, she sounded sulky and defensive. She remembered Bumblestripe's teeth and claws flashing above her, and felt sick. She had been in danger, she knew, but she didn't want to admit it.

"If Bumblestripe had hurt you, not only would you have

been injured, but *he* would have been less reliable as a fighter the next time something attacked him unexpectedly," Lionblaze explained. "He'd be held back by the memory of accidentally hurting one of his own Clanmates when she was just an apprentice."

"And think about how upset the whole Clan would be. A warrior hurting an apprentice? Every cat would be horrified and perhaps even distrustful of Bumblestripe," Cinderheart added, her voice soft but certain. "A Clan where cats don't completely trust one another is a *weak* Clan."

Spotpaw looked down at her paws, feeling heavy and tired suddenly. "I didn't think about any of that."

Cinderheart brushed her cheek against Spotpaw's. "We know you didn't mean to do anything to hurt your Clan," she meowed. "But good warriors have to think about the consequences of their actions."

Lionblaze let his tail fall reassuringly across Spotpaw's shoulders. "When Darktail came to the lake," he told her, his eyes darkening at the memory, "he came at a time when ShadowClan cats didn't trust one another. Rowanstar was a good warrior, but he was a weak leader. Apprentices were disobeying their mentors. Cats were challenging his leadership. Darktail offered them a life where they didn't have to follow the code, and some of the ShadowClan cats listened. That put first ShadowClan, then all the Clans, in danger."

"But that's not going to happen again," Spotpaw argued. She watched her claws work in and out of the moss at the bottom of her nest. Surely a little playing around wouldn't lead to a problem like Darktail for her whole Clan. Would it?

"Not as long as every cat in the Clan does their best to be a loyal warrior," Cinderheart agreed. "Including you."

"I do want to be a loyal warrior." A pang shot through Spotpaw's chest. She hadn't meant to cause any *real* trouble. "But I'm just an apprentice."

"StarClan watches over all of us, even apprentices," Lionblaze meowed. "They'll guide our paws, but we have to listen to them. One of the ways we do that is by following the code."

"A strong Clan depends on strong warriors," Cinderheart added. "Every warrior who follows the code sets an example for every other warrior. You're a smart cat, Spotpaw. I know you can be a good example to the other apprentices, and to the kits in the nursery."

Spotpaw cocked her head doubtfully. "I'm not an example. I'm one of the youngest 'paws. I don't think Shellpaw or Plumpaw or most of the other apprentices would listen to me."

"Your littermates pay attention to everything you say," Cinderheart purred encouragingly. "And Stempaw followed you straight into trouble."

That's true! Spotpaw's pelt began to tingle with excitement. *He did follow me, even though he's older.* She could imagine the other apprentices looking at her with respect as she became the best hunter and fighter, learning all the Clan could teach her and obeying the code perfectly. Dizzyingly, she pictured herself as leader one day, all of ThunderClan following her. She wouldn't be a weak leader. She'd be as strong as Bramblestar, as strong as Firestar.

"I'll do it," she announced, sitting up straight with determination. "I'll be good."

Leafshade gave Spotpaw an approving nod as they came into camp. "Good job patrolling, Spotpaw," she purred. Warmth spread through Spotpaw's chest. She'd paid careful attention to everything Leafshade had taught her, and she'd been the first to spot a ShadowClan patrol on the other side of the border.

It had been three sunrises since she'd gotten in trouble, and Spotpaw had been trying hard to be a good apprentice, to be the *best* apprentice. She still had to clean out the leader's den, but she could tell that Leafshade wasn't mad at her anymore, and Cinderheart had licked Spotpaw's ears this morning and told her how proud she was.

As the other cats in the returning patrol began to spread out around camp—Leafshade toward the warriors' den; Plumpaw and her mentor, Mousewhisker, to the fresh-kill pile—Stempaw looked up from the sunny spot where he'd been cleaning his fur.

"Hey, Spotpaw," he called. "Want to share a vole?"

I guess I'm hungry. . . . Spotpaw took a few steps toward him, then changed her mind. It was more important to be a good apprentice than to spend time with Stempaw. And she hadn't finished her apprentice duties.

"I still have to change Bramblestar's bedding," she meowed apologetically. Stempaw flicked his ears in acknowledgment, but she thought he looked a little disappointed. Except for a few words exchanged in the apprentices' den, they'd barely had a chance to talk since they'd gotten into trouble.

Spotpaw held her tail high as she climbed up the rock tumble to the leader's den, proud of being so responsible. Inside, the fresh moss with which she'd lined Bramblestar's nest the previous day was clawed and scattered, as though Bramblestar had scrambled out of his nest in a hurry. Hooking a ball of moss with her claws, she began to clear the floor, tossing moss out onto the Highledge.

She was pulling another load of moss outside when Flipkit, followed by his littermates Bristlekit and Thriftkit, darted up to her. "What're you doing?" he asked.

"Cleaning out Bramblestar's den," Spotpaw told him, then straightened up, trying to look noble. "Part of an apprentice's duties is making sure every cat has a clean, soft nest. If our Clanmates sleep well, they'll be better warriors."

"Uh-huh." Thriftkit looked at the pile of old moss, the tip of her tail twitching eagerly. "Can we have some of this to play with?"

"Help yourself," Spotpaw purred, and all three kits dived into the moss and started batting pieces back and forth. Thriftkit wriggled onto her back and tossed a clump of moss into the air. "Wait, just take a little bit. Don't scatter it everywhere."

"Kits," Fernsong called from the clearing below, "leave Spotpaw alone. She has work to do." Spotpaw shot him a grateful look as Thriftkit and Flipkit scrambled to their paws and bounded down the rocks toward their father, taking a ball of moss with them.

Only Bristlekit remained for a moment, gazing up at Spotpaw with wide blue-green eyes. "When I'm a 'paw, I'm going to help my Clanmates, too," she announced. "Just like you."

Spotfur blinked, then purred. "Thanks," she answered. "I'm sure you'll be a great apprentice."

She was still feeling warm and happy as she put soft new moss into Bramblestar's nest. *Turns out it's easy to be a good influence.*

"Oh, hi, Spotpaw." Bramblestar stuck his broad tabby head through the den entrance.

"Hi." Spotpaw looked down at her paws, suddenly feeling shy as the ThunderClan leader came into his den. He hadn't been around before when she was tidying his nest, and she didn't think she'd ever been alone with him.

"You did a great job in here," Bramblestar told her, looking around. "I'm sorry it was such a mess this morning. I was in a hurry."

"That's okay," Spotpaw meowed awkwardly. "You've got a lot to do."

"Still, I remember how long it takes to clean up after other cats. When I was an apprentice, my mentor, Firestar—well, he was Fireheart when I first became his apprentice—always made a huge mess in the warriors' den. All the 'paws complained about it," Bramblestar told her.

"*Firestar* was your mentor?" Spotpaw asked, amazed. Firestar had died before she was born, but she'd heard plenty of stories about the huge ginger tom. He had started out as a kittypet and led ThunderClan through many battles, then saved them from the wicked traitor Tigerstar, before leading the Clans from the destroyed forest to their new territory here at the lake, where he'd battled the evil dead cats of the Dark Forest. Bramblestar must have learned so much from having a mentor like that. "Did he teach you how to be leader?"

"Well . . ." Bramblestar hesitated. "He taught me everything an apprentice needs to know. And I've tried to live up to the way he led the Clan."

"Right." Spotpaw tried to imagine Leafshade someday becoming leader, being able to say she'd been her apprentice. She couldn't—Leafshade was a good warrior, and a good mentor, but Spotpaw didn't think she even *wanted* to be leader. "But he was always special, wasn't he?"

Bramblestar looked out onto the clearing, where the kits were still tumbling under Fernsong's watchful eye. Squirrelflight was organizing a hunting patrol and Cloudtail and Brightheart were sharing tongues while Mousewhisker and Plumpaw split a sparrow. "Firestar made ThunderClan what it is now," he meowed softly. "I'll always try to follow his example. I hope I'm half the leader he was."

Spotpaw stared at him admiringly. Even Bramblestar, who led ThunderClan so wisely, wanted to be a better leader and looked up to another cat.

Her parents were right: What mattered most was being loyal to your Clan, and following the code, and setting a good example. *That* was how to make sure the Clan stayed strong.

CHAPTER 3

♣

The ThunderClan camp flooded a moon later.

It had been raining for days, a bleak steady rain that made the cats' fur constantly damp and the ground slippery underpaw. Spotpaw could hear it beating down outside as she curled in her nest in the apprentices' den, nose tightly tucked between her paws. Her sister Flypaw shifted beside her, and Spotpaw opened her eyes for a second, blinking into the dim grayness that came just before dawn, then closed them again. A drop of rain plopped from the cave entrance, hitting the edge of her nest, and Spotpaw shuffled away from it, eyes still shut.

The sound of the rain intensified, and, on the other side of the den, Eaglepaw grumbled wordlessly in her nest. More rain pattered at the den's entrance, a soothing rhythm easing Spotpaw back toward sleep.

Then the moss under her was suddenly cold and wet, shocking her eyes wide open. "Ugh!" She leaped to her paws, shaking water out of her fur.

"Watch it!" Flypaw complained, and then scrambled upright too. "Why is it wet in here?"

In the dim light, Spotpaw could see a broadening stream of

water spreading across the den floor. All the apprentices were on their paws now, exclaiming in disgust.

"It's been raining so much," Stempaw meowed. "Let's see what the rest of camp is like." Yowls of complaint were coming from outside, too, muffled by the steady beat of the rain.

Spotpaw poked her head out of the den, then squirmed out between the bramble tendrils that shielded its entrance, Stempaw behind her.

Outside, the rain beat down so hard that it felt like the paws of an enemy warrior hitting her back. Water streamed down the rock walls that enclosed the camp, making muddy puddles in the clearing. Ivypool and Fernsong were in deep discussion, huddled beneath the bramble bush that protected the nursery, the kits peeking out around their legs. Graystripe and Millie were peering out of the elders' den, their eyes worried.

Cinderheart emerged from the warriors' den and ran to the apprentices, her paws sending up splashes. "Bramblestar is evacuating camp," she yowled over the sound of the rain.

"Is it really that bad?" Spotpaw asked. The clearing was soaked, but the puddles weren't deep.

"Just in case," Cinderheart explained. "He wants to get to higher ground. The camp flooded badly once, and the whole Clan was caught in it." She looked past Spotpaw and Stempaw at the other apprentices clustered at the mouth of their den. "Stay together!" She raised her voice so all of them could hear. "Bramblestar will lead us out when every cat's ready."

She turned and dashed toward the medicine den, where the

three medicine cats were emerging, bundles of herbs clutched in their jaws. Squirrelflight was rounding up the warriors, while Daisy, Ivypool, and Fernsong coaxed the kits out of the nursery.

Spotpaw padded farther into the clearing, puddles sloshing over her paws. *The water's rising fast,* she thought uneasily.

"Kits, keep under our bellies to stay dry," she heard Daisy instruct, and Daisy, Ivypool, and Fernsong straightened up, stretching their legs to make as much room beneath themselves as they could. Bristlekit, Thriftkit, and Flipkit scurried out of the den and sheltered under them, rain already soaking their fur. Bristlekit and Thriftkit looked excited, but Flipkit's tail was drooping, his golden eyes wide with worry.

More and more cats gathered in the clearing as Squirrelflight and Cinderheart ran from one den to another, checking all the nests to make sure every cat was ready to evacuate. Spotpaw shifted from paw to paw: The water sloshing against her legs was freezing. Snappaw pressed against her side, shivering. "This is weird," he muttered. Spotpaw could see fear in her littermate's eyes.

She ran her tail over his back comfortingly. "We'll stick with the Clan and all take care of one another," she meowed, careful to keep her own anxiety out of her voice. "Everything's going to be fine." Snappaw's shoulders relaxed slightly, and Spotpaw realized she felt better, too: Reassuring her littermate had made her feel stronger.

It looked like all the cats of ThunderClan were in the clearing now, hunching against the rain, tense and alert.

Bramblestar strode past her, his broad shoulders clearing a path through the crowd of anxious cats.

"ThunderClan," he meowed, loudly enough that every cat could hear him over the rain, "follow me." He ducked into the tunnel and ThunderClan streamed after him. Spotpaw watched as her Clanmates hurried past her, their tails touching one another's shoulders to keep together, their faces set against the driving rain. They didn't know exactly where they were going, but they trusted Bramblestar to take them there.

Spotpaw trusted him, too. She was cold and a little afraid, but she knew, as surely as she knew the steady beat of her own heart, that Bramblestar would look after them. All she had to do was follow his orders. She caught Leafshade's eye and started forward obediently with the other apprentices.

The rain was coming down harder than ever, obscuring her vision and filling her ears with noise. She dug in her claws as she waded through the mud toward the camp entrance, trying to keep her balance. A hard lump—a rock, maybe—caught under her paw, and she stumbled to one side.

Something soft broke her fall with a frantic squeak. Spotpaw looked down to see Flipkit pinned beneath her, his small face terrified. He was trembling.

"Sorry!" she yelped, trying to scramble off the kit. It took a few heartbeats of floundering in the mud, splashing them both, before she managed it. "Are you okay? Where are your parents?"

Flipkit looked up at her and opened his mouth in a wail of dismay. "They left me!"

"They wouldn't have left you on purpose," Spotpaw told him comfortingly. Fernsong was the most indulgent father in the Clan, spending most of his time in the nursery with his kits, and Ivypool was a loving mother.

But looking at the cats hurrying past them out of camp, Spotpaw realized how they could have gotten separated from Flipkit. The driving rain blurred her vision, so that she could barely tell one cat from another, and now that she was off to one side, she didn't think any of them could see her. If a kit stumbled or hung back instead of staying safely under his mother or father, he could be left behind.

"Why didn't you keep up?" she asked, exasperated.

Flipkit's meow was shaky. "I *couldn't*! I'm stuck!"

"You are?" Spotpaw stared down at Flipkit. The water that lapped at her knees was almost up to his belly. He tried to move, and she saw his short legs straining. His paws were encased in mud, too heavy for him to move. "You must have stepped in a mud hole," she realized. "Don't worry, I'll help you."

Sliding her paws next to his, she began to claw the mud away. *Ugh!* It was cold and clammy, and she could feel it sticking to the bottom of her claws, clotting between her toes. Pulling back her ears in disgust, she kept scraping away. Out of the corner of her eye, she could see fewer and fewer cats in the clearing. *We have to hurry!*

"There!" she declared at last. "Try to pull your paws out." Flipkit strained, but as soon as he got one paw out of the mud, the others sank deeper. "Okay," Spotpaw decided. "I've got you." Bending forward, she took the loose fur at the back of his neck in her mouth, the way parents did with their kits, braced herself, and lifted. At first he seemed impossibly heavy, thick mud clinging to his paws, but then with a jerk Flipkit was free, hanging from her jaws.

She dropped him beside her. "Oof," she teased. "You definitely weigh more than prey." Flipkit gave a short purr of laughter, and Spotpaw sighed in relief. At least he wasn't scared and miserable anymore. "Okay," she meowed again. The last few warriors were disappearing into the thorn tunnel. "We'd better hurry. Get beneath my belly so I can protect you."

Flipkit was too tall for this. Since Spotpaw wasn't a full-grown warrior, his head bashed into her stomach. She stiffened her legs and stretched up, making herself as tall as possible. Flipkit ducked down, hunching his shoulders and holding his tail straight out. "Let's go," he decided at last.

"Great, now *yowl* if I'm about to leave you behind," Spotpaw told him.

It was slow going through the thorn tunnel. Spotpaw tried to keep her legs straight and her paws under her, but also to look down at Flipkit frequently to make sure he wasn't falling behind. Their paws slipped and scrambled on wet rock and mud as they climbed out of the ravine. Water soaked through her fur, wetting it as thoroughly as if she had tried to swim across the entire lake.

When they came out of the ravine, the rest of Thunder-Clan was out of sight. The rain was more blinding than ever outside the shelter of the tunnel. Trying to blink water out of her eyes, Spotpaw looked around. Trees, rocks, mud. No cats. And there was no sense in trying to scent their trail in this rain.

"Where'd every cat go?" Flipkit asked, peering out from under her. His voice was shaking.

Spotpaw swallowed hard. *I have to be brave for Flipkit.* "We'll find them," she declared. "Look around, see if you see any sign of which way ThunderClan went."

She scanned the ground, looking for some mark—surely, even in this driving rain, a whole Clan couldn't pass without leaving a trail. But there was nothing. . . .

"Look!" Flipkit yowled excitedly, and Spotpaw followed his gaze. A long scrape in the mud, clearly made by a paw. Another, heading uphill.

Higher ground, Spotpaw thought. "Good work, Flipkit!"

As they went uphill, she and Flipkit spotted more signs of the Clan's passing: bent grass, a muddy paw print, underbrush shoved aside.

At last, they heard the sounds of ThunderClan making camp among the bushes.

"Pull those branches this way."

"Is there any point trying to hunt in this weather?"

A terrified yowl. *"Flipkit!"*

"He's here!" Spotpaw yowled back. Ivypool burst through the brush just in front of them, frantic.

"Thank StarClan," she gasped. "Flipkit, are you all right?"

"Spotpaw and I found you!" he exclaimed, running out

from under Spotpaw's belly. "I was scared, but Spotpaw helped me!"

"I'm so glad." Ivypool nuzzled Flipkit, then rubbed her cheek gratefully against Spotpaw's. "Thank you so much. I don't know what I'd have done if we couldn't find him." She nodded back in the direction from which she'd come. "Come on, I'll show you where we're making camp, and then get Flip-kit back to Fernsong."

The temporary ThunderClan camp was as waterlogged as the rest of the territory, but they'd be less likely to get washed away on this higher ground. Cherryfall and Leafshade were standing guard over where most of the Clan rested beneath a tangle of bushes, while Bramblestar walked among them, checking that every cat was safe. He dipped his head to Spot-paw as she passed. "Well done," he told her.

Despite her cold, soaking-wet fur, Spotpaw felt a warm glow in her chest. Flipkit was safe. And Bramblestar had noticed how she'd helped her Clan.

Most of her Clanmates were curled together, taking what shelter they could beneath the thin branches above. She glanced at Leafshade before plopping down next to Stempaw: She wasn't allowed to train with him now; was she allowed to sleep next to him? But Leafshade blinked at her approvingly.

Shivering, she pressed her side against Stempaw's. He wasn't any warmer, though. He seemed asleep, but as she settled beside him, he half opened one green eye. "What hap-pened?" he asked. "Where were you?"

Spotpaw yawned, suddenly heavy with exhaustion. "Flipkit

was stuck," she murmured. "But I got him here."

Stempaw draped his tail across her back. "Spotpaw," he purred sleepily. "You saved Flipkit. You're amazing."

"Rise and shine, Spotpaw." Stempaw's voice sounded amused. Spotpaw opened her eyes and blinked at the light, so much brighter than it usually was when she woke in the morning in the apprentices' den. It was late morning . . . and the sun was shining.

"It stopped raining!" she yowled, scrambling to her paws. She was the last to wake—the other cats were already up and about. Everything around them was still wet, but the sky was clear blue for the first time in what felt like moons.

She and Stempaw stood shoulder to shoulder for a heartbeat, looking toward ThunderClan's ravine. Birchfall, Finleap, and Snappaw were just coming back into the temporary camp, mice dangling from their mouths, and Spotpaw raised her tail to her littermate in greeting.

It felt good to be next to Stempaw. It felt natural. *Maybe we'll be mates one day,* Spotfur thought dreamily, and then shook out her fur, irritated with herself. She was way too young to be thinking about that. *I don't even have my warrior name yet. Right now, I need to concentrate on being the best Clanmate I can.*

But, one day, when I am a warrior . . . maybe.

"A strong Clan depends on strong warriors," Cinderheart had told her. She was right. The Clan had worked together to evacuate camp, and every cat was okay. And *she* had protected

Flipkit. Thank StarClan she had found him before she left camp. *StarClan guided my paws.*

"Spotpaw! Stempaw!" Spotpaw's other littermate, Flypaw, called. "Twigbranch says we'd better start cleaning out the apprentices' den if we want dry nests tonight."

Stempaw sighed. "Ugh. Cleaning up camp's going to be a *lot* of work."

"It's okay," Spotpaw meowed, feeling a glow of pride in her Clan. "As long as we stick together, we can do anything."

CHAPTER 4

❧

Spotfur shivered, hunching her shoulders against the leaf-bare cold. The fresh-kill pile was almost empty. Only a single shriveled shrew remained.

"Thornclaw, Lilyheart, Spotfur," Squirrelflight called. "I want you to go on a border patrol. Mark the ShadowClan border well."

Flicking her tail at the deputy in acknowledgment, Spotfur headed for the other warriors. *The other warriors.* She'd earned her warrior name recently enough that she still got a thrill from it: She was not a 'paw anymore, but a full warrior.

Lilyheart was looking dubiously at the fresh-kill pile. "Can we wait for the hunting patrol to come back?", she asked. "I'm starving."

Thornclaw snorted. "You'll be better off hunting while we patrol. Once they've fed the elders and the queens, there won't be anything left. Prey's been short for a moon."

"I'll send out more hunting patrols," Squirrelflight promised. "We won't let the fresh-kill pile stay empty."

Spotfur stared at the shrew again, her stomach tight. *I hope we do find some prey.* In the chill of leaf-bare, there seemed to be less to hunt with each sunrise.

"Well, look at that," Cloudtail meowed admiringly, and Spotfur glanced up to see the hunting patrol returning through the camp entrance. Lionblaze had several mice—they must have found a nest. Molewhisker was carrying a robin, and Stemleaf, most impressively, had a large squirrel, big enough to feed three cats, dangling from his mouth.

Spotfur's mouth watered. This was enough prey that the nursing queens and the elders would eat well and there would still be food for other cats. If a few more hunting patrols went out today, maybe there would be enough for every cat to have a full belly.

Stemleaf's eyes met hers across the clearing, and she twitched her whiskers in greeting. After dropping the squirrel on the fresh-kill pile, he headed toward her.

"Hi, Stemleaf!" Bristlepaw darted in front of him. Spotfur rolled her eyes, amused. Bristlepaw was an eager apprentice—maybe a little *too* eager, sometimes. *Was I like that?*

"How did you catch *that*? Did you have to climb a tree?" Bristlepaw was asking Stemleaf. "Rosepetal won't show me how to hunt in trees yet; she says I have to wait until it's not so icy."

"Rosepetal's a great mentor," Stemleaf meowed. "She'll teach you how to get up a tree in a heartbeat, just like she taught me. When you're hunting with a patrol, you all do it together—one cat goes up the tree and the others stay on the ground in case the squirrel jumps down. Clanmates work together."

Bristlepaw's ears pricked with excitement as Stemleaf stretched out, showing her the proper careful leap to take down prey in a tree. "And then, pounce!" he added. "You'll get it!"

He's such a good Clanmate, Spotfur thought, affection swelling in her chest. Stemleaf looked up and his eyes met hers. He took a step forward, as if he was going to join her.

"Like this? Will you show me again?" Bristlepaw asked eagerly, and Stemleaf blinked apologetically at Spotfur, then looked back to Bristlepaw.

"Come on, Spotfur," Thornclaw called out, and, with a tiny sigh, Spotfur turned away from Stemleaf and joined the rest of her patrol. *I'll talk to Stemleaf later.*

The sun was low in the sky when they returned. Spotfur groaned as she sank down next to Stemleaf outside the warriors' den.

"Are you okay?" he asked, looking her over critically. "Were you limping?"

"Ugh." Spotfur flexed her sore paws, sheathing and unsheathing her claws. "The ground is so hard. I don't think I'll ever get used to it." As leaf-bare drew on, the hard-frozen ground was more and more unforgiving under her paws, sending a cold ache up her legs.

"I know," Stemleaf agreed. He hunched his shoulders, puffing out his fur to stay warmer. "Do you think leaf-bare is always like this? We were so young last leaf-bare, I don't even remember. Prey wasn't running so badly then, was it?"

Spotfur had hazy memories of curling against Cinderheart

in the nursery, cozy with Flykit and Snapkit on either side. She knew it had been cold outside, but she didn't remember this bone-aching iciness that lingered even when she was in the warriors' den with warm Clanmates beside her. And she didn't remember the constant hunger that seemed to follow them all—no cat was starving, but none of them ever had quite enough. "I don't think it was," she meowed. "Even Graystripe says he doesn't remember there ever being a leaf-bare this cold. Maybe old bones feel it more, but I don't think that's it."

Stemleaf's usually bright eyes were anxious. "What if it stays like this?"

"StarClan will guide our paws," Spotfur meowed, but she felt a catch in her throat that wasn't usually there. It had been a long time since the medicine cats had been able to commune with StarClan. She'd heard Alderheart talking to Squirrel-flight about it, both their faces dark with worry.

"Yeah." Stemleaf's ears twitched. "I'm sure StarClan will come back when the Moonpool thaws."

They shared an uneasy look. The Moonpool had never frozen solid before, and StarClan had never gone so long without sending the Clans some kind of sign.

"They will," Spotfur tried to sound sure. *StarClan would never abandon us.* "I'm just worried, though. If they can't reach us right now, StarClan can't keep us from making the wrong choices."

"We'll just have to look after each other, I guess," Stemleaf reassured her. His side pressed against hers, warm and solid.

Tension drained out of Spotfur's shoulders. *We can. We*

will. She remembered the stream of cats, tails pressed to one another's shoulders, as they'd evacuated the ThunderClan camp when she was an apprentice. And how all the Clans had worked together to find SkyClan a territory of their own. *We'll be all right until StarClan comes back, as long as we stick together,* she thought.

The ground was so cold against her belly that she was about to suggest to Stemleaf that they go out on a hunt of their own to stay warm, when a sharp voice came from the other side of the clearing.

"How could you be so careless?"

Spotfur looked up to see Dewnose glaring at his apprentice, his gray-and-white tail slashing angrily. Thriftpaw was staring at the ground, her paws shaking. Beside them, Alderheart looked as if he'd rather be anywhere else. "It was an accident, Dewnose," he muttered.

"Of course it was an accident," Dewnose snarled. "She's not a traitor, she's just a fluff-brain. Digging through the medicine-cat stores when you've got your back turned!"

"I just thought I could help Baykit!" Thriftpaw wailed. "I remembered what Jayfeather gave me when I had the same cough."

Alderheart shook his head. "You must never try to give any cat medicine, especially not a kit," he told her seriously. "Without a medicine cat's training, you might give them too much, or the wrong thing, and make them sicker."

"*And,*" Dewnose put in furiously, "not only did you try to treat a kit yourself, but you messed up the medicine cats' supply of marigold petals, too. What are they supposed to do *now*? Marigolds don't bloom in leaf-bare."

Thriftpaw bowed her head, ashamed.

"I might be able to find some dried petals left on the plants by the lake," Alderheart offered. "Thriftpaw can come help me look in the morning."

"She can go by herself *now*," Dewnose meowed sternly.

Spotfur and Stemleaf exchanged a look. *It's getting late. And it's awfully cold.*

"I'm sure it can wait until tomorrow." Alderheart sounded taken aback.

"She needs to fix what she did wrong," Dewnose argued. "That's how she'll learn."

Alderheart looked doubtful, but finally nodded.

"Okay." Thriftpaw's eyes were wide, but she straightened up, holding her head high. "I'll make this right," she meowed earnestly.

As the apprentice headed out of camp, Spotfur turned to Stemleaf. "She shouldn't go out there all by herself," she argued. "She hasn't even been an apprentice for very long." *Should I go after her?* Two cats would be much better off searching the lakeshore at dusk than one.

"Dewnose is her mentor; he gets to decide her punishments," Stemleaf answered, but he looked worried, too. "If he thinks it's safe, I'm sure she'll be all right."

Spotfur paced, watching the camp entrance anxiously.

It was dark, and Thriftpaw still hadn't returned.

"He shouldn't have sent her off by herself," Spotfur muttered. On the other side of camp, she could see Dewnose looking just as worried as she felt. The older warrior's head had dropped to his paws, and his eyes were fixed on the tunnel into camp.

"She's probably just looking for the marigold," Stemleaf meowed. "I'm sure she's fine." But his tail was twitching uneasily.

Spotfur shivered. Was it getting *colder*? Thriftpaw was too young and inexperienced to be out in the snow by herself after dark. *I can't let her stay out there alone.* Having made up her mind, she headed for Dewnose.

"We have to go find Thriftpaw," she told him abruptly. "She's not safe."

"She's *my* apprentice," Dewnose snapped back. Then he bowed his head. "But you're right. I'll go look for her."

"*You* shouldn't go alone, either," Spotfur insisted. Owls and foxes hunted at night. She glanced back at Stemleaf, hoping he would agree, and he got to his paws. "We'll come with you."

"I will, too." Honeyfur had been listening quietly, her green eyes worried, and now she rose and joined them. "We'll find her."

As they left the ravine, more snow began to fall. "This is going to wash away her scent trail," Spotfur meowed.

"Let's head for the lakeshore," Stemleaf suggested. "That's where she was supposed to go to look for the dried-up marigold."

They picked their way through the snow in a single file,

fierce wind clawing at their fur. Spotfur hunched low, trying to shield herself behind Honeyfur. All scents were half hidden under the smell of snow, and, except for the sound of the wind, the night seemed ominously silent. Spotfur wasn't used to being out of camp at night, and the darkness was confusing. She had to stop for a heartbeat and look around to get her bearings.

At the edges of the lake, the water had frozen into crackling ice. Honeyfur poked at it with a tentative paw. "She wouldn't have gone out on the ice, would she?"

"Why would she?" Spotfur meowed, suppressing a shudder at the thought. "The dead marigold plant is right here." Snow covered the remains of plants around the shore. Spotfur squinted at them, trying to make out any paw prints that might show Thriftpaw had been there, but the snow was falling faster and it was impossible to tell.

"Thriftpaw!" Dewnose yowled, and the rest of them joined in. "Thriftpaw!" There was no reply. Their own voices seemed muffled by the snow falling all around them.

Finally, they fell silent. Dewnose's tail drooped as he looked from side to side, desperately scanning the shore. "What if we don't find Thriftpaw?" he meowed. His amber gaze was agonized. "If anything's happened to her, it's my fault."

"We'll find her," Spotfur insisted, but her heart was sinking. *Thriftpaw could be anywhere.* How *would* they find her in the snowy darkness?

Dewnose sighed. "When I was a 'paw, Whitewing always gave me punishments that fixed whatever I'd done wrong.

That's what I was trying to do. I never thought it might be dangerous."

Stemleaf was staring back toward camp. "Thriftpaw knew the most likely place to find dried-up marigold petals was here, right?"

"Right." Honeyfur's ears twitched. "Can you think of anywhere else?"

"No," Stemleaf meowed. "But she would have gone from camp to here, and from here back to camp. We know the route she would have taken."

Hope flared in Spotfur's chest. "That's right! Even if she got lost, she wouldn't have wandered too far. We need to try to retrace her paw steps."

Together, they turned and padded back toward camp. The wind was at their backs this time, forcing them forward.

"Thriftpaw!" they yowled. Spotfur tried to look everywhere, her eyes searching the underbrush. "Thriftpaw!" she yowled again, her throat straining as she fought to make her voice heard above the wind.

Halfway to camp, Honeyfur stopped. "This is hopeless," she growled, frustrated. Spotfur's stomach twisted. *She's right. We're never going to find Thriftpaw in this.* The snow and the darkness turned the landscape around them into unfamiliar shadows.

Any of this—the snow, the wind, the bitter cold—could kill Thriftpaw, she realized, her mouth suddenly dry. *We can't stop searching for her.*

I'm not giving up. Just looking wasn't good enough. They needed to *think*.

"If Thriftpaw couldn't get home, what would she do?" she asked slowly. "She'd want to find somewhere where she would feel safe."

Stemleaf's fur was wet with snow, making him seem smaller and thinner than usual. "Where would she go that felt safe?"

"Somewhere a little like a den." Spotfur thought back to being an apprentice, curled safely in her nest, darkness and warmth and the soft sound of the other apprentices breathing nearby. "Somewhere sheltered."

Honeyfur shook her head. "I can't think of anywhere like that between the lake and camp."

Somewhere sheltered. Honeyfur was right that there was nothing like the little cave of the apprentice den out here. The leaf-bare underbrush wouldn't be thick enough to hide beneath, and tree roots would only shield part of her from the snow. Then Spotfur remembered. "The fallen tree! The one near where the apprentices learn to fight!" Back in leaf-fall, an old beech tree had fallen. There was a hollow beneath its trunk. "If she couldn't make it back to camp, I bet Thriftpaw would try to get there."

Dewnose nodded. "We were hunting near it just yesterday. I'm sure she'd think of it."

They hurried in that direction, their paws slipping on the wet ground. *Please let her be there,* Spotfur thought.

"Thriftpaw! Thriftpaw!"

Silence. The shape of the fallen tree was a dim blur up ahead.

Then there was a frightened yowl. "I'm here!"

* * *

Back at camp, Jayfeather nosed Thriftpaw all over, licking her fur dry as he scolded her and Dewnose equally: Dewnose for being such a mouse-brain as to send an apprentice out alone into the snow at night, and Thriftpaw for being stupid enough to listen to Dewnose *and* to get lost on her own Clan's territory. Shyly, Thriftpaw gave him the wilted marigold petals she had carefully carried all the way from the lakeshore, and Jayfeather paused in his lecture, taken aback.

"Very well," the blind medicine cat meowed at last. "Eat this feverfew, just in case, then go to your den and rest."

Dewnose thanked Spotfur, Stemleaf, and Honeyfur for their help, his meow rough with emotion, then escorted Thriftpaw to the apprentices' den, insisting that she lean on him. He'd apologized several times since they'd found her for sending her out on such a night.

"Dewnose feels pretty bad," Stemleaf commented as he and Spotfur turned in to the warriors' den.

Heading for her nest, Spotfur stretched, her tired muscles sore. "He should," she answered. "Thriftpaw might have really gotten hurt."

"I know." There were older warriors sleeping closer to the warm center of the den, and Stemleaf lowered his voice. "But he didn't actually do anything wrong, did he? Apprentices are supposed to get appropriate punishments, and he sent her to get the herb she ruined."

"He wasn't breaking any rules," Spotfur agreed. She climbed into her nest and snuggled down into the moss and feathers at the bottom. "Maybe we need a rule that will make sure punishments don't put cats in danger."

"Maybe." Stemleaf's nest was next to hers. He curled up and looked at her, his head on his orange-and-white paws. "But how could we change them? We don't make the decisions."

"Bramblestar does. I'm sure he'd listen to what we had to say," Spotfur told him. "He's a good cat. A good leader."

"Okay. We'll try." Stemleaf stretched, arching his back. "I'm proud that we found her," he added quietly. "We work well together, don't we?"

"Yeah." Spotfur dropped her voice even more. "It was scary that Thriftpaw was lost. But we figured it out together. And I liked that." *I liked working with you.*

She was happy to hunt or patrol with any of her Clanmates. But Stemleaf was special. She brushed her tail across the space between them, and felt his tail twining together with hers. She closed her eyes. *Tomorrow, we'll change the rules. Together.*

"I don't think you should bother Bramblestar." Shellfur flicked his tail. "He's too important to spend time listening to you."

"No cat asked you," Spotfur snapped back. She wished that Stemleaf's littermate hadn't overheard them planning. He wasn't as bossy now as when they'd been apprentices, but he was still sure he knew best.

Shellfur directed a pointed look toward Stemleaf. "Don't let her get you in trouble again."

Stemleaf's whiskers twitched. "It's as much my decision as Spotfur's," he meowed calmly. "I see the problem, too, and I think we should do something about it. I don't want to imagine what could have happened to Thriftpaw."

Spotfur swallowed and turned her back on Shellfur. "Let's do it," she meowed. Shoulder to shoulder, she and Stemleaf padded to the rock tumble below Bramblestar's den. Outside, they hesitated, their paws wet with snow.

"Should we . . . call him?" Stemleaf asked.

Spotfur took a deep breath. *Bramblestar's nice,* she reminded herself. *And he's a good leader. He'd want us to come to him about this.* "Bramblestar?" she meowed politely.

"What?" The ThunderClan leader thrust his broad tabby head out of his den and looked at them quizzically. "Something going on?"

Spotfur's mouth was dry. She looked at Stemleaf.

"We wanted to talk about what happened with Thriftpaw yesterday," Stemleaf began.

Bramblestar nodded, then leaped down, landing in front of them. "That must have been frightening," he meowed. "Dewnose told me how helpful you both were in finding her."

"She was lost." Spotfur realized that had sounded more abrupt than she'd meant it to. "She shouldn't have been out there alone."

Bramblestar flicked his ears. "Maybe not," he meowed. "But Dewnose was doing what he thought was right, and we can't blame him for the weather getting worse."

"No," Spotfur answered, frustrated. Why wasn't she

making herself clear? "I'm not blaming Dewnose. But I—*we*— think that there should be a rule about being sent out of camp alone. At least during a leaf-bare like this one."

Stemleaf nodded. "Apprentices shouldn't be punished that way. It's too dangerous."

Bramblestar gazed at them both for a few heartbeats, his amber eyes intent. "You're right," he agreed at last. "I've been letting mentors use their own judgment, but Squirrelflight and I will tell them to keep their apprentices from leaving camp alone, at least until newleaf comes. And no cat should be sent out alone as punishment."

"Thank you," Spotfur meowed, light-headed with relief. Bramblestar was taking them seriously, as if they weren't two of the most junior warriors in the whole Clan.

Bramblestar dipped his head to them. "I appreciate you coming to me about this," he told them quietly. "It's clear you're both eager to help your Clan."

He padded off into the clearing, heading for Squirrelflight's side. As soon as he was out of earshot, Spotfur turned to Stemleaf, delighted.

"He listened to us," Stemleaf purred. "That was easier than I thought it would be."

Spotfur let her tail rest against his side. "We *do* work well together, don't we?"

CHAPTER 5

♣

The cold of leaf-bare was fiercer than ever, but the sun was shining. Spotfur was eager and alert: It was so *good* to feel the sun on her pelt after days of heavy clouds looming over the forest. The last border patrol had just left camp, and Squirrelflight was organizing the remaining warriors to hunt. As prey got scarcer and scarcer in the brutal weather, she'd taken to sending out three or four patrols at a time to hunt in different parts of ThunderClan territory.

"Twigbranch," she began, "take a patrol toward the abandoned Twoleg nest."

"Okay," the gray she-cat replied cheerfully. She called, "Hey, Bristlefrost, do you want to hunt with us?"

There was a pause, and Spotfur turned to see the new warrior standing a little apart from the other cats, a strange expression on her face. "No, thanks," she answered slowly. "I . . . er . . . there's a thorn in my bedding and I need to get it out."

Huh? That was no reason to refuse to hunt. And Bristlefrost had always been eager, such an enthusiastic apprentice that Bramblestar had let her take her assessment and become

a warrior before either of her littermates. Spotfur turned
to Stemleaf in confusion, but he hunched his shoulders and
avoided her gaze.

"Um. Stormcloud, then, do you want to patrol with us?"
Twigbranch pressed on, even as Rosepetal, her tail slashing,
dragged Twigbranch out of sight.

"Sure," Stormcloud answered.

Stemleaf was about to step forward and volunteer himself,
but Spotfur laid her tail across his back before he could move.

"Do you know what's up with Bristlefrost?" she asked
softly. "That was weird."

Stemleaf shifted from one paw to another. "She's . . .
unhappy," he meowed at last. "And I think it's because of me."

"Because of *you*?" Spotfur echoed, puzzled. Stemleaf had
always treated the other cat like a younger sister. Why would
Bristlefrost suddenly be unhappy because of him?

Stemleaf looked even more uncomfortable. "She said . . .
after she passed her assessment, Bristlefrost told me she hoped
one day we could be mates. That she had feelings for me."

"Oh." Spotfur's stomach dropped.

"And I, well, I told her that couldn't happen. Because
I already knew which cat I want to be my mate." Stemleaf
looked at her, then away.

A wave of dizziness hit Spotfur. Did he mean . . . Stemleaf
was looking at her again. "Me?" she meowed, her voice faint.

Stemleaf blinked at her. "Of course. It's always been you."

Despite the cold, Spotfur felt suddenly, amazingly warm.
"Me too," she meowed, the words rushing out. "You're the

only cat I've ever felt like this about."

They stared at each other. Then Stemleaf took a step forward and pressed his cheek to hers. He smelled familiar, and comforting, and wonderful.

"Spotfur," a sudden yowl rang out, and she jerked back. "You're with us." Another hunting patrol had gathered around Birchfall, ready to set out.

"Coming," she meowed, and stepped away from Stemleaf, still looking at him. "I have to go."

His whiskers twitched. "Go on, then," he meowed. "We'll have time to talk when we get back."

Yes. She turned and hurried toward the others, her paws light. *We'll have the rest of our lives together.*

It was a long, hard hunt and they returned with only a few skinny voles and sparrows, but Spotfur still felt a glow of happiness despite the cold. She dropped her vole on the fresh-kill pile and looked around to see if Stemleaf's patrol had returned yet.

She saw Bristlefrost first, curled up quietly with Rosepetal, and a pang of regret shot through her. She couldn't be sorry that Stemleaf loved her—that was the *best* thing she could think of—but she was sorry that it hurt Bristlefrost. The younger warrior looked sad, and something else that made the hair along Spotfur's spine prickle . . . frightened?

She saw Stemleaf coming from the warriors' den and forgot Bristlefrost for a moment. Her heart thudded in her chest as she took a step toward him.

"Spotfur," Squirrelflight called from behind her, her voice weary. "Bramblestar's in the medicine den. Take him some prey; he'll need to eat."

Spotfur turned to see the ThunderClan deputy standing with Jayfeather at the edge of the clearing, both their faces sharp with worry.

"Sure," she answered, turning back to the fresh-kill pile. "Is he sick?"

Squirrelflight closed her eyes for a heartbeat and took a deep breath. "He's not well." As Spotfur inspected the fresh-kill pile, Squirrelflight turned back to Jayfeather and continued their low-voiced discussion.

Spotfur selected a vole a little fatter than the rest and headed toward the medicine den. As she passed him, Stemleaf fell into step beside her. "Bramblestar decided to lead our hunting patrol," he whispered. "He was acting really weird, and then he suddenly fainted."

Fainted? Spotfur made a concerned noise around the vole.

"It was bad," Stemleaf meowed. "When we got him back to the medicine den, he started convulsing. The medicine cats don't know what's wrong with him. He's been resting for a while, though."

As they reached the entrance to the medicine cat den, Stemleaf leaned forward and quickly pressed his cheek against Spotfur's. "I'll talk to you later," he whispered. She felt warm all the way through, even as she pushed her way through the bramble tendrils that covered the den's entrance.

Inside, Bramblestar was huddled in a nest, his face turned

away from the rest of the camp. Alderheart, who was Bramble-star's son as well as a medicine cat, was beside him, eyes fixed anxiously on his father.

He looked up as Spotfur entered. "Squirrelflight sent you?"

Spotfur nodded, stepping closer to Bramblestar's nest and dropping the vole beside him. "Is he awake?" she asked softly. From here, she could feel heat coming off of Bramblestar's body, startling against the leaf-bare chill of the den. "He's burning up," she meowed.

The ThunderClan leader abruptly raised his head toward her, his eyes blazing. Spotfur flinched backward. "Why are you here?" he asked, his voice unusually rough.

"I brought you some fresh-kill," she told him, glancing toward Alderheart.

Bramblestar blinked. "Is that poisoned prey?"

Spotfur bristled in surprise. "What? Of course not!"

"Bramblestar," Alderheart began soothingly, but Bramble-star cut him off with a growl. Spotfur felt sick and horrified at the suggestion.

"Prove it," Bramblestar demanded. "Taste the prey."

Confused, Spotfur looked at Alderheart again. "Do it," the medicine cat urged. "He needs nourishment to fight this sickness."

Spotfur dipped her head and took a small bite of the vole, warm blood spreading over her tongue. "It's good," she meowed when she'd finished, and pushed it toward Bramble-star.

Bramblestar shook his head, his eyes blurred with confusion. "Spotfur?" he meowed. "I'm sorry . . . I don't know what's happening to me. I feel like . . ." He paused. "I keep forgetting where I am." He looked lost.

"You'd better go," Alderheart told her quickly. "He's not himself."

No, he's not. Spotfur backed toward the entrance, unable to turn away from her leader's confused stare. How could this be the same cat who had listened so thoughtfully when she and Stemleaf had come to him about Thriftpaw? She barely recognized him.

Outside she found Stemleaf and her littermate Snaptooth waiting for her. "How is he?" Stemleaf asked at once. "Was he awake?"

"He was *weird*," Spotfur told them. "Scary. And then it was like he was lost."

She told them what had happened.

"You said he was feverish, right?" Stemleaf asked. "That's probably why he was acting strange."

"Yeah." Spotfur breathed in, calmed by the scents of her brother and her . . . what was Stemleaf now? Friend, still? Someday mate? She felt like she wasn't communicating exactly how alarming Bramblestar had been. He had looked at her as if she were a stranger, some rogue he had to guard against. "I'm not doing a good job of explaining how scary he was. But you didn't see him."

"Sickness makes every cat weird." Snaptooth flicked his

golden tabby tail dismissively. "Remember when we were kits and I got that fever? I thought I was an eagle for a while." He purred with laughter. "You and Flywhisker had to talk me out of jumping out of a tree to prove I could fly."

"Right . . ." Spotfur tried to purr, too. She remembered how confused Snaptooth had been, but he hadn't acted as different from his regular self as Bramblestar had, or as desperate.

"It's nothing to worry about." Snaptooth blinked reassuringly at her, then headed for the warriors' den. Spotfur stayed beside Stemleaf.

"Are you okay?" he asked, looking at her intently.

"I'm not overreacting," she insisted miserably. "It felt like there was something seriously wrong with Bramblestar. He must be very sick."

"I don't think you're overreacting." Stemleaf pressed his side against hers, warm and comforting. "You wouldn't. But don't forget, Bramblestar's got nine lives. He's safer than we are, even when he's sick. He's bound to be all right."

"I guess," Spotfur mewed. But a tendril of cold worry curled through her. StarClan hadn't spoken to the Clans for moons. *What if Bramblestar dies and they won't bring him back?*

Bramblestar got sicker and sicker, until he lay motionless in the medicine den, unresponsive no matter what was going on around him.

"What's going to happen to him?" Flywhisker whispered, sitting shoulder to shoulder with Spotfur by the apprentices' den.

Spotfur swallowed. "I don't know," she murmured.

She and Flywhisker watched Squirrelflight pacing through camp, her face tight with worry, her tail twitching. *Squirrelflight's barely holding the Clan together,* Spotfur thought. *What will we do if Bramblestar dies?*

The next day, Bramblestar didn't wake at all. Alderheart came out at sunhigh to nibble on a mouse, looking exhausted. "He just tosses and turns," he told Spotfur sadly. "His fever isn't coming down." Spotfur exchanged a look with Stemleaf, her heart sinking. *Is this the end?*

She and Stemleaf and the rest of ThunderClan spent most of that day waiting nervously in the clearing, wondering when news would come from the medicine den. *Will Bramblestar ever wake up again?*

She was crouched by herself near the medicine den, scratching lines in the dirt with her claws and listening for any sound that might indicate how Bramblestar was doing, when Stemleaf approached her. He sat down beside her, a determined look on his face.

"I want you to be my mate," he meowed bluntly.

Spotfur blinked. "Uh—" It seemed wrong to talk about this right now.

"I was waiting, but then I realized Bramblestar wouldn't *want* us to wait," Stemleaf told her. "If bad things are going to happen, I want you beside me. And if good things are going to happen, I still want you beside me. No cat knows what's coming, but we never do. I don't want to wait any longer."

Spotfur stared into his intent green eyes, and warmth

rushed through her. Stemleaf was right. No matter what, they wanted to be together. "Okay," she meowed softly. "Me too. Yes."

Stemleaf pressed his side against hers, and they stayed there, quiet together, as the sun got lower and lower in the sky.

Near sunset, a border patrol brought Tigerstar, Shadow-Clan's leader, and Shadowpaw, the ShadowClan medicine-cat apprentice, into camp. They claimed that Shadowpaw had received a vision from StarClan. If they made Bramblestar a nest in the snow and left him there overnight, he would get better.

Won't he get sicker? Spotfur wondered, her chest tight with apprehension. *And why would StarClan give a message about Thunder-Clan's leader to ShadowClan?*

Squirrelflight said no. It was a ridiculous idea.

But they tried everything their own medicine cats could think of, and nothing helped. Bramblestar grew weaker still. Alderheart and Jayfeather, thin and exhausted, rarely left the medicine den. Squirrelflight paced the camp late at night and barely spoke.

What if Bramblestar can't come back? Has StarClan forgotten us? That couldn't happen, could it? Spotfur knew that every cat in the Clan was wondering it, but she whispered it only to Stemleaf.

"There's only one thing left to try," Alderheart argued at last. Shadowpaw's plan. Jayfeather snarled at the idea of putting Bramblestar out in the cold, but finally, after a Gathering where Shadowpaw spoke of another vision from StarClan, Squirrelflight, too, agreed. The treatment might have a slim chance of saving Bramblestar, but it was the only chance they had.

Finleap and Molewhisker carried Bramblestar out to the moor, followed by Alderheart and Jayfeather—Jayfeather still objecting to the plan in a hoarse, angry voice—so that the ThunderClan medicine cats could watch over their leader.

"I don't know," Finleap told them on his return. He worked his paws restlessly against the ground, his tail drooping. "Shadowpaw made a nest for him in the most exposed part of our territory. He'll be covered with snow. How can this help?"

"It's got to help," Spotfur meowed. She ached with anxiety. "Shadowpaw is a medicine-cat apprentice. It *must* be a real message from StarClan." Shadowpaw seemed like a nice cat, and they'd been at peace with ShadowClan for a while. Surely no medicine-cat apprentice would lie about something like this.

But he was so young. What if he was wrong? She licked at her paws nervously. But Shadowpaw was supposed to have received visions from StarClan before, when no other cat had been able to hear them, and he had known that Bramblestar was sick when no cat outside ThunderClan should have known.

"I didn't want to leave him there," Molewhisker confessed. "If he—if this doesn't help . . . I'll feel like it was my fault."

"It wouldn't be your fault," Stemleaf meowed firmly. "It wouldn't be Alderheart's or Squirrelflight's either, even though they made the decision. It's the only chance left."

Spotfur lay awake all night in her nest near the entrance to the warriors' den. Her tail touched Stemleaf's, but they didn't speak. She could hear the other warriors shifting in their nests. No cat was sleeping tonight. Regularly, a shadow passed in front of the den entrance: Squirrelflight, pacing through camp, her fur wet with snow, ignoring the bitter cold.

It must be colder out on the moor, Spotfur thought.

As the gray light of dawn began to illuminate the camp, ThunderClan's warriors padded out into the clearing to wait together. Squirrelflight slipped silently out of camp, and they all watched her go, knowing she was heading for the moor.

"Maybe he's recovered," Snaptooth whispered. "Maybe he and Squirrelflight will come back together."

"I hope so," Spotfur answered. Her mouth was dry, and she couldn't take her eyes off the camp entrance.

The sun climbed higher and higher. Some cats shared tongues quietly, but there was no conversation. No cat ate, and no cat organized hunting or border patrols. It seemed like they were all breathing together—shallow, nervous breaths— as they waited and worried.

Finally, the brambles at the camp entrance shook. Some cat was coming into the ravine. Spotfur rose to her paws, vaguely aware of Stemleaf getting up beside her.

Squirrelflight came into camp alone. Her green eyes were wide and staring, and she stood still, her sides heaving as she gasped for breath.

When she finally spoke, her voice was strained. "Bramble-star is dead."

* * *

It was past sunhigh when four of ThunderClan's warriors bore Bramblestar's ice-crusted body back into camp. Every cat in the Clan watched, some silent, a few yowling with grief. Squirrelflight huddled near the entrance to the warriors' den, unmoving, her fur soaked with snow. Her daughter, Sparkpelt, pressed close against her, while Whitewing and Sorrelstripe hovered nearby, but she didn't seem to notice any cat. She stared bleakly at Bramblestar's still form as Bristlefrost and the other warriors carefully lowered him to the ground.

If only I could have done something, Spotfur thought helplessly. She had seen how sick Bramblestar was, that first day in the medicine den. But nothing had helped. Shadowpaw must have been wrong about his visions. StarClan *had* abandoned them. She felt like something was tearing apart inside her. Bramblestar had been a wise leader, kind and strong and steady. What would they do without him?

When darkness fell, all the cats of ThunderClan gathered to sit vigil for their dead leader. Sparkpelt and Alderheart, along with Jayfeather and Lionblaze—the kits Bramblestar had raised—sat close to him on one side, Squirrelflight on the other. They and the warriors who had known Bramblestar best spoke of his bravery and of how well he had guided the Clan.

Spotfur, farther back in the crowd of warriors, huddling between Stemleaf and Snaptooth, kept losing track of what was being said. Even when Jayfeather snarled at Squirrelflight, "Why did you let Shadowpaw kill him?" she barely heard.

She couldn't pull her eyes away from Bramblestar's body. He was so *still*. Her heart pounded, and with every beat, waves of sick disbelief washed through her. *How can he be dead?* He had been ThunderClan's leader her whole life.

At last, the junior warriors spoke their memories of Bramblestar, one by one. Spotfur barely listened as Flywhisker spoke—something about how Bramblestar had encouraged her as an apprentice—and then cleared her own throat. "He was kind to me," she meowed. "He *listened*, even though I was young and inexperienced."

Sorrow flooded through her, and she sat down in silence. Soon the vigil was over. The elders, led by Graystripe, stepped forward solemnly to pick up Bramblestar's body. They would bury him outside camp.

Then Bramblestar moved, a slow shiver of his side.

A murmur of disbelief ran through the gathered cats. *It must have been the wind in his fur,* Spotfur told herself. She had seen the ice covering Bramblestar's body. If he was going to come back with his next life from StarClan, surely it would have happened right away. She had always been told that it took only a few breaths for a leader to move from one life to another.

Bramblestar's side moved again, his muscles shifting. Spotfur turned to Stemleaf and found him staring, hope dawning in his eyes. "Did you see that?" he asked. Together, they turned back.

"This can't be," Thornclaw whispered, his voice taut with hope.

Bramblestar raised his head and blinked groggily, then rolled onto his belly. He looked around at the Clan.

Spotfur gasped, disbelief and joy warring inside her. She had been wrong. StarClan had never abandoned them.

Bramblestar's alive!

CHAPTER 6

Spotfur stretched, then licked lazily at her foreleg, enjoying the sun's warmth soaking into her pelt. Patches of snow lingered at the shadier end of camp and below the Highledge, but the air was warmer than it had been for moons, and the sky was a clear pale blue.

Everything's going to be all right, she thought cheerfully. Stemleaf was on the other side of the clearing, sharing a squirrel with his sisters, Eaglewing and Plumstone, and he flicked his ears companionably at her when their eyes met.

Mmm, squirrel, she thought. Now that newleaf had begun, prey was running well and the hunger of leaf-bare was only a memory. Just as she began to consider getting up and investigating the fresh-kill pile, a hunting patrol led by Cinderheart came into camp, more prey dangling from their mouths.

Maybe a mouse, she thought, cocking her head to eye the plump mice Finchpaw was carrying. As Spotfur got to her paws, Squirrelflight appeared at the entrance to Bramblestar's den, then scrambled down the rockfall to the clearing.

"Good hunting!" she praised. "ThunderClan will eat well today."

Behind her, Bramblestar jumped down from the Highledge, his paws hitting the ground with a quiet thump. Anxiety fluttered in Spotfur's chest, replacing her earlier good mood. Since he'd awakened with his new life, Bramblestar had been unpredictable. Maybe it was hard to adjust to being alive again, after he'd been dead for so long.

"Lilyheart," he meowed, scanning the hunters. "Where is your prey?"

The small tabby peeked past the rest of her patrol. "I didn't catch anything," she answered quietly. Spotfur tensed more at the nervousness in Lilyheart's eyes.

The tip of Bramblestar's tail twitched. "No?" he asked. "Why not?"

"I . . ." Lilyheart blinked, and Cinderheart, dropping her prey on the pile, stepped in.

"She helped in hunting most of the things we caught. You know how a patrol hunts together, Bramblestar."

Bramblestar glanced at her dismissively. "What I'm hearing is that she caught nothing herself." He stalked closer to Lilyheart. "A warrior who doesn't hunt for her Clan is letting the Clan down. She's not following the code." Spotfur shifted her paws, wishing she could defend Lilyheart. It wasn't fair to blame her, especially when, just as Cinderheart had said, she'd doubtless helped catch the prey the patrol was carrying.

"I *tried*!" Lilyheart objected. She looked like she wanted to run away and hide.

"Bramblestar," Squirrelflight broke in. "Lilyheart's a good warrior. Not every warrior can catch prey every time they go on a hunting patrol. And we've got plenty."

Narrowing his amber eyes, Bramblestar looked around at the gathered cats. "The code tells us to put our Clan first." He raised his voice, his words ringing out over the clearing. "A true warrior would keep hunting until she had prey to feed her Clan. Every cat must serve the Clan if we're all going to be safe."

Lilyheart stared down at her paws. "I'm sorry," she whispered.

"You can prove your determination to do better by *doing* better," Bramblestar told her. "Sleep on the moor tonight, and come back to camp tomorrow, once you've caught at least a few pieces of prey." Spotfur gasped silently, her dismay mirrored in her Clanmates' faces. Was Bramblestar really going to send Lilyheart out alone for punishment? Didn't he remember what he'd promised after Thriftpaw had gotten lost in the woods?

"On the moor!" Squirrelflight meowed indignantly. "There's still snow on the ground there. Can't she just do an extra hunt tomorrow?"

"It depends how well she wants to serve her Clan. And if she believes what the code tells us—that her leader's word *is* the code." Bramblestar was watching Lilyheart with his eyes narrowed.

"I'm not sure it's a good idea for any cat to be out there alone at night," Squirrelflight argued.

Lilyheart swallowed hard. "I'll do it," she meowed.

Bramblestar nodded. "Good. Maybe you *can* be loyal to ThunderClan."

As Lilyheart headed back to the camp entrance, Spotfur's pelt prickled uneasily. Why was Bramblestar so much harsher now? Just a few moons ago, he'd agreed with her and Stemleaf that sending a cat out of camp alone at night wasn't a fair punishment. He'd been harsh and snappish since he'd started his new life, but he'd never gone against a rule he'd decided on before his death. Why would he punish Lilyheart that way? Why would he punish her at all?

Across the clearing, her eyes met Stemleaf's, and she could tell his thoughts matched hers. *This isn't right.*

"We have to have faith that Bramblestar knows what he's doing," Cinderheart meowed. She scented the air. "Do you smell rabbit?"

Spotfur wanted to yowl with frustration. She'd convinced her parents to come out on a patrol with her so that they could talk in private, but it didn't seem like they were hearing what she said at all.

Lionblaze's ears pricked up. "I could go for some rabbit," he mused.

"Aren't you worried about how Bramblestar's acting?" Spotfur asked. How could they not see a problem? "He's so much harsher than he ever was before. And if he's not scolding some cat for something, all he wants to do is curl up in his den with Squirrelflight. He's even gotten *Bristlefrost* to do half the deputy duties so that Squirrelflight doesn't leave his side."

The younger warrior was doing her best, but it was *ridiculous* to ask some cat who'd had their warrior name for such a short time to take on that kind of responsibility. Maybe Bramblestar didn't notice the way some of the senior warriors' pelts spiked when such a young cat gave them orders, but Spotfur did.

Cinderheart and Lionblaze exchanged a look.

"Spotfur," Cinderheart began, "Bramblestar's been through a lot. He's just lost a life. It's natural he would want his mate by his side." She blinked at Lionblaze lovingly.

That's true, but . . . "The way he woke up . . . that wasn't the way it's supposed to go when a leader gets a new life, is it? Maybe something happened to him in StarClan."

Spotfur had never seen a leader begin a new life before, but she'd heard stories about how it worked—there ought to have been only a few heartbeats between one life ending and the new one beginning. And he should have woken strong and refreshed. Spotfur shuddered, thinking of the hours when Bramblestar had lain cold and still, ice gathering in his fur, saw again the dazed, dull look in his eyes when he'd finally awakened.

Cinderheart's blue eyes were sad. "StarClan has gotten so far away from us," she meowed. "Maybe it was hard for Bramblestar to find his way home."

Reluctant sympathy stirred in the back of Spotfur's mind. She imagined Bramblestar wandering, somewhere between their ancestors in StarClan and his own cold body.

"That's still no excuse for the way he's treating other cats," she argued stubbornly. "He's always been a kind leader. Why would he punish Lilyheart like that?"

"I don't like the way Bramblestar's acting either," Lionblaze meowed, his paws shifting as he thought. "But he's earned a lot of trust. He's led ThunderClan through all kinds of trouble. He raised me and my littermates like a father. And he's always wanted the best for all of us. I have to give him a chance."

"We must choose to follow Bramblestar and believe in him," Cinderheart added gently. "I'm sure he'll get back to being himself again. Can you try to believe that, too?"

Looking between her parents, Spotfur could see the sincerity in their faces. And they were right. Bramblestar had proved over and over that he was a good leader, that he only wanted to guide and protect his Clan. Surely he deserved a little time to recover from what had happened to him.

"Okay," she agreed, a swell of relief running through her at the thought that Bramblestar might soon be himself again. "I'll try."

Cold raindrops trickled through Spotfur's pelt and she shook herself irritably, fluffing her fur. Beside her, Lionblaze's golden fur was marked with dark trails of rain, while Bristlefrost ducked her head to keep water out of her eyes. It had been raining all day, and the heavy gray clouds overhead showed no sign of clearing. *Still,* Spotfur thought, *going on this border patrol is better than being in camp right now.* The day before, Bramblestar had announced that he and Squirrelflight, as the

Clan leaders, would take the first pick of the fresh-kill pile, before even the elders and queens, and every cat was bristling like they had a burr stuck in their pelt.

The warrior code said that elders and queens with kits ate first. Giving elders the first of the prey was how the Clan honored warriors who had spent their lives serving their Clans, while making sure nursing queens ate well was a way to preserve the Clan's future. It was one of the most important rules of the warrior code.

Why would Bramblestar suddenly change things? Spotfur wondered, pushing her way through tall, wet grass. The code *did* also say that the Clan leader's word was the code, so whatever Bramblestar said must be right. But he'd never insisted on special treatment before. Squirrelflight had looked surprised and uncomfortable at his announcement, but she'd gone along with it.

Will this change Lionblaze's mind about Bramblestar? Spotfur wondered. Her father was stalking next to her, scenting the air. He didn't look like he was thinking about anything except borders and prey, but he'd been angry yesterday. He'd argued with Bramblestar. Her chest tightened with anxiety—if even Lionblaze thought Bramblestar was doing something wrong, it must be true.

"Let's patrol the SkyClan border first," Bristlefrost suggested. "It's more sheltered beneath the trees."

At least Bristlefrost hasn't lost all her common sense, Spotfur thought. The younger warrior watched Bramblestar with worshipful eyes and seemed to take his word as StarClan's will, but she kept her head when they were on patrol.

Streams of water dripped steadily off the tree canopy above them. "She has a point," Spotfur meowed. "It might stop raining. Then we could check the WindClan border without getting drenched."

Lionblaze eyed the heavy clouds overhead and snorted. "We're going to get drenched anyway," he meowed. "We might as well check the scent line before it's completely washed away."

He headed out onto the moor and, with a sigh, Spotfur followed, Bristlefrost trailing behind. The full force of the rain hit Spotfur's back as she moved out from under the trees, but at least it wasn't freezing cold. "It's good to see rain instead of snow," she meowed to Lionblaze.

Lionblaze shook his head, raindrops flying from his ears. "I think I prefer snow."

"At least there's warmth in the air," Spotfur reminded him, hurrying across the grass.

"Not much," Lionblaze retorted. "But the prey's returning, which is worth a little rain."

"Thank StarClan," Spotfur remembered the constant low ache of hunger she'd felt all through leaf-bare.

Lionblaze glanced up at the sky, his eyes narrowing. "You're wasting your breath. We don't even know that they're listening anymore."

"Of course they are!" Spotfur meowed, horrified. Maybe the Clans hadn't been able to hear StarClan while the Moonpool was frozen solid, but she had to believe that StarClan had been watching over them the whole time. They had brought

Bramblestar back when it seemed like all hope was lost, hadn't they? Surely it wouldn't be long before they spoke to the medicine cats the way they always had. Anyway: "The thaw has set in properly now. There's no reason why they can't."

Lionblaze's shoulders hunched. "It might take a while for them to reach us again."

Spotfur's pelt prickled anxiously. That couldn't be true, could it?

"Perhaps they're waiting for us to follow the warrior code properly," Bristlefrost's voice broke in from behind them. Spotfur turned to frown at her. What was she implying?

"We've always followed the warrior code," Lionblaze's voice was cold. "At least, some of us have."

Lionblaze and Bristlefrost stared at each other for a long moment. With relief, Spotfur caught a familiar scent. "I can smell rabbit," she meowed, breaking the tension.

Lionblaze raised his head, sniffing the air. "So can I." They exchanged glances, then looked out across the stretch of heather between them and the WindClan border.

There! A gray rabbit, still thin from leaf-bare's hunger, was nibbling grass between two bushes. Spotfur crouched, then skulked forward, keeping low. Out of the corner of her eye, she could see Lionblaze doing the same.

They were close enough to see the quick movement of the rabbit's sides as it breathed and the twitch of its ears when it suddenly caught their scent and bolted. Spotfur and Lionblaze dashed after it.

Spotfur slipped on the wet heather as she bounded after the

rabbit, then caught her balance and ran faster, her nose full of its tantalizing scent. There was a flash of white belly as it drew up on its hind legs, then veered frantically in another direction. Weaving through the bushes after it, her father leaping ahead of her, rain flying in her face, her paws felt lighter than they had for days.

At last, the rabbit was trapped between them and, with a leap, Lionblaze brought it down. Meowing a quick thanks to StarClan, he picked the rabbit up and carried it back toward Bristlefrost.

"Good hunting," Spotfur purred, and Lionblaze dipped his head to her.

Bristlefrost ran to meet them halfway, her face frightened. "You caught that on WindClan land!" she yowled, as soon as they were close enough to hear.

Spotfur's heart sank, and she looked around. It wasn't true, was it? But there was the line of furze that marked this part of the WindClan border, just a few tail-lengths away. They had definitely crossed it in their hunt.

Lionblaze dropped the rabbit. "We couldn't help it," he meowed guiltily.

Spotfur nodded in agreement. They hadn't done it on purpose. They'd just been following their prey. *ThunderClan* prey. "It was only on WindClan land because we chased it there." She glanced back toward the moor. She wished the stream that separated part of WindClan and ThunderClan's territories ran here, too—they couldn't have missed that border.

Lionblaze and Bristlefrost were still arguing. "StarClan

will know," Bristlefrost meowed desperately.

"StarClan would never be angry at a warrior for feeding his Clan," Lionblaze decided with finality, and picked up the rabbit. "This will make a good meal for Graystripe, Cloudtail, and Brightheart."

Belly twisting with anxiety, Spotfur padded after Lionblaze. As she scent-marked the ThunderClan side of the border, she wondered whether Lionblaze was right. Surely StarClan wouldn't punish them for a well-intentioned accident. . . .

"If Harestar comes here, and accuses us of invading his land, is that what you're going to tell him? That you wouldn't have done it if he kept his borders better marked?" Bramblestar was furious. The fur along his spine rose as he growled at them. Lionblaze snarled back, pointing out that sometimes borders were accidentally crossed. Behind Bramblestar, Spotfur could see Bristlefrost, her paws working anxiously against the ground.

Of course Bristlefrost told him, Spotfur thought. She and Lionblaze would have told their leader themselves, if he'd been the old, steady, thoughtful Bramblestar. This new Bramblestar was unpredictable. *Untrustworthy.* Worry curled inside her at the thought. If they couldn't trust their leader, who could they trust?

"You know StarClan has been silent these past moons," Bramblestar hissed. "We're supposed to be following the warrior code so that they'll come back. How do you think they'll feel about warriors crossing borders without permission? Do you think they'll come back if we can't even obey such a simple rule?"

"StarClan isn't going to abandon us just because I crossed the WindClan border," Lionblaze growled.

As they argued, Spotfur felt her anxiety turn to anger. What right did Bramblestar have to decide what would make StarClan angry? He was treating Lionblaze like the younger cat was some kind of rogue, when just a few days before, Lionblaze had been defending him! She pressed her shoulder against her father's.

"You broke the code, even though I've told you it must be followed," Bramblestar snarled, his face barely a whisker's length away from Lionblaze's.

Spotfur couldn't hold back any longer. She'd held her tongue when Bramblestar snarled at the rest of the Clan, but she wasn't going to let him talk to her father that way. "Every cat here has broken the code at some point," She glared at Bramblestar. "Some of us worse than others."

Bramblestar's amber eyes were on her now, so angry that Spotfur felt the urge to bow her head and back away, but she firmed her shoulders and stared boldly back.

"What's that supposed to mean?" Bramblestar asked, flexing his long claws.

"I mean that Squirrelflight once lied to every cat, pretending her sister's kits—her sister the *medicine cat's* kits—were hers. She lied on purpose and she lied for moons. If you can overlook that, then you can overlook us crossing a border without realizing." Spotfur heard Squirrelflight's sharp inhale and felt Lionblaze—who *was* one of those kits—tense by her side, but she kept her eyes locked on Bramblestar's. It wasn't fair to them to bring up these painful parts of their past, she knew, but Bramblestar had to realize that he was being a hypocrite. Why should he get to choose who was allowed to break the code?

StarClan had forgiven Leafpool and Squirrelflight. Squirrelflight had told ThunderClan that when she and Leafpool had been injured in a rockfall and were hovering between life and death, StarClan had debated about the things the two had done and decided the sisters belonged in StarClan, despite the ways they'd broken the code.

Spotfur couldn't imagine that StarClan would ever turn their backs on good warriors, even if they had done something so against the code. What was a little accidental border crossing compared to that?

For a heartbeat, Spotfur thought Bramblestar was going to spring at her. But then he stepped back, pelt smoothing. "Don't concern yourself with Squirrelflight," he meowed. "As deputy, she's served her Clan selflessly. I'm Clan leader and I decide who deserves punishment. Unless you think being granted nine lives by StarClan doesn't mean anything?"

He's right. StarClan had approved Bramblestar as their leader. Spotfur dropped her gaze. There was a moment of silence. She could feel the eyes of the whole Clan on her. *Is everyone mad at me?* Surely some of her Clanmates must be as frustrated with Bramblestar as she was.

"For the next quarter moon," Bramblestar began, "no cat is to talk to Spotfur."

Spotfur's head jerked up and she stared at Bramblestar. She had never heard of *talking* being used as a punishment. Was she supposed to hunt and sleep and eat alongside warriors—alongside her own kin—in total silence?

But Bramblestar wasn't looking at her anymore. He was staring at Lionblaze. "*You* are banished from the camp for a quarter moon."

Spotfur's eyes widened. *Banished? Lionblaze is such a loyal warrior. How can Bramblestar send him away?*

"It's not right," Stemleaf whispered.

Shadows were growing long across camp as the sun sank behind the trees. No cat had spoken to Spotfur since Bramblestar had declared the punishments, since Lionblaze had squared his shoulders and walked out of camp, although Cinderheart looked at her sadly and Bristlefrost kept catching her eye in what seemed to be an agony of guilt. Even now that the camp was getting dark, she and Stemleaf lay facing away from each other, their faces carefully blank, so that no one would notice they were talking.

"I know," Spotfur murmured back. "These punishments—sending cats away and now not letting anyone talk to me—it's like they're meant to drive us apart." Resentment stirred in her as she thought of her father's shocked face. "Bramblestar is Lionblaze's father in all the ways that matter. Why would Bramblestar treat him like this?"

"Ever since he got his new life," Stemleaf whispered, even more quietly, "there's been something wrong with Bramble-star."

"Yes." Admitting it felt as liberating as if she'd pulled her fur free of brambles. Her tail swept across the muddy ground. "We can't be the only cats feeling this way. Something has to change."

CHAPTER 7

❧

"Wait for me!" Spotfur yowled, happy to hear her own voice. She'd spent the quarter moon of her punishment ringed by silence—not speaking, not spoken to—until she'd worried that she'd forget how to talk. Since her punishment had ended the day before, she'd made more noise than usual, just to hear herself. Lionblaze hadn't returned yet from his exile, but she was sure he would be back soon, and she was eager to see her father again.

Snaptooth and Flywhisker turned back from the camp entrance, their gazes warm. "Come on, then," Flywhisker called. "We're going to see if we can find some mice down by that big oak tree."

Spotfur followed her littermates through the thorn tunnel. Once outside, Flywhisker bumped her shoulder cheerfully into hers. "I'm glad we can talk to you again," she purred.

Snaptooth nodded. "Now everything can go back to normal."

Spotfur's spine stiffened. She and Stemleaf had decided they'd talk to other cats about how strange Bramblestar was acting, and who better to start with than her own littermates?

Now that she had an opportunity, her pelt prickled uneasily. "Actually," she began, "I wanted to talk to you both about that."

Flywhisker was staring into the underbrush, her tail quivering. "Talk about what?" she asked distractedly. "I think there are a couple of shrews under there."

"About things going back to normal," Spotfur mewed. Her voice sounded hesitant to her own ears, and she swallowed, then spoke more firmly. "You don't really think the way Bramblestar's been acting is *normal*, do you?"

Flywhisker, startled, lost interest in the underbrush. She and Snaptooth exchanged a look.

"What do you mean?" Snaptooth asked cautiously.

"What he's been doing," Spotfur meowed. "He's so angry all the time. He's obsessed with the code, but then he makes sure he eats first, and he stops Squirrelflight from doing her deputy duties, and he acts like it's our fault StarClan hasn't been talking to the medicine cats. Stemleaf and I think that if enough cats stand up to him, he'll see he needs to change. . . ." Her voice trailed off. Snaptooth and Flywhisker were both staring at her in horror.

"Bramblestar's the Clan leader," Snaptooth argued. "StarClan gave him nine lives."

Flywhisker shook her head. "If we turn against Bramblestar, StarClan might *never* come back."

Was this the way all her Clanmates felt? "So you'd follow Bramblestar no matter what he did?"

"He's our leader," Snaptooth repeated, his gaze steady. His

fur was fluffing as if he was ready to fight. "I'm a loyal warrior, and you should be, too."

"I *am* loyal," Spotfur meowed, stung. "But being loyal isn't just following one cat. It's working together to make our Clan better. Even if that means standing up to Bramblestar."

Flywhisker was frowning. "Don't do this, Spotfur," she pleaded. "It sounds like you're trying to rebel against our leader. That's a good way to get yourself hurt. To get other cats hurt."

"I'm not trying—" Spotfur began indignantly, but Flywhisker cut her off.

"Don't you remember what we've always heard about Darktail and ShadowClan? The apprentices and young warriors of ShadowClan didn't want to listen to Rowanstar. They didn't want to follow the code. And it was easy for a rogue to take control. Because some of the Clan wasn't loyal."

"It's not that I don't want to follow the code," Spotfur objected. "But I think what Bramblestar has been doing lately is *against* the code."

"I don't agree," Flywhisker meowed, her tabby tail flicking from side to side. "And you'd be a mouse-brain to act against Bramblestar. You've seen how he's punishing cats who break the code. How do you think he'd treat a cat who tried to turn his own Clan against him?"

Snaptooth narrowed his eyes. "Are you sure this isn't just because he punished you?" he asked. Flywhisker cocked her head to one side, and both of Spotfur's littermates waited for her answer.

"Of course not," Spotfur meowed. Her voice sounded sulky, and weaker than she would have liked. Why wouldn't they listen to her? Clearly disbelieving, her littermates exchanged another look, and then Snaptooth flicked his golden tail and turned away.

"Let it go, Spotfur," he meowed. "Let's race to the oak tree."

"You can't catch me!" Flywhisker, clearly glad of the subject change, took off without waiting for them to be ready.

"No fair!" Snaptooth dashed after her.

It's no use, Spotfur thought, trailing after them. Her littermates didn't see, or at least wouldn't acknowledge, the disturbing things Bramblestar had been saying. *But maybe it's because Bramblestar's behavior hasn't affected them yet.*

Maybe another cat who had been experienced a harsh punishment would be more likely to listen to her.

Spotfur and Stemleaf found Thriftear alone at the edge of camp.

"Can we talk to you?" Spotfur asked quietly, looking around to make sure no other cat was in earshot. Cloudtail and Brightheart were sharing tongues near the elders' den, Graystripe chatting with them, while Finchpaw and Flamepaw were busily pulling old moss from the den to change the elders' bedding. Fernsong had just taken a sparrow from the fresh-kill pile.

Things looked normal, but there was a subdued air over the whole camp. *It's because of Bramblestar,* Spotfur thought. *Every cat's afraid to put a paw wrong.*

Thriftear certainly looked afraid. Her pale amber eyes shifted between Spotfur and Stemleaf, and then she glanced over her shoulder nervously. "What do you want to talk about?" she asked at last.

"Bramblestar, and what's wrong in ThunderClan," Spotfur told her. She and Stemleaf whispered their concerns to the younger warrior, watching to make sure no cat came within earshot.

"Do you agree that Bramblestar's changed?" Stemleaf asked. "And that we should be working together to make ThunderClan the way it used to be?"

Thriftear ducked her head. "Bramblestar is acting strange," she agreed. Then her chin came up and her eyes narrowed suspiciously. "Are you trying to make me say something bad about Bramblestar so you can tell him about it?"

"Of course not!" Spotfur meowed, shocked. Then she saw where Thriftear was looking. Bristlefrost was watching them from the other side of camp, her blue-green eyes wide.

Spotfur's pelt prickled along her spine. No wonder Thriftear's thoughts had immediately gone to betrayal. Every cat knew that Bristlefrost was reporting her Clanmates' missteps back to Bramblestar. Thriftear was Bristlefrost's littermate, but even that didn't mean she'd be safe. Since Bristlefrost had told Bramblestar about Lionblaze and Spotfur crossing the border, their leader had been calling her into his den all the time, no doubt to question her about which cats weren't following the code. Every cat knew that she would tell Bramblestar anything he asked.

They couldn't trust Bristlefrost.

Spotfur couldn't hate her either, though. Bristlefrost was the same eager cat she'd been as an apprentice, desperate to serve her Clan and be the best warrior she could. Spotfur knew exactly how she felt. Only Spotfur didn't think that following Bramblestar's lead was the best way to serve ThunderClan now.

She felt cold at the thought. It wasn't *right*. They needed a leader they could trust.

"Okay," Thriftear murmured shakily. "I think there's something wrong with what Bramblestar is doing. But there isn't anything *we* can do about it."

"There is," Spotfur meowed automatically. *But what, exactly?* She looked to Stemleaf and he nodded. "We'll figure it out."

"We've had to be careful," Spotfur explained. "We can't just walk up to every cat and ask what they think of Bramblestar. But a lot of us don't agree with the way he's running things now."

Twigbranch and Finleap were huddled close together, shoulder to shoulder, and Stemleaf sat beside them, his eyes scanning the underbrush to make sure their discussion stayed private. They were by the lakeshore, and there were no other cats in sight. Newleaf was truly here now: A balmy breeze off the water ruffled the four ThunderClan cats' fur, and the air was full of the scent of growing plants and healthy prey. *If it weren't for Bramblestar,* Spotfur thought, *maybe we could enjoy it.*

Twigbranch looked miserable. "I know I switched Clans for a while," she meowed. "But is that really breaking the code? I've never been disloyal."

Spotfur purred in sympathy. After SkyClan had come to the lake, Twigbranch and her sister, Violetshine, had discovered that their parents were SkyClan cats and that their father and other kin were still part of that Clan. It was understandable that both she-cats had chosen to join SkyClan—they'd never known their kin before. But Twigbranch had returned to ThunderClan, bringing Finleap with her, because she'd realized ThunderClan was her true home. Her commitment to her Clan was stronger than ever. She'd chosen it over her kin.

How could StarClan not understand that? Spotfur wondered. *They* must *understand.* "StarClan is just cats like we are," she meowed. "They're Clan cats who have died. They can't blame you for needing to spend time with your kin—especially not when you ended up choosing your Clan."

"But they named me as a codebreaker!" Twigbranch wailed.

Shadowsight, the ShadowClan medicine cat who had saved Bramblestar, had had a vision, the first communication from StarClan in a long time. In that vision, StarClan had given him the names of cats who had broken the warrior code, who must be dealt with or, they prophesied, the Clans would suffer.

"That whole list of codebreakers seems weird to me," Stemleaf mused. "I mean, they named Lionblaze and Jayfeather because their *parents* were codebreakers. Does StarClan really think they broke the code by being born?"

"Whatever StarClan thinks, *Bramblestar* is taking the list very seriously," Finleap meowed, laying his short tail comfortingly over his mate's back. "You heard the oath he made them swear. If Twigbranch—if any of them—break the code at all, he's going to exile them for good."

Spotfur thought of the smug expression on Bramblestar's face as he'd forced the three cats to swear their oath. "He was so happy to do it. The other leaders were upset at the idea that StarClan wanted them to punish their codebreakers. But it seems like Bramblestar can't wait to exile cats."

Stemleaf nodded. "Think of how he already exiled Lionblaze from camp for a quarter moon. You crossed the border, too, but he only punished you with silence. And he punished Sparkpelt for going to look for Lionblaze."

Spotfur shuddered. When Lionblaze still hadn't returned two days after the end of their punishments, Sparkpelt had gone to look for him. When Bramblestar had found out, he'd punished her by sending her to the abandoned Twoleg nest alone to find catmint. She'd come back wounded. "He didn't even care that she got attacked by dogs. She's his own daughter." She shook her head. "He's never been like this until now."

Finleap shuffled his thin brown paws. "I wasn't even born in this Clan. What if Bramblestar wants to exile me next? I don't want to go back to SkyClan. I'm a ThunderClan cat now."

Twigbranch looked sadder than ever. "I don't think Leafstar would even take me back. StarClan didn't name any codebreakers in her Clan, and I'm sure that's the way she likes it."

"Even if she would take me back, I wouldn't go to SkyClan without you," Finleap told her, pressing his shoulder to hers.

Spotfur flicked her tail, breaking in as the pair nuzzled closer to each other. "The point is, Bramblestar has been getting worse lately. He'll punish any cat who's not perfect, codebreaker or not. And the other leaders are listening to him when he says he speaks for StarClan, so soon it'll be the same in every other Clan. ThunderClan is falling apart. If we let it keep happening, it won't matter which Clan you were born into, because there won't be a ThunderClan anymore."

"Certainly not the ThunderClan we believe in," Stemleaf added. "We're going to meet with cats from other Clans who see what's happening, too. We need to make a plan." He fixed a serious stare on Finleap and Twigbranch. "Are you with us?"

CHAPTER 8

I didn't expect so many cats to show up, Spotfur thought. She and
Stemleaf had been approaching cats privately for a few days,
choosing the ones who seemed most worried about the way
things were going in the Clans. They'd invited them to a
secret moonhigh meeting at the greenleaf Twolegplace. But
most cats they'd talked to, even the ones who had spoken up
when Bramblestar denounced the codebreakers, had seemed
surprised and suspicious. She and Stemleaf hadn't known if
any of them, especially cats from other Clans, would want to
come.

Now, as the moon drifted high overhead, they huddled
together in a small hollow surrounded by bushes. And cats
from every Clan had joined them: their own Clanmates
Finleap and Twigbranch, and Dappletuft and Sneezecloud
from RiverClan; Breezepelt, Smokehaze, and Slightfoot
from WindClan; Cloverfoot, Whorlpelt, and Blazefire from
ShadowClan; and Rootpaw, Frecklewish, and Blossomheart
from SkyClan. Tree from SkyClan, too, although they hadn't
invited him—his son, Rootpaw, must have brought him. Spotfur wouldn't have thought that Tree would be interested, so

she hadn't bothered to approach him. The odd former loner always seemed to have one paw out of the Clans. But his mate and kits were part of SkyClan, after all; she supposed it made sense that he cared.

As the cats settled in a circle, she could feel that every eye was on her and Stemleaf. The cats looked wary, their tails twitching. Spotfur had never seen this many cats from different Clans together outside a Gathering. Her stomach twisted. *Will they listen to us? They wouldn't be here if they didn't think there was something wrong.*

Stemleaf cleared his throat, looking a little anxious. "Thanks for coming," he began. "I know it was hard to get away from your Clans. But I think it's really important that we're here."

Breezepelt looked at him with a challenge in his amber eyes. "Do you really think we can stop what's happening to the Clans?"

Whorlpelt dug his claws into the ground. "Nothing *would* be happening to the Clans if it weren't for Bramblestar."

"He's the one who wants to make an example of the code-breakers," Sneezecloud agreed, the tip of his tail twitching.

Frecklewish shifted uneasily. "He does seem to have Star-Clan on his side."

Cold shot through Spotfur. How could that be true? The StarClan she believed in wouldn't harshly punish cats this way. Their ancestors weren't hawks waiting to swoop down on living cats; they were their kin.

Frecklewish and Stemleaf were discussing Shadowsight's

latest vision, another warning about codebreakers, but a sudden sound distracted Spotfur. A crackle of shifting twigs came from a nearby bush, and she tensed, her ears pricking. But there was no glow of eyes from the darkness, and the noise didn't come again. Tasting the air, she smelled only the sharp scents of the other Clan cats around her. *Probably just the wind.*

She turned back to the discussion just as Rootpaw meowed unsurely, "Perhaps StarClan doesn't want the codebreakers to suffer as much as Bramblestar does. Perhaps they only want them to acknowledge that they've broken the code."

Spotfur thought of her father. "Not every codebreaker knows what they've done wrong."

There was a swell of angry voices as the cats began arguing, some outraged, some distressed. No cat could agree on how codebreakers should be punished, or even if that was truly what StarClan wanted. Spotfur winced at the noise. Every cat had started off speaking with hushed voices, but as they got more upset, they forgot this was supposed to be a *secret* meeting. Stemleaf laid his tail across her back but remained focused, his green eyes flashing from one speaker to another.

At last, he broke in. "Well, if Bramblestar weren't yowling about punishment all the time, the Clans could find a better way to deal with the codebreakers."

Cloverfoot's eyes narrowed. "What are you suggesting?"

Stemleaf lifted his head. "Bramblestar is trying to make us act like Darktail's Kin. He wants us to turn on one another. But warriors aren't cruel. They never have been. Bramblestar must have bees in his brain. We have to get rid of him before he spoils the Clans forever."

There was a moment of silence. Spotfur pressed her ears back. Even now, it was shocking to think of actually getting rid of their leader. But this was where they'd always been heading, wasn't it?

Her breath caught in her throat. It was impossible for her to imagine ThunderClan without Bramblestar. But what would ThunderClan become if he stayed?

The other ThunderClan cats seemed to feel the same way. As Stemleaf and the cats from other Clans argued about whether banishing Bramblestar was even possible, she and Twigbranch and Finleap stared at one another miserably.

Finally, Finleap meowed in a small, shaking voice, "The old Bramblestar would never have acted like this. I wish he'd pull himself together and be normal again."

That was the heart of the problem. *Is it possible that he could still change back to his old self?*

Rootpaw half rose and suggested, with an odd urgency, "Perhaps he can't be normal again. Perhaps something happened when he was dead."

Spotfur blinked, confused. "Do you think StarClan said something to him while he was dead?"

Rootpaw was trembling. He stared at his father, his eyes beseeching, and Tree stepped forward. "Something happened while he was dead, but I don't think it was anything to do with StarClan. The cat that came back isn't Bramblestar."

Huh? Spotfur looked around at the other cats in the circle, but their faces seemed as confused as she was.

"What do you mean?" Stemleaf asked.

Tree raised his chin as if bracing himself for a fight. "It can't be Bramblestar. Because I've seen Bramblestar's ghost in the forest. I've spoken to it."

"You saw his ghost?" Stemleaf asked, stunned.

"You *spoke* to it?" Spotfur added. Her mind spun. It didn't make any sense. Bramblestar was no ghost; he was warm and solid and busy punishing codebreakers—or any cat who displeased him.

Every cat knew that Tree was peculiar. It was best not to take what he told them too seriously. But Bramblestar *had* changed. . . .

Frecklewish, one of the SkyClan medicine cats, began to argue, and Tree turned toward her. "The Bramblestar who came back isn't the *real* Bramblestar. Some cat is using his body to harm the Clans. The real Bramblestar is a ghost. He can see what's going on, but he can't contact StarClan. I'm the only cat he can talk to."

Shock and sorrow flooded through Spotfur at the thought. If it was true, how *horrible*.

She remembered the loneliness of the quarter moon when no cat was allowed to speak to her. They'd been able to see her, though, had known she was there. How much worse to walk through your Clan's camp unseen and unheard. If what Tree told them was true, Bramblestar had not only been suffering that dreadful loneliness and separation from his Clan; he'd had to witness an intruder in his own body, an enemy using *his* voice to punish and bully his Clanmates. A stranger getting close to his mate. Her eyes met Stemleaf's, and she saw her own horror reflected there.

The other cats were arguing about Shadowsight, and whether he could be behind this theft of Bramblestar's body. *He did insist on putting Bramblestar out in the snow,* Spotfur thought. *That's when he died, so that must be when the other cat stole his body.* But it was hard to reconcile the sheer evil of a plan like that with the shy innocence that shone so clearly from the young Shadow-Clan medicine cat.

Most of the others seemed to think so, too, especially the ShadowClan cats who knew him best. "I don't think Shadowsight is capable of anything dishonest," Cloverfoot meowed, frowning. "But he might have made a mistake."

As Frecklewish answered her, another slight crackling sound came from the far side of the hollow, and Spotfur's head shot up. But again she saw nothing.

"Okay, we'll find out more about Shadowsight's visions before we decide what to do next," Stemleaf announced, getting to his paws. "We'd better get back to our Clans before any cat notices we're missing."

Spotfur rose and, side by side with Stemleaf and the others, began to cross the hollow. For the first time in a while, she felt hopeful. The idea that Bramblestar wasn't really Bramblestar was horrifying, but at least now they knew what was wrong. There were other cats who would work with them to fix everything—they weren't alone fighting against their leader.

The bushes rustled again, and suddenly Spotfur caught

sight of wide blue-green eyes peering out of the darkness. Bristlefrost!

"Run!" Twigbranch screeched. "It's Bramblestar's spy! Get out of here! She'll report us!"

Spotfur whipped around and bent her hind legs, ready to leap away. Her heart was pounding. If Bristlefrost reported this meeting to Bramblestar, it would all be over. *I'll be exiled.* But Bristlefrost yowled desperately behind them. "I won't report you! I came here to . . ."

Spotfur paused, turning back toward her. Bristlefrost lifted her muzzle. "I came here to join you!" she declared.

Beside Spotfur, the other cats shifted uneasily. Was she lying? Bristlefrost had always been so loyal to Bramblestar. She'd reported back to him on violations of the code—with the idea that it would strengthen the Clan and be better for every cat, maybe, but she'd always told. Could she really have changed her mind?

Stemleaf questioned her, his eyes narrowed, and Bristlefrost claimed she had heard only the last part of their meeting. "I know Bramblestar's not really Bramblestar," she told them. "You want to get rid of him."

Spotfur put her ears back. *Is this a trick?* But beside her, Stemleaf's eyes were locked with Bristlefrost's. Her gaze was pleading, as if she was desperate for him to understand.

Suddenly, Spotfur felt like the outsider. Did Bristlefrost still have feelings for Stemleaf? "How did you find out about this meeting?" Spotfur asked abruptly.

Bristlefrost turned away from Stemleaf and directed the

same desperate look to Spotfur. "I heard you talking about it with Stemleaf."

"So you were spying again?" Spotfur snapped, then felt guilty, then annoyed with herself for feeling guilty. Bristlefrost might seem sincere, but she'd also reported back to Bramblestar on Spotfur and on other Clanmates. *No one spoke to me for a quarter moon!*

Bristlefrost's eyes widened even more as she tried to explain again that she hadn't been spying; she had just overheard. And she'd had to come to the meeting, because she knew that Bramblestar had changed.

Rootpaw had always liked Bristlefrost. He spoke up. "We're going to ask Shadowsight about his visions," he told her. "He might be able to give us a clue about who the impostor is."

Spotfur had never seen Bristlefrost look so sad. "Then what? We have to expose Bramblestar," she mewed. "It's the only way we'll be safe. We need the support of more powerful cats."

Frecklewish bristled, seemingly indignant at the idea that any cat could be more powerful than a medicine cat, but Bristlefrost went on. "There's another cat in ThunderClan who already suspects Bramblestar's not Bramblestar. If we can persuade her to join us, we might be able to get rid of the impostor without a fight."

A powerful ThunderClan cat who already suspects? Spotfur tried to imagine who it could be. Bristlefrost had said "she." *Cinderheart? Ivypool?* "Who are you talking about?"

Bristlefrost lifted her chin defiantly, as if she expected

not to be believed. "Squirrelflight."

She explained, backed up by Rootpaw and Tree. The real Bramblestar had sent a message to Squirrelflight through Tree. Squirrelflight had already been sure that *something* was wrong with her mate, and the SkyClan cats had persuaded her of the truth.

Squirrelflight would need the support of her Clanmates— they were all agreed on that.

"And we can't risk Bramblestar getting hurt," Spotfur added. "Bramblestar's ghost will want his body back."

Bristlefrost's eyes were more desperate than ever. "We have to do something. The impostor tried to kill Sparkpelt."

Bristlefrost had investigated the abandoned Twolegplace after Sparkpelt had been attacked. Some cat had been luring dogs there with fresh-kill for days. As Bristlefrost explained that she thought Bramblestar had sent Sparkpelt into a trap he'd set, Spotfur felt as if an owl had her in its talons, pressing her sides together so that her breath grew short. *His own daughter . . .*

Not his daughter. But Squirrelflight's daughter. She'll have to act.

Spotfur felt hope expand in her chest. If Squirrelflight, Bramblestar's mate, the deputy of ThunderClan, was on their side, then things might turn out all right after all.

A moon later, things were worse than ever.

"Maybe Tigerstar's right," Stemleaf whispered, weaving a bramble tendril through a hole in the wall of the warrior's den. "Maybe killing Bramblestar is the only way."

"Shh!" Spotfur hissed, glancing over her shoulder to make sure there was no cat within earshot. "We can't talk about this here!"

I don't really want to talk about it at all.

Squirrelflight was in exile, hiding out in the abandoned Sky-Clan camp on ShadowClan's territory along with Lionblaze, Jayfeather, and Twigbranch, as well as Crowfeather, the Wind-Clan deputy, and Mothwing, the RiverClan medicine cat. Despite Squirrelflight's efforts to convince the other leaders, Tigerstar was the only leader who was willing to fight whatever cat was pretending to be Bramblestar—Leafstar, the SkyClan leader, thought that Bramblestar was wrong to punish code-breakers but wasn't willing to risk her Clan by openly opposing him. And Mistystar and Harestar, leaders of RiverClan and WindClan, were on Bramblestar's side. That was why they'd exiled Mothwing and Crowfeather as codebreakers.

Tigerstar believed the false Bramblestar had killed Shad-owsight, even though Bramblestar claimed he had run away. The young medicine cat had been missing for days now. It wasn't hard for Spotfur to believe he might be dead.

But murdering a leader . . .

It was wrong. It was wrong to kill any cat, wasn't it?

"Do you think the others are right?" she murmured to Stemleaf, weaving another twig into the wall. "If Bramble-star's body is killed, will he have a chance to take it back from whatever cat stole it?"

Stemleaf shook his head hopelessly. "There's no way for us to know."

Spotfur looked around the camp. Flamepaw was pulling a tick off Cloudtail's side, his ears pinned back in disgust. Alderheart and his new "apprentice," Flipclaw, were sorting through herbs outside the medicine den. Cinderheart, her tail drooping, was nibbling sadly at a sparrow—she'd had little appetite since Lionblaze was exiled.

No cat was happy, it seemed to her. But the Clan was in one piece. "If we act against Bramblestar, whether it's attacking him or trying to drive him out," she murmured, more softly than ever, "won't ThunderClan be torn apart?"

Before Stemleaf could answer, Bristlefrost slipped through the thorn tunnel into camp. Her ears were pressed back and her tail was twitching nervously.

"Are you okay, Bristlefrost?" Cinderheart asked, getting to her paws. Bristlefrost just stared at her, apparently too upset to speak.

"Wasn't she out with Bramblestar?" Stemleaf whispered. Bramblestar had been searching for Squirrelflight for the last quarter moon with increasing desperation—he might have exiled her, but clearly, he had been hoping she'd come back, asking to be forgiven. This time, he'd taken Bristlefrost with him.

Behind Bristlefrost, Bramblestar padded slowly out of the tunnel, his tail dragging along the ground behind him. Spotfur stared. Bramblestar's eyes were dull and his fur was dirty and unkempt. She had never seen him looking this way before.

"Bramblestar?" Cinderheart asked tentatively.

The muscular tom padded to the center of the clearing. "Squirrelflight's dead," he announced flatly. "A monster killed her on a Thunderpath by the Twolegplace." As if the words had taken the last of his strength, he collapsed onto the ground and began to wail.

Exclamations of shock and grief went up all around them.

"I can't believe it!" Honeyfur's tail drooped sadly.

"She never should have been sent away!" Thornclaw growled.

Spotfur stared at Stemleaf, her eyes stretched wide with horror. "How can Squirrelflight be dead?" she asked numbly.

"She's not," Bristlefrost whispered. She had made her way over to them, unnoticed in the commotion. She looked exhausted. "Faking her death was the only way to get him to stop looking for her."

Spotfur frowned, then nodded. "If he'd kept looking, he might have found the exiles' camp," she realized. "We were all in danger."

It was a smart plan. This false Bramblestar, whoever he really was, was their enemy. And Bristlefrost's tricking him like this proved that she was on their side.

In the center of the clearing, Bramblestar dug his claws into the earth and moaned. Spotfur felt like a heavy weight had landed on her back. She couldn't help feeling sorry for him. She could think of nothing worse than believing Stemleaf was dead. Whoever this cat was in Bramblestar's body, his grief was real.

* * *

A few days later, the rebels met again and learned that Shadowsight had been found—alive, but terribly injured—by SkyClan, and cared for by their medicine cats. *Some* good *news at last,* Spotfur thought. But every cat was still worried.

"At best, Bramblestar lied about Shadowsight just running off," Tree told them. "At worst, he had something to do with the attack."

The cats argued about whether such a thing was possible. Would Bramblestar ever attack another cat, especially a medicine cat? Or would whichever cat was inside him?

"He would," Stemleaf's voice was low, meant for just the cats closest to him, and Spotfur nodded. The impostor *hated* the cats of ThunderClan, she was sure of it.

Crowfeather's yowl rose above the other cats' arguing. "Things have gone too far." The former WindClan deputy's voice was full of certainty. "I don't like it, but it's clear what we need to do: kill Bramblestar."

Spotfur felt sick. *Are we really going to do this?*

Pandemonium broke out—meows of horror and meows of agreement. At last, Squirrelflight pleaded that they had to wait. "At least until we find out for sure what happened to Shadowsight. Surely we can delay until he regains consciousness and we can find out what he knows. There are too many unanswered questions for us to act now."

Spotfur's heart sank still further. Squirrelflight might only be asking for time, but she could see in the ginger cat's desperate eyes that she'd never agree to kill Bramblestar's body, no matter which cat was in it.

And, meanwhile, the impostor was tearing the Clans apart. More and more cats were being sent into exile. He'd tried to kill Sparkpelt. He'd tried to kill Shadowsight. How much longer could the Clans survive?

Stemleaf spoke up. "You're right, Squirrelflight." Spotfur stared at him. Her mate wasn't looking at any cat, but gazing at his paws, and his voice shook a little. *He's lying,* she realized. "We should wait until Shadowsight wakes up to do anything."

Tigerstar agreed, demanding a promise from the cats who had argued most fiercely for Bramblestar's death that they would wait.

Stemleaf avoided every cat's eye for the rest of the meeting, but as they headed out of the exiles' camp, he stopped.

"What's going on?" Spotfur asked.

"I don't think we have time to wait, do you?" Stemleaf told her. His gaze was clouded with worry. "Things are getting worse and worse."

"Why did you agree with Squirrelflight, then?" Spotfur asked.

Stemleaf shook his head. "She's never going to agree to kill Bramblestar's body. She can't bear the idea of losing the last link to her mate, even if he's already gone. She might even warn him. It can't be an official decision because the others will tell her."

Spotfur watched Tigerstar hurry away with the SkyClan cats, no doubt to visit Shadowsight in their medicine den. Squirrelflight and Crowfeather were still arguing in the clearing of the exiles' camp. Stemleaf was right; they couldn't turn to any of these older cats. "Then we need to make a plan of our own."

A few days later, they were ready. They walked side by side through the forest, their pelts brushing together. Spotfur leaned even closer to Stemleaf, taking comfort in his scent.

I can't help being scared. It felt as if something large were twisting in her chest, making it hard to breathe. If she and Stemleaf led an attack on Bramblestar, it might save ThunderClan. But what if they failed? *Whatever happens, everything is going to change.*

Reaching the border, they paused. Spotfur swallowed. Once they crossed back into ThunderClan's territory, the plan would feel so much more real.

Stemleaf leaned into her, his tail twining with hers. She turned to look into his eyes.

"Do you think StarClan will come back?" he asked. "If we kill Bramblestar and protect our Clan?"

"I don't know," Spotfur answered. Was reaching StarClan even the goal anymore? She just wanted ThunderClan to be united again, like it had been when she'd been an apprentice. "I've always tried to be a good warrior," she told Stemleaf, and he nodded, his eyes dark with sympathy. Spotfur remembered when her parents had encouraged her to be an example to others of what a Clanmate should be. *What kind of good Clanmate attacks her leader?*

He's not my leader. This is the way a loyal warrior saves her Clan. The twisting in her chest settled, and she felt cold with determination. "I *do* know this is the only way. I don't like it, but I believe that Bramblestar's death will be the best thing for ThunderClan."

Stemleaf pressed his cheek against hers. "It'll be dangerous."

Spotfur closed her eyes and breathed in his scent. "Tomorrow, everything will change."

Later that night, they curled in one nest, their heads pillowed on each other's sides, breathing together. "StarClan will come back," Spotfur whispered. *Please, StarClan, if you're still watching us, come back.*

Stemleaf pressed even closer, his fur warm and soft, his scent sweet. "It's going to be all right," he murmured. "Tomorrow."

CHAPTER 9

❧

"Okay." Spotfur looked around at the assembled cats. "Is every cat clear on the plan?" A light drizzle was falling, chilling her to the bone, and she shuddered. *It's not just that I'm cold,* she realized. *I'm frightened of what we have to do.*

The four cats beside her looked back at her with grim, resolved faces. She knew they felt the same way.

Conefoot blinked at her solemnly. "You're going to convince Bramblestar to come out of camp with you and Stemleaf. When you get him far enough, we'll"—the ShadowClan tom winced—"attack."

Dappletuft and Kitescratch glanced at each other uneasily, then nodded, their gazes hardening. "Mistystar won't like it if she finds out," Dappletuft meowed. "But even if I can never go back to RiverClan, this is the right thing to do."

Spotfur met Stemleaf's eyes, seeing her own thoughts mirrored in his gaze: If ThunderClan found out they were behind Bramblestar's death, they'd be driven out. Plotting to kill their own Clan leader was not just breaking, but *shattering* the warrior code. For a moment, she felt terribly sad. Bramblestar had been so kind, such a wise leader. She remembered how carefully he'd listened when they'd gone to him about Thrift-paw's punishment, his amber eyes clear and thoughtful. She would have never imagined that one day she'd be attacking the cat with those eyes.

It'll be worth it, she thought. *Someday, they'll know we were working to protect the Clan.*

They padded forward through the familiar woods, and each step sent an ache through Spotfur's heart: the gentle patter of the light rain through the birch and oak leaves, the musty scent of the woods and the underlying scent of prey, the softness of the moss and new grass beneath her paws— all of this was *ThunderClan* territory, as familiar to her as her own fur.

She brushed her tail against Stemleaf's side. "If we succeed," she murmured, "are we going to lose all of this? Our home?"

Stemleaf shook his head. "No," he answered, his voice strong. "One day, the Clans will all understand why we had to do this. Then we can come home. We'll raise kits in Thunder-Clan."

Something in Spotfur's chest warmed, picturing this—kits with Stemleaf's fiery fur and her own blue eyes, playing in the camp clearing, safely surrounded by ThunderClan. She could see it so clearly.

That's why we have to do this. For our kin and our kin's kin. So the Clans can be safe.

As they got closer to the ThunderClan camp, Stemleaf paused. "Where should we have them hide?" he asked Spotfur.

Spotfur thought about how far they were likely to be able to lure Bramblestar out of camp. "We'll have to tell him we've found signs of the exiles coming around," she suggested. "And we'll want to make sure we're out of the path of any patrols, so it can't be near the border. Near the lakeshore maybe? They could hide under the bushes there until we get close."

"Shh!" Conefoot's ears pricked up. "Do you hear that?" The cats froze, listening.

"I want to know what you think, Bristlefrost," a voice meowed in the distance. "I have my doubts about Berrynose."

Spotfur's eyes widened. "It's Bramblestar!" she gasped quietly.

This changed everything. No cat had to hide, or find a way to lure Bramblestar out of camp. They could act *now*. "Wait here," she whispered. Quietly, she crouched and slunk forward, keeping downwind of where Bramblestar must be. *How many cats are with him?* This could make their plan either easier or impossible.

Peering through the underbrush, she saw the muscular tom looming over Bristlefrost, his shoulders hunched and his teeth bared. "Surely all that loyalty must be an act," he snarled. "Don't you think so?"

A wave of revulsion swept over Spotfur at the sight of him. How had she ever thought this fox-hearted cat with the contemptuous gaze was really Bramblestar? It was an insult to ThunderClan's true leader.

She waved the others forward with her tail. They'd never have a better chance than this, Bramblestar far from camp with only Bristlefrost beside him. "Now," she told them. "We have to be bold. For all our Clans." She narrowed her eyes and extended her claws. There was no turning back now.

"Well," Bristlefrost was saying, "I don't really know—"

She broke off with a gasp of horror as her eyes met Spotfur's. Alerted, the false Bramblestar whipped around. It took him only a heartbeat to realize they were on the attack. With a snarl of rage, he leaped toward them.

"Now!" Spotfur screeched, and met him in midair.

She clawed at the impostor, but a kick from his powerful hind legs sent her reeling backward, and she landed hard on the ground. The others were all around him now, scratching and grappling, and she scrambled back to her paws to launch herself at him again.

Dappletuft swiped at Bramblestar's throat, claws extended for the kill, but the older cat blocked his paw, then struck a blow that staggered the RiverClan warrior.

"Bristlefrost," Bramblestar screeched, "get help! There must be a patrol nearby!"

Will she fight on our side? Bristlefrost agreed with the rebels, Spotfur knew, but she'd taken Squirrelflight's side when the deputy had argued against killing him. Spotfur didn't dare take her eyes off the false Bramblestar, looking for an opening to attack again, but she pricked her ears for Bristlefrost's response. There was a moment of hesitation, and then the pounding of Bristlefrost's paws, running away.

It would have helped to have another set of claws on their side, but Spotfur had no time to think about it. At least

Bristlefrost wasn't fighting against them. Stemleaf had leaped onto Bramblestar's back and was clinging on as the massive leader thrashed. Dappletuft and Conefoot harried the ThunderClan leader on each side as Kitescratch clawed at his hindquarters. Dashing in, Spotfur swiped at Bramblestar's eyes, but the impostor dodged so that she left a deep scratch across his nose instead. Blood ran down his muzzle.

Bramblestar threw himself violently to one side, almost dislodging Stemleaf from his back, and slashed a massive paw across Dappletuft's chest. Bright red blood flooded across the RiverClan warrior's gray-and-white fur, and his blue eyes clouded. His mouth opened in a soundless wail as he stumbled and fell to his knees.

With screeches of horror, the other cats redoubled their attack. Spotfur's vision was full of fur and claws as she scratched and bit. Bramblestar was trying to back away from them now, but there was nowhere to go. The rebels surrounded him.

This is for everything you've done, Spotfur thought, her mind humming with a bloodthirsty joy, and she slashed at his face again. *Give me back my leader.*

There was a furious howl, and a tortoiseshell pelt shot past her, knocking Conefoot off his paws. *Leafshade,* Spotfur realized, her heart sinking. The patrol Bramblestar had been hoping for had found them.

Spotfur snarled and leaped at Bramblestar again, but claws were pulling her backward, throwing her down, and as she kicked up, her hind legs clawed at the belly of another cat: *Shellfur,* she realized, Stemleaf's littermate. He had her pinned, his green eyes—the same shade as Stemleaf's—blazing with fury, when suddenly he faltered, his gaze fixing on something else.

Spotfur wriggled out from underneath him, getting her paws under her just in time to see Bramblestar strike. Stemleaf was on the ground, and the impostor's claws flashed as he slashed them across Stemleaf's throat. Beside her, Shellfur gasped.

Get up. Stemleaf thrashed, deep red blood soaking his fur. He gave a strange, gasping meow, and then he was still.

Get up! Spotfur thought again.

Conefoot was down, too, Spotfur realized, as she ran toward Bramblestar. Leafshade and Kitescratch were locked together, yowling as they struggled. Bramblestar turned to meet Spotfur. She could see the drops of blood—*Stemleaf's blood*—spattered across his foreleg.

She leaped for his throat, teeth meeting in his fur, but he knocked her back.

Snarling, more warriors burst out of the undergrowth. Berrynose, Sorrelstripe, Dewnose, and Snaptooth, with Bristlefrost leading the way. Spotfur's eyes widened in horror. *We've lost. Bristlefrost betrayed us.*

"It's over!" Kitescratch yowled, running toward her. Blood was streaming from his shoulder, but he was still on his paws. "Let's go!"

Spotfur backed away from the other cats, from Bramblestar. There were three still shapes on the ground. Dappletuft. Conefoot. *Stemleaf.* She couldn't breathe.

Kitescratch barreled into her, shoving her backward. "We can't help them," he mewed. "Spotfur, we have to *go*."

He was right. It was too late to do anything for the others. *For Stemleaf.* Spotfur drew in a long, shuddering breath, turned, and, side by side with Kitescratch, began to run.

CHAPTER 10

We failed. I can't go back to ThunderClan.

I can't go back to ThunderClan, and Stemleaf is dead.

Spotfur stared blankly at her paws, ignoring the voices around her in the exiles' camp. She could still imagine those kits with Stemleaf's fur and eyes the same color as her own, safe and happy in ThunderClan. *That will never happen now.*

She took a long, shuddering breath, and squeezed her eyes shut. In her mind, she saw the blood on the grass, saw Bramblestar's claws come down onto Stemleaf's throat.

"I told you to *wait*," Tigerstar's angry voice broke through her daze. "It wasn't time yet, and now Bramblestar will be warier than ever. And we've lost our eyes in ThunderClan's camp."

"Finleap's there," Twigbranch argued. "And Bristlefrost."

Spotfur's mouth was dry and her voice sounded strained even to her own ears. "Bristlefrost ran for help," she told them. "She defended Bramblestar."

"I'm not sure we can trust her anymore," Kitescratch agreed. "She didn't fight us, but she didn't fight *for* us."

"*I* asked her to protect Bramblestar," Squirrelflight broke in. "Bristlefrost made me a promise, and she was only trying to fulfill it. She's a loyal warrior."

Lionblaze hissed in frustration. "I love Bramblestar, too. He raised me. The *real* Bramblestar. But he's gone, and you're protecting the cat who killed him."

Squirrelflight was unmoved. "I still believe we can get him back," she meowed. "I'm not giving up on him."

"Whether you've given up on him or not, this attack has only made things harder," Jayfeather hissed.

Squirrelflight sighed. "I can't fault Spotfur and Kitescratch and the others for their bravery," she meowed. "They did what they thought was right. Now all we can do is make sure that Stemleaf, Dappletuft, and Conefoot didn't die in vain."

Spotfur cringed. *Nothing could be worth losing Stemleaf.*

Later that day, Spotfur curled at the edge of the exiles' camp alone, her eyes half-slitted against the light of the setting sun. The chill of evening was spreading through her, but she didn't have the energy to move.

Soft paw steps approached, and Squirrelflight spoke. "Can I sit with you?"

Spotfur shrugged, and the former ThunderClan deputy sat down beside her, her side brushing Spotfur's. She was warm and solid.

Spotfur rested her head on her paws. She felt empty, drained of all her horror and sorrow, with nothing left but weariness. "Thank you," she murmured at last. "For what you said. I know you didn't want us to attack Bramblestar at all.

If I had listened, maybe Stemleaf would still be alive." Guilt washed over her, and she shut her eyes for a moment.

"I still don't want to attack him," Squirrelflight meowed. "We're going to figure out a way to save the *real* Bramblestar. But I know you were fighting for ThunderClan. Bramblestar himself would appreciate that." She lowered her chin onto her own paws, and Spotfur shifted to meet her eyes. Squirrelflight's gaze was clear and gentle. "You were very brave," she told Spotfur. "And so were Stemleaf and the others."

Grief stabbed through Spotfur. "Stemleaf's *dead*," she meowed. "I don't know what to do now."

Squirrelflight brushed her tail across Spotfur's back. "I know it's hard, but you'll get stronger every day. You're a young cat with a long life ahead of you."

Spotfur winced—*a long life without Stemleaf*—and Squirrelflight pressed her shoulder against hers. "Which is what Stemleaf would have wanted," she went on. "For you to have a long, happy life. And to keep fighting. We'll take back ThunderClan one day and turn it back into what a Clan should be."

Spotfur gave a half *mrrow* of broken laughter. "With some impostor as leader?" she asked. "What if the real Bramblestar never comes back?" Squirrelflight, she realized, was grieving her mate, too, even if she still had hope. It seemed to Spotfur that Bramblestar was probably lost forever.

Squirrelflight's voice was steady. "I don't know. But ThunderClan is more important than any one cat. Whatever happens, I'm going to fight for it."

Spotfur swallowed hard. That was all she and Stemleaf had ever wanted: to be the best warriors they could, and to protect their Clan. Someday they would reach StarClan again, and maybe Stemleaf would be able to see how they had helped.

His death would mean something. They'd fought for the future, side by side.

Those kits that she and Stemleaf had planned for, tumbling happily in the ThunderClan camp, their flame-colored pelts gleaming in the sun, they'd never be born. But *other* kits would be born. Kits who deserved the safety of the kind of Clan Spotfur had grown up in.

Whatever became of Spotfur, the future of ThunderClan still mattered. A new sort of strength began to flow into her, and Spotfur lifted her head. *I will still try to be the best Clanmate I can.*

She and Stemleaf had planned together for the future, but the future of the Clans had never been just about them. Spotfur was still alive, and she had something to live for, something to try to protect.

"One day," she echoed to Squirrelflight, something warming inside her, "one day, we'll take back our Clan."

WARRIORS

BLACKFOOT'S
RECKONING

Special thanks to Clarissa Hutton

ALLEGIANCES

THUNDERCLAN

LEADER   **FIRESTAR**—ginger tom with a flame-colored pelt

                 APPRENTICE, BRAMBLEPAW (dark brown tabby tom with amber eyes)

DEPUTY   **WHITESTORM**—big white tom

MEDICINE CAT   **CINDERPELT**—dark gray she-cat

WARRIORS   (toms and she-cats without kits)

                 DARKSTRIPE—sleek black-and-gray tabby tom

                 APPRENTICE, FERNPAW (pale gray she-cat with darker flecks and pale green eyes)

                 LONGTAIL—pale tabby tom, dark black stripes

                 MOUSEFUR—small dusky-brown she-cat

                 APPRENTICE, THORNPAW (golden-brown tabby tom)

                 BRACKENFUR—golden-brown tabby tom

                 APPRENTICE, TAWNYPAW (tortoiseshell she-cat with green eyes)

                 DUSTPELT—dark brown tabby tom

                 APPRENTICE, ASHPAW (pale gray tom with darker flecks and dark blue eyes)

                 SANDSTORM—pale ginger she-cat

                 GRAYSTRIPE—long-haired gray tom

                 FROSTFUR—beautiful white she-cat, blue eyes

                 GOLDENFLOWER—pale ginger she-cat

CLOUDTAIL—long-haired white tom

LOSTFACE—white she-cat, ginger splotches

QUEENS (she-cats expecting or nursing kits)

WILLOWPELT—very pale gray she-cat, unusual blue eyes

ELDERS (former warriors and queens, now retired)

ONE-EYE—pale gray she-cat, the oldest cat in ThunderClan, virtually blind and deaf

SMALLEAR—gray tom with very small ears, the oldest tom in ThunderClan

DAPPLETAIL—once-pretty tortoiseshell she-cat, lovely dappled coat

SPECKLETAIL—pale tabby she-cat

SHADOWCLAN

LEADER **TIGERSTAR**—big dark brown tabby tom, unusually long front claws, formerly of ThunderClan

DEPUTY **BLACKFOOT**—large white tom, huge jet-black paws, formerly a rogue cat

MEDICINE CAT **RUNNINGNOSE**—small gray-and-white tom
APPRENTICE, LITTLECLOUD (very small tabby tom)

WARRIORS **OAKFUR**—small brown tom

BOULDER—skinny gray tom, formerly a rogue cat

RUSSETFUR—dark ginger she-cat, formerly a rogue cat
APPRENTICE, CEDARPAW (dark gray tom)

JAGGEDTOOTH—huge tabby tom, formerly a rogue cat

APPRENTICE, ROWANPAW (ginger tom)

QUEENS   **TALLPOPPY**—long-legged light brown tabby she-cat

WINDCLAN

LEADER   **TALLSTAR**—black-and-white tom, very long tail

DEPUTY   **DEADFOOT**—black tom with a twisted paw

MEDICINE CAT   **BARKFACE**—short-tailed brown tom

WARRIORS   **MUDCLAW**—mottled dark brown tom

WEBFOOT—dark gray tabby tom

TORNEAR—tabby tom

ONEWHISKER—brown tabby tom

APPRENTICE, GORSEPAW (very pale gray-and-white she-cat with blue eyes)

RUNNINGBROOK—light gray tabby she-cat

QUEENS   **ASHFOOT**—gray she-cat

MORNINGFLOWER—tortoiseshell she-cat

WHITETAIL—small white she-cat

RIVERCLAN

LEADER   **LEOPARDSTAR**—unusually spotted golden tabby she-cat

DEPUTY   **STONEFUR**—gray tom, battle-scarred ears
              APPRENTICE, STORMPAW (dark gray tom
              with amber eyes)

MEDICINE CAT **MUDFUR**—long-haired light brown tom

WARRIORS   **BLACKCLAW**—smoky black tom

              HEAVYSTEP—thickset tabby tom
              APPRENTICE, DAWNPAW (pale gray she-cat)

              SHADEPELT—very dark gray she-cat

              MISTYFOOT—gray she-cat, blue eyes
              APPRENTICE, FEATHERPAW (silver tabby
              she-cat with sky-blue eyes)

              LOUDBELLY—dark brown tom

QUEENS   **MOSSPELT**—tortoiseshell she-cat

BLOODCLAN

LEADER   **SCOURGE**—small black tom with one white
              paw

DEPUTY   **BONE**—massive black-and-white tom

CATS OUTSIDE CLANS

BARLEY—black-and-white tom who lives on a
farm close to the forest

RAVENPAW—sleek black cat who lives on the
farm with Barley

PRINCESS—light brown tabby, distinctive
white chest and paws, a kittypet

SMUDGE—plump, friendly black-and-white
kittypet who lives in a house at the edge of the
forest

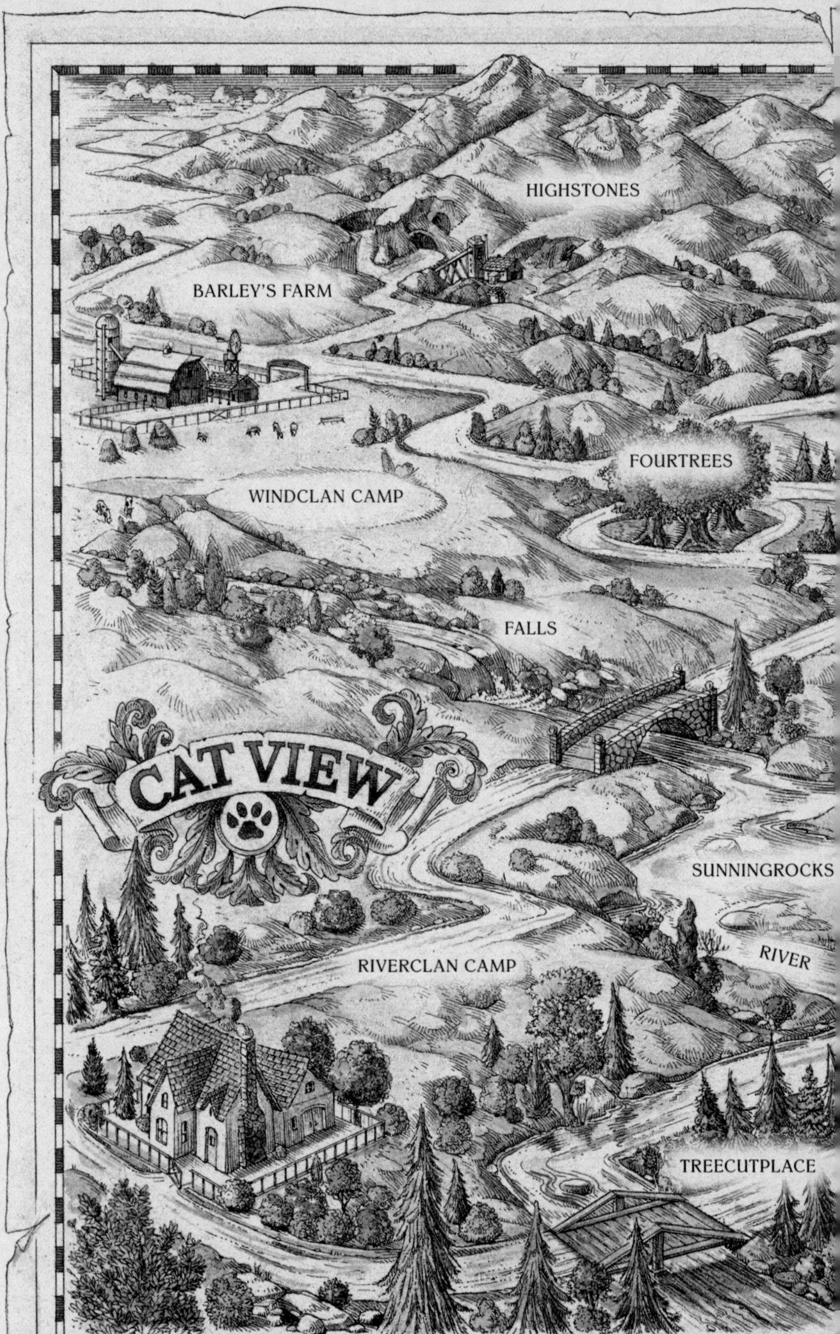

CAT VIEW

HIGHSTONES

BARLEY'S FARM

FOURTREES

WINDCLAN CAMP

FALLS

SUNNINGROCKS

RIVER

RIVERCLAN CAMP

TREECUTPLACE

CARRIONPLACE

SHADOWCLAN
CAMP

THUNDERPATH

OWLTREE

GREAT
SYCAMORE

THUNDERCLAN
CAMP

SNAKEROCKS

SANDY
HOLLOW

TALLPINES

TWOLEGPLACE

KEY
To The
CLANS

THUNDERCLAN

RIVERCLAN

SHADOWCLAN

WINDCLAN

STARCLAN

NORTH

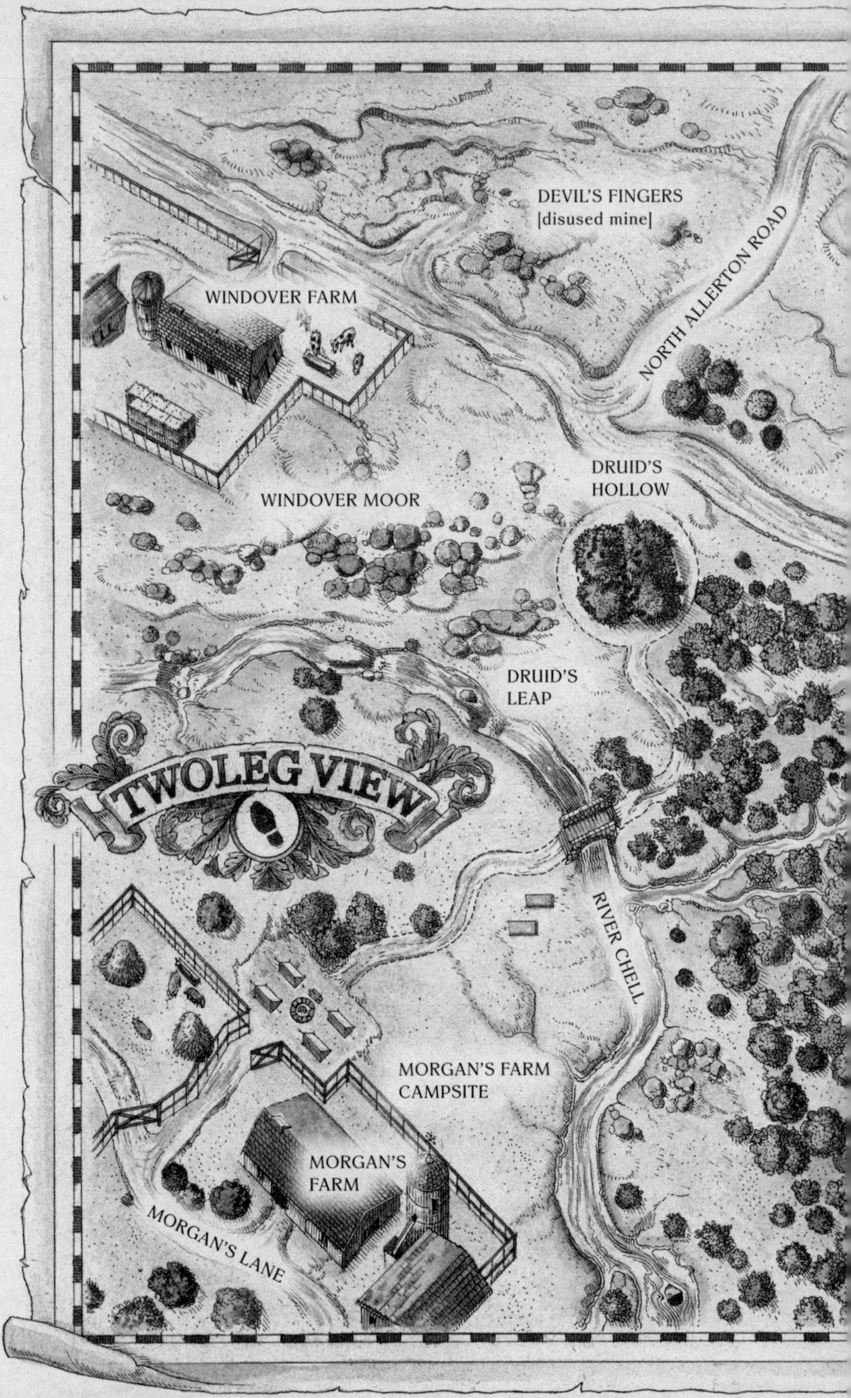

DEVIL'S FINGERS
[disused mine]
NORTH ALLERTON ROAD
WINDOVER FARM
DRUID'S
HOLLOW
WINDOVER MOOR
DRUID'S
LEAP
TWOLEG VIEW
RIVER CHELL
MORGAN'S FARM
CAMPSITE
MORGAN'S
FARM
MORGAN'S LANE

NORTH ALLERTON
AMENITY TIP

WINDOVER ROAD

WHITE HART WOODS

CHELFORD FOREST

CHELFORD MILL

CHELFORD

DECIDUOUS WOODLAND

CONIFERS

MARSH

CLIFFS AND ROCKS

HIKING TRAILS

KEY To The TERRAIN

NORTH

CHAPTER 1

"Scourge! Scourge is dead!"

As the cry rang out from somewhere behind him, Blackfoot dug his teeth into the matted fur of the BloodClan tabby he was fighting. His opponent didn't seem to hear, and continued growling and struggling against him. Her paws ripped at his sides, but he ignored the stinging scratches and bit down harder onto her throat. *Can it be true?*

"Scourge is dead!" Another BloodClan cat yowled in horror.

The tabby heard it this time. She jerked back in shock as the wail went up all around them; Blackfoot lost his grip on her. They both turned and saw Scourge's small form sprawled lifeless, blood coating the front of his body. *It is true.* For a moment, Blackfoot and the tabby stared at each other. Then, her eyes widening, she turned and ran. With a snarl, Blackfoot followed.

All the BloodClan cats were running. Without their leader, they were abandoning their attack on the Clans' territory. Panicked, they streamed out of Fourtrees as fast as they could, Clan cats chasing close behind. Blackfoot raced after them.

Tallstar of WindClan ran beside him, snarling at the fleeing invaders, while on his other side, Tallstar's Clanmate Morningflower bared her teeth ferociously. Cats of all four Clans joined the pursuit, all swept up in a fierce vengeful joy.

With a last swipe, Blackfoot clawed at the tabby she-cat's hindquarters as they reached the end of Clan territory, sending her yowling into the forest. She and the other BloodClan invaders were running back toward the Twolegplace they had come from. Blackfoot didn't think that they would return. Without Scourge, the tiny, bloodthirsty leader who had wanted the Clans' territory for his own, they were nothing but rogues.

And what is ShadowClan, without Tigerstar? Blackfoot's own leader had been killed by Scourge, after he tried to make a bargain with the BloodClan leader to battle against his own enemies within the Clans. Tigerstar had been determined to lead every cat in the forest. He had planned every move that TigerClan—the Clan he had formed by combining Shadow-Clan and RiverClan—had made. *What will we do without him?* Blackfoot bristled at his own unwelcome thought, then shook his pelt as if to shake the idea away. He could feel a trickle of warm blood through his fur, and glanced down at a row of stinging scratches on his shoulder.

ShadowClan will do what we always do, he told himself. *We'll survive.*

Turning back to Fourtrees, he saw that cats were gathering in small Clan groups, centered around their medicine cats or their leaders. A few bodies—both warrior and rogue—dotted the ground, and Blackfoot bristled as he passed Darkstripe's corpse sprawled in the dirt. The black-and-silver striped gray tabby's face was still twisted in a snarl. Darkstripe had left ThunderClan, following Tigerstar to ShadowClan, but once Tigerstar was dead, he had turned against the Clans entirely and fought for the rogues.

Traitor. There was nothing worse than a cat who abandoned his Clan, and Darkstripe had done it twice. Blackfoot snarled at the dead cat for a moment before moving on. They would leave Darkstripe there for now; ShadowClan certainly didn't owe him a warrior's vigil.

Without looking back, he crossed the clearing to where Runningnose, ShadowClan's medicine cat, was surrounded by their Clanmates.

"If you keep that scratch clean, it shouldn't leave a scar," the small gray-and-white tom was saying to Oakfur, who had a long bloody wound across his chest. "Come to my den in the morning and I'll put more marigold on it."

The warrior nodded. "Thanks, Runningnose."

Blackfoot looked around at the ShadowClan warriors. Littlecloud, Runningnose's apprentice, was licking clean a gash on Tallpoppy's side. Russetfur's hindquarters were scratched, but it seemed that the bleeding had already stopped. Those were the worst injuries he could see. *Thank StarClan.*

"Every cat's okay?" he asked, just to make sure.

"We were lucky," Rowanclaw meowed, glancing at the bodies that dotted the grass.

"We fought well," Russetfur corrected, raising her head

proudly. Blackfoot purred in approval.

Tawnypaw, Oakfur's apprentice, was crouched beside her littermate, Bramblepaw, their heads close together in conversation. Blackfoot's eyes narrowed at the sight. *Should I drive Bramblepaw away?* Both apprentices were Tigerstar's kits, but the young tom was a ThunderClan apprentice, while Tawnypaw had chosen to join her father in ShadowClan when the busybodies in ThunderClan had questioned her loyalty. With Tigerstar gone, ShadowClan needed to be stronger and more united than ever.

But today the Clans had fought side by side. And Bramblepaw and Tawnypaw were both Tigerstar's kits. Blackfoot didn't want to prevent them from sharing their grief; he didn't want to give Tawnypaw any reason to reconsider her loyalty to ShadowClan. And with Tigerstar gone, Blackfoot mused, it was time for him to begin thinking like a leader. He'd been Brokenstar's deputy before serving the same role under Tigerstar. *If StarClan agrees . . . ShadowClan is mine to lead.*

But instead of making him feel powerful, the thought filled Blackfoot with doubt. *Do I have it in me to lead?* It felt as if he were suddenly carrying the full weight of ShadowClan on his shoulders. He was the one who would have to make the decision, would have to make all the choices for his Clan from now on. *I've always had some other cat to show me the way.* He missed Tigerstar, sharply and suddenly. The huge dark brown tabby had always known what to do.

Motion caught his eye, and he looked up to see the RiverClan cats following Leopardstar out of the clearing. The dappled golden tabby stared straight ahead as she led her Clan, her head held proudly. She did not even glance at Blackfoot.

I see her plan, Blackfoot thought, his tail twitching with irritation. Leopardstar had chosen to follow Tigerstar. She had willingly joined RiverClan to ShadowClan, forming TigerClan, because she thought it would make her stronger. She'd done everything that Tigerstar had told her, because she'd believed that together the two Clans could overpower the other Clans and rule the whole territory.

But now Tigerstar was dead, defeated at Scourge's claws, and she and her warriors were abandoning ShadowClan. If the other Clans wanted revenge for what Tigerstar had done, she would surely prefer that they not remember that RiverClan had been his ally—that, for a while, she and Blackfoot had stood proudly on either side of Tigerstar.

There was a soft hiss behind him. Blackfoot turned to see Russetfur glaring after the RiverClan leader with disdain. "Fox-heart," the dark ginger warrior muttered, and Blackfoot nodded in agreement.

"Tigerstar never should have trusted her," he growled.

Another cat, a big flame-colored tom, was limping slowly toward them, and Blackfoot stiffened. *What does Firestar want?* He lifted his head as the ThunderClan leader got closer.

"Firestar," he meowed in greeting. "So, we won the battle after all." His pelt prickled. This cat had long been a thorn in Tigerstar's paw. Firestar had once been a kittypet before he joined ThunderClan, but he had risen in the Clan until finally he'd driven Tigerstar out and taken his place as deputy.

"Yes, we did," Firestar agreed. "What will you do now, Blackfoot?"

Blackfoot's eyes narrowed. Wasn't it obvious? *Does Firestar doubt that I could be leader?* He'd never really imagined leading ShadowClan, but it was his right. "Take my Clan home and prepare for a journey to Highstones. I'm their leader now. We have much to do to recover, but life in the forest will go on as usual."

"Then I'll see you at the next Gathering."

Blackfoot was irritated by the rush of relief that ran through him. Firestar's opinion shouldn't matter. But life would be easier if ThunderClan and WindClan accepted him, and Tallstar, the WindClan leader, would follow Firestar's lead. Leopardstar, he felt sure, wouldn't want to pick a fight—she'd be too busy trying to live down the TigerClan episode to be starting new trouble.

Firestar was staring at him. "You would do well to learn from the mistakes of your predecessors," he went on coolly. "I saw what you did to Stonefur at the Bonehill."

Blackfoot's relief turned to shame, a hot, heavy weight in his chest.

I was a loyal deputy. I was following my leader's orders, he told himself. *That's what a good deputy does.*

But the weight in his chest was still there.

At a flick of Firestar's tail, Bramblepaw got to his paws, pressed his muzzle briefly against his sister's flank, and padded to his leader's side. Tawnypaw gazed after him longingly for a moment, then looked up at Blackfoot again, waiting for his orders. Blackfoot felt a small rush of relief. *I was right not to break them up. She's still one of ours.*

Blackfoot nodded to his own cats, and they rose and gathered around him. "Come on," he meowed. They followed him out of the clearing, Runningnose bringing up the rear.

The next morning, Blackfoot stretched and shivered as he emerged from the warriors' den. A pale sun was barely breaking through the cloud cover, and the air was chilly. He glanced at the entrance to the leader's den beneath the big oak tree and felt a stirring in his chest. It hadn't felt right to sleep there the night before . . . *but tomorrow, that will be mine.* It was still hard to believe.

Runningnose was waiting for him in the clearing. "Ready?" the medicine cat asked. "You slept in a bit, and the wind is strong today. It may slow us down. We ought to start making our way to Highstones."

"Let's just go." Blackfoot glanced toward the fresh-kill pile, which he was not permitted to go near before journeying to Highstones. He somehow felt simultaneously hungry, and too unsettled to consider eating. He would never admit it to Runningnose, but he was nervous about sharing tongues with StarClan. He knew he'd been a perfect deputy . . . but perhaps not always a perfect cat. *Will StarClan judge me worthy of being leader?* He had to believe that they would, but thinking about what his ceremony might look like caused icy claws of panic to rake at his pelt.

Runningnose gave him a hard stare. "Are you ready?" he asked.

Blackfoot wasn't sure what the medicine cat meant. *Am I ready to make the trek to Highstones? Or am I ready to lead?* "Why wouldn't I be?" he replied shortly, matching Runningnose's sharp expression.

Runningnose turned away, not answering his question. "Let's go, then," he said, walking away before Blackfoot could answer. Blackfoot smoothed his pelt and followed.

At the entrance to camp, Russetfur was standing guard, looking tired but alert. She dipped her head respectfully as they approached. "Good luck on your journey."

He blinked fondly at her. For a long time last night, as he'd waited for sleep, Blackfoot had one thought repeating in his head: *If I'm going to be leader, I'll need a strong deputy.* And finally, one name had sprung to mind. Now, meeting Russetfur's candid gaze, he knew the decision he'd made was the right one. The dark ginger she-cat might have started life as a rogue, but there was no warrior more loyal to ShadowClan. "Thank you," he told her. "While I'm gone, I'd like you to choose today's patrols and send them out."

Russetfur's eyes went wide in surprise. "Okay."

"I trust you to watch over ShadowClan until I return," Blackfoot continued.

Her ears pricking, Russetfur meowed slowly, "Do you mean . . . ?"

"Yes," Blackfoot purred. "When I come back from the Moonstone, I will name you ShadowClan's deputy. I can't imagine a better choice." Sudden joy lit the other cat's eyes, and Blackfoot's pelt warmed all the way through. *Maybe I will be a strong leader,* he thought. *At least my first decision was the right one.*

That feeling of satisfaction helped Blackfoot keep up a steady pace on the long journey to Highstones, despite the hunger gnawing at his stomach and the ache in his injured shoulder. Runningnose had treated his wounds with comfrey root and bound his shoulder with cobwebs, but it still hurt.

The sun was setting, sending long shadows across the ground, when they finally reached Highstones. The earth was cold beneath Blackfoot's paws, and he looked up the sloping path nervously, taking in the gaping dark hole that was Mothermouth.

"Are you ready?" Runningnose asked again.

The appearance of Mothermouth made this all too real. Again, Blackfoot wondered whether he'd heard doubt in Runningnose's mew. He wanted to challenge the medicine cat, yowling *of course I'm ready,* but instead Blackfoot only nodded, his chest tight with anxiety. He couldn't pretend confidence to Runningnose when his own mind churned with doubts. *How will StarClan receive me?* He had accompanied other cats to Highstones before, but he had never entered Mothermouth, had never seen the Moonstone. He'd never been brave enough to ask Tigerstar or Brokenstar what it looked like; it would have felt like overstepping his role. This was sacred knowledge reserved for leaders and medicine cats. He followed Runningnose up the rocky slope, his heart pounding, then paused for a moment at the cave entrance, peering into the darkness.

"Follow me." Runningnose touched his tail lightly to Blackfoot's back. "It's time for us to learn what awaits you at the Moonstone."

As they entered, the dim light from the entrance was quickly swallowed in darkness. Blackfoot padded behind Runningnose, alert to the medicine cat's scent and the sound of his quiet paws, relying on them to guide him in the dark.

The tunnel sloped downward and the air grew stale, but Blackfoot breathed it in gladly, his doubts shrinking as his chest filled with pride. *This is really happening. I am going to lead ShadowClan!* They were still grieving the loss of Tigerstar. But they were fierce, and loyal to one another. If he led them wisely, Blackfoot could make them the strongest Clan in the forest once again. *Will I be enough?*

He felt that same shiver of doubt, but pushed it away.

I'll have to be.

The darkness grew colder and colder as the tunnel continued to descend. The chilly stone was rough beneath Blackfoot's paws, and the walls of the tunnel closed in tighter, so that his whiskers brushed against them as he went.

At last, he caught the scent of prey somewhere in the distance. *There must be an opening in the rock far overhead,* Blackfoot thought. Ahead of him, Runningnose stopped.

"We're here," the medicine cat told him softly. "Now we wait for moonhigh."

His pelt brushed against Blackfoot's as he sat, and Blackfoot folded his paws under himself to sit too. As they waited,

Blackfoot's mouth went dry and he could feel his own heart pounding harder. *I'm going to be a good leader,* he told himself. But the faces of dead cats were passing before his eyes: young Badgerpaw, so eager to prove himself; Brokenstar, with his cold, fierce gaze; Tigerstar, full of anger and determination. Stonefur, his eyes wide in horrified disbelief. Blackfoot swallowed hard. He hadn't saved any of those cats.

But I followed my leaders. I followed the code. I was a loyal deputy. I did what I was supposed to do.

He couldn't push away the prickle of unease.

What will StarClan say about everything I have done?

Suddenly, a blinding light flooded the cave. Startled, Blackfoot jumped back. Just ahead, an enormous stone towered over them, huge enough to crush them both like ants. Blackfoot felt suddenly tiny, insignificant. The stone seemed to glow with a power of its own, glittering as if it were made from a thousand shards of ice.

As much as he'd wondered about this place, nothing had prepared him for this moment.

"The Moonstone," Runningnose meowed reverently. "Lie beside it and touch it with your nose, and your future will become clear. I'll watch over you while you share tongues with StarClan."

Hesitantly, Blackfoot skulked forward. He glanced back at Runningnose, hoping for encouragement, but the medicine cat just nodded him along. It was hard to tell what Runningnose was thinking. Blackfoot finally settled beside the stone, his eyes stung by its brightness. Taking a deep breath, he leaned forward, closed his eyes, and touched his nose against the Moonstone.

A shock of cold shot through him. His body jerked in sudden pain, and then his legs and tail grew heavy. He was afraid to try to move, sure he would be unable to. It felt like he was dying. He had never been so cold, not even during the harshest leaf-bare. He shook in terror.

Why didn't Runningnose warn me about this? Has StarClan decided to punish me?

Time seemed to pass, but he felt nothing but the cold and the pain, and heard nothing but his own racing, insistent heartbeat. He wondered whether he would survive. Then, just as suddenly as it had all began, the sound and the pain dropped away. Now he couldn't hear anything, not even Runningnose's breathing. Timidly, he opened his eyes.

The cave was gone. The Moonstone was gone. A warm breeze ruffled his fur. He tipped back his head and parted his jaws to take a deep breath of fresh air.

He was at Fourtrees, near the Great Rock, but Fourtrees did not look the way it had the day before. There was no sign of battle, and the scents were those of early greenleaf—prey and warm earth and growing plants. The oak trees above him were lush and full, and Silverpelt twinkled overhead out of a clear sky.

Wait . . . Silverpelt? Blackfoot blinked and looked above. *Is it meant to be moonhigh in StarClan too? And where are the cats to greet me?* As he got to his paws, Silverpelt seemed to drift closer and closer, growing ever clearer, and suddenly he realized with a thrill of fear that these were not just stars, but cats. Star-Clan was coming toward him. His heart pounded harder, and he panted in fear, his breath short. Their eyes blazed at him as they came closer, and he felt as if they could see straight through his pelt to his mind and heart beneath. They knew everything. All his doubts and fears were exposed. Blackfoot gritted his teeth against the whimper that wanted to escape his throat. *I won't show fear.*

The cats of StarClan gathered around him, both strangers and cats he knew. There were so many of them that he couldn't see where the crowd ended, just starry glimmers stretching away from him on all sides. Nightstar was there, raising his tail in greeting, and Whitethroat, who had died on the Thunderpath, flicked his ears in a friendly gesture. But other cats were watching Blackfoot coldly.

A snow-white she-cat stepped forward out of the crowd. Blackfoot recognized her: Sagewhisker, who had been ShadowClan's medicine cat when he was an apprentice.

He dipped his head. "Sagewhisker."

Tiny stars sparkled in the medicine cat's fur as she greeted him solemnly. "Blackfoot, I know that you are uncertain."

"I—" Blackfoot hesitated. He wanted to argue, but he knew he couldn't lie to her. "I am. But I am loyal. I would put my Clan before anything else."

A soft hiss came from the crowd of cats around him, and he flinched, trying to see which cat had made it. But he couldn't:

Blazing eyes and starry fur surrounded him. Any one of them looked furious enough to have hissed at him. He felt himself shrink.

"ShadowClan has suffered," Sagewhisker told him. "But so have *all* the Clans, and part of that is ShadowClan's fault. The next leader of ShadowClan must be strong and honorable, or ShadowClan will fall into oblivion."

Blackfoot felt his eyes widen. Surely the danger had passed? Scourge was dead. Tigerstar, too. The Clans would be at peace again. Then his stomach twisted—the Clans weren't fighting right now, but there was no trust between them. He remembered how Leopardstar had turned away from him, and the cool hostility of Firestar's words.

"If ShadowClan falls," Sagewhisker went on, "the other Clans will fall, too, even StarClan. There must be a balance in the forest. Do you really think you're up to the task? Can you be the strong and honorable leader ShadowClan needs?"

Blackfoot swallowed. "I will do my best," he answered, his voice hoarse. "Like I said, I would do anything for Shadow-Clan. Everything I *have* done has been for ShadowClan."

Sagewhisker nodded. "Very well. The next few moments will be a test of sorts, then. Each cat will give you a gift. The gift may come with a memory, and not all these memories will be welcome."

Blackfoot felt his mouth go dry. There was so much he didn't want to remember. He struggled to swallow. "I'm ready," he said, hoping it was true.

Sagewhisker met his eye. "If at any point it becomes too

much," he said, "you can tell us to stop. You can leave, and live as you always have, and there will be a new leader for Shadow-Clan. Do you understand?"

Blackfoot stared at him. He was burning to know whether this was what every cat's leader ceremony was like, or whether they were testing *him*, specifically. He remembered what Runningnose had said: *Your future will become clear.*

So it was up to him. "I understand," Blackfoot said.

Sagewhisker flicked his ear. "Good. Let us begin."

The glimmering crowd of StarClan parted, and two cats stepped forward. Blackfoot blinked. "Hollyflower," he breathed, meeting the gray-and-white she-cat's gaze. *My mother.* "I've missed you."

Her blue eyes were warm. "My kit," she purred proudly. "The next leader of ShadowClan." But then her tail drooped as she looked to the cat beside her, then back to Blackfoot. "There's something you should know," she meowed.

Blackfoot turned to the mottled white tom standing with his mother. "It's all right," he told him. "I've known for a long time. Hello, Blizzardwing."

Almost instantly, he felt the cats around him recede, as the camp of his kithood surrounded him. . . .

CHAPTER 2

The medicine den was cold. Blackpaw curled his body tighter and squeezed his eyes shut, his belly aching horribly. *I never should have listened to Fernpaw.* He and his littermate had found a dead frog near the edge of camp, and he'd been so hungry!

"I'm sure it's fine," Fernpaw had told him as he'd poked the frog with a slender tortoiseshell paw. "It can't have been dead for long, or we would have seen it earlier."

"Maybe . . ." Blackpaw had meowed doubtfully. He'd taken a sniff. The frog had *seemed* okay. His stomach had rumbled, reminding him how long it had been since he'd eaten. At last, he'd taken a bite, teeth sinking into the frog's rubbery flesh.

Big mistake! he thought now, remembering. He settled deeper into his nest in the medicine den. This was his second night here. He felt a *little* better. Maybe in the morning Sagewhisker would say he was ready to go back to the apprentices' den. And then he'd have something to say to Fernpaw about her terrible advice.

Their mother, Hollyflower, had stayed close while he'd been sick, and, without opening his eyes, he sniffed the air, taking in her comforting scent. *Yes, she's still here.*

There was another cat here, too, he realized. The new scent wasn't Sagewhisker's, nor was it her apprentice, Yellowfang's. It was a tom . . . who *was* that?

"What are you doing here?" Hollyflower asked quietly. There was a strange, unhappy note in her voice, and Blackpaw pricked up his ears.

"I was worried." The low voice was familiar. *Blizzardwing?*

Why was the warrior visiting the medicine den in the middle of the night? What was he worried about? Without moving, Blackpaw cracked his eyes open just a slit.

Hollyflower and Blizzardwing were barely more than shadows, facing each other at the entrance to the medicine den. But every line of Hollyflower's body was tense, as if she was ready to fight.

Why would Hollyflower want to fight Blizzardwing? Blackpaw wondered. He didn't know the older warrior well, but he'd always seemed pleasant enough.

"You don't need to be concerned." Hollyflower's meow was cold. "Aren't you worried some cat might see you here? You wouldn't want them to get any ideas, would you?"

Blizzardwing sighed. "Whatever you think, I *do* care about the kits. They're mine, too, you know?"

Blackpaw felt as if he'd been kicked in the chest. He gasped, then quickly muffled himself by pressing his snout to his flank. *Blizzardwing's kits?* But . . . Blizzardwing didn't have kits. He had a *mate*, Featherstorm. A mate who wasn't Hollyflower.

Hollyflower hissed. "Blackpaw and Fernpaw and Flintpaw are *mine*. You left me to raise them alone because you didn't want to tell Featherstorm the truth. I don't need help from any cat, and especially not you."

Shock ran through Blackpaw's body, and he screwed his eyes shut tighter. He didn't want them to know he was awake. He had always wondered who his father was. Fernpaw and Flintpaw and he had talked it over all the time, even when they were tiny kits.

"Nightkit and Clawkit's father is Toadskip," Fernkit had reasoned, her small face screwed up in thought. "He comes to the nursery all the time. *We* must have a father, too."

"We *must*," Blackkit had agreed. "But who?"

Flintkit had asked Hollyflower, but she had only shaken her head and licked soothingly at the fur on his back. "You don't need a father," she'd told them. "All you have to know is that you are part of ShadowClan." Something about the way she'd said it had kept them from asking again.

Now he knew it was *Blizzardwing*! The pain in Blackpaw's stomach intensified, making him feel even more nauseous. Blizzardwing had known that he was Blackpaw and his littermates' father, and he hadn't told them, hadn't told any cat, because he was afraid of his mate finding out.

They hadn't mattered enough.

Hot anger flooded through Blackpaw. He wanted to leap to his paws and attack Blizzardwing, tear at the tom's pelt with his claws. And, confusingly, part of him also wanted to rush over and press his muzzle to Blizzardwing's, to ask him to stay. He'd always wanted to know his father. He cracked his eyes open, wanting to see how Blizzardwing was reacting to Hollyflower's angry hisses.

"We don't need anything from you." Hollyflower's voice was cold, and Blackpaw saw Blizzardwing's ghostly shape turn away. He tucked his face beneath his paw, feigning sleep, and heard Hollyflower cross the medicine den and lie down.

How am I going to ignore this the next time I speak to Hollyflower? I should let Fernpaw and Flintpaw know.

But he didn't want his littermates to have to feel this way.

I can't tell them.

He thought back to what Hollyflower had said back in the nursery. *I don't need a father. All I need to know is that I am part of ShadowClan.*

Three sunrises later, Blackpaw's stomach was feeling better. All morning, he'd been trying not to think about the conversation he'd overheard between Hollyflower and Blizzardwing. Sometimes he could convince himself that the whole thing had probably been a dream brought on by the bad prey. But late at night, in his nest in the apprentices' den, he knew that it was true. Blizzardwing was his father. And Blizzardwing had been careful that no cat would ever find out.

Blackpaw hadn't told any cat.

It was just past sunhigh and the apprentices were play fighting near the edge of camp. Nearby, Brokenkit was batting around a wad of moss by himself, the bent tail that gave him his name sticking out behind him.

Brokenkit is always playing by himself, Blackpaw realized. Was he lonely? His father, Raggedpelt, was proud of the kit, but his mother's identity was a secret and his foster mother, Lizard-stripe, didn't like him much. She let her own kits pick on him and blamed him if he complained. Every cat knew she was impatient to be back in the warriors' den, not raising an extra kit as well as her own, but at least she seemed a little proud of her own kits. Blackpaw didn't blame Brokenkit for keeping away from them.

"Back, you rotten ThunderClan fox-heart! Get off our territory!" Clawpaw yowled, throwing himself at Flintpaw, who dodged and flung a blow at the brown tom. With a startled blink, Blackpaw turned back to the apprentices' game.

"Ambush!" Fernpaw leaped onto Clawpaw's back, knocking him down. Clawpaw flipped over and shoved her away with his hind paws.

With a playful hiss, Blackpaw pounced on Nightpaw from behind, pinning the black tom to the ground beside his brother. "We will defeat you, wicked invader!" Holding Nightpaw down with both front paws, he meowed. "Do you surrender?"

Nightpaw glared up at him, his tail twitching, and coughed before catching his breath. "Never!"

"I can stand here all day," Blackpaw told him, pricking Nightpaw lightly with his claws. He was heavier than the black-furred apprentice, and Nightpaw squirmed ineffectually under his paws.

He glanced up from the other apprentice's angry face just

as Blizzardwing crossed the clearing to the fresh-kill pile. The older tom's eyes met his for a moment, and Blackpaw's breath caught in his throat.

Nightpaw suddenly twisted beneath him, and, startled, Blackpaw fell heavily to the ground. Scrambling back to his paws, he saw that Blizzardwing had turned away and was carrying a vole to Featherstorm.

"Ha!" Nightpaw meowed, coughing. "I beat you!"

"I guess I should have been paying better attention," Blackpaw answered dully.

"You have to be alert!" Flintpaw scolded him. "What if this had been a real battle?"

Clawpaw flicked his tail, looking smug. "Maybe being half-Clan means you three can only be half warriors."

"We're going to be great warriors!" Fernpaw meowed indignantly.

"And we're *not* half-Clan!" Blackpaw snarled, his fur bristling. "We're completely ShadowClan!"

Flintpaw and Fernpaw exchanged a glance. "Well, we don't *know* that," Flintpaw meowed hesitantly. "But no cat could be more loyal to ShadowClan than we are."

"We *do* know it!" Blackpaw insisted. He wanted to slash at the other apprentices with his claws, even his littermates. If only he could tell them the truth! "Every bit of me is Shadow-Clan!"

Clawpaw sniffed. "Who's your father, then?" he asked. "He was probably some kittypet. I'm surprised Cedarstar hasn't kicked you out."

"He knows we'll be twice the warriors you and Nightpaw are," Fernpaw hissed. "It doesn't matter who our father is."

It does *matter! He* is *a ShadowClan warrior!* Blackpaw wanted to yowl it right in Clawpaw's face.

But what would happen if every cat knew? Blizzardwing would be ashamed—ashamed that Blackpaw and his litter-mates existed. His mate, Featherstorm, would be hurt and embarrassed. And what about Hollyflower? Would the other cats be angry with her? Was there a punishment for having kits with another cat's mate? What if they drove *her* away from ShadowClan?

Swallowing his anger, Blackpaw turned his back on the other apprentices. "I don't want to play anymore," he muttered. He stomped away and sat down alone near the apprentices' den.

Brokenkit was still batting the moss nearby. When Black-paw sat down, he stopped. "Why do you care what *they* think?" he asked, gazing at Blackpaw with sharp orange eyes. "Claw-paw's a mouse-brain."

"He is a mouse-brain," Blackpaw agreed, a sudden surge of affection swelling inside him for the kit. "And he's making fun of me because of something he doesn't know anything about."

Brokenkit flicked his tail. "Who cares?" he meowed. "Other cats don't matter. You just need to know what you want, and figure out how you can make them help you get it." He swiped at his ball of moss again.

That's a little creepy. No wonder Brokenkit was always alone, if he didn't think other cats mattered. But with Lizardstripe always letting her own kits pick on Brokenkit, Blackpaw understood why he felt that way. He was probably lonely. *He's like me. He only has one parent who cares about him.*

"It's just that I know that he's wrong," Blackpaw tried to explain.

Brokenkit looked up. "You know who your father is? Is he a ShadowClan cat? You should have told them who it was. That would shut Clawpaw up."

Blackpaw froze. He couldn't tell any cat the truth. *I shouldn't have even told Brokenkit that I knew.* "It's a secret," he told him at last.

"Your father's in ShadowClan, but he doesn't want any cat to know who he is?" Brokenkit seemed to take Blackpaw's silence as agreement. His eyes narrowed. "Maybe one day you'll be a great warrior, and then you can teach your father a lesson."

Blackpaw imagined spitting the truth into Blizzardwing's face. He didn't need him—Brokenkit was right about that, anyway—but maybe one day he would be better than his father. And this weird little kit might be the only cat who understood how he felt about that. He brushed his tail over Brokenkit's back. "Maybe you're right."

Blizzardwing and Hollyflower gazed at Blackfoot sadly, their starry tails drooping, as the visions of his kithood faded.

"What did you see?" Blizzardwing asked.

Blackfoot shook his head, hoping to clear it. "The moment I overheard you in the medicine-cat den," he explained. "The moment I first knew you were my father."

"I can't believe you knew for so long," Hollyflower's voice was soft.

"I'm so sorry that I hurt you," Blizzardwing meowed. "But thank you for keeping our secret. Do you want this life?"

Blackfoot stared as his father. *Do I?* The memory had been painful, but it didn't change anything. And Blackfoot wouldn't be the first Clan leader to have unusual parentage. "I do," he said.

Blizzardwing stepped forward, the faint stars in his fur seeming to shine more brightly, and touched his nose to Blackfoot's forehead. The touch burned like cold fire, and Blackfoot held back a gasp.

"With this life, I give you acceptance. Accept your past so that you may leave it behind as you and your Clan move forward."

Warmth flooded through Blackfoot's body. He felt as if a weight had been lifted off his back. The future was before him, separate from his past. A cool breeze blew back his whiskers. He could step forward and know, without any doubt, that his Clanmates would be with him, waiting for his command.

They are *giving me nine lives,* he thought, *and I can handle it. Star-Clan knows that everything I've done was for the good of my Clan. Maybe I have nothing to be ashamed of after all.*

CHAPTER 3

❦

Blizzardwing and Hollyflower turned away, Hollyflower with one last affectionate glance over her shoulder. As they rejoined the rest of StarClan, another cat rose and padded toward him. Blackfoot recognized him at once.

"Raggedstar," he greeted him with respect, dipping his head. This cat had been his Clan's deputy and then leader, prior to Brokenstar. Blackfoot had always looked up to him.

"Hello, Blackfoot," the former leader greeted him warmly. He bent to touch his scarred nose to Blackfoot's forehead. Blackfoot managed not to flinch this time, anticipating the burning cold of his touch. Almost immediately, the StarClan cats faded, and the past took shape around him

"Not even a whiff of WindClan today," Blackfoot meowed cheerfully to his patrol as he led the way back into camp.

"They know better than to come onto *our* territory," Rowanberry answered, switching her brown-and-cream-furred tail. Beside her, Nutwhisker purred in agreement.

Blackfoot's chest swelled with pride as they passed through the narrow tunnel between the brambles and into

ShadowClan's camp. By patrolling, he helped to keep the camp, and all the cats in it, protected. And here the camp was, busy and safe. *This is what being a warrior is all about.*

In the center of camp, Runningpaw, the medicine-cat apprentice, was laying out herbs to dry in the sun. Archeye and Crowtail were sharing tongues and gossiping in front of the elders' den. Mousewing and Boulder sat side by side, gulping down prey. It was so peaceful! Nutwhisker nudged Blackfoot cheerfully with his shoulder as he and Rowanberry brushed past on their way to the fresh-kill pile, and Blackfoot flicked his ears at them.

"If I *ever* see you doing that again, I'll make sure you're squeezing ticks off the elders for a moon!" The harsh yowl broke through the calm of the clearing, and Blackfoot turned to see Ashheart scolding Brokenpaw at the edge of camp. She looked as if she was barely holding herself back from charging at him. The muscular apprentice was glaring back at the she-cat, his tail slashing angrily. Behind them, Deerpaw shifted anxiously from paw to paw. There was a long, bloody scratch across his shoulder.

"You can't tell me what to do!" Brokenpaw snarled back defiantly.

Ashheart's face twisted in fury and she raised a paw in threat, her claws extended.

"Wait!" Without pausing to think, Blackfoot hurried toward them. He pushed in front of Brokenpaw, blocking Ashheart. "You can't attack an apprentice."

"I don't need your protection," Brokenpaw meowed indignantly.

"The punishment fits the crime. He was tearing into Deerpaw with his claws out," Ashheart told Blackfoot. "He knows better than to use his unsheathed claws in training."

Brokenpaw growled. "How are we going to fight other Clans if we're afraid to get blood on our paws?"

He's going to make a fierce warrior, Blackfoot thought with admiration. But all warriors were supposed to set good examples for the apprentices, so he meowed, "We don't get our *Clanmates'* blood on our paws, Brokenpaw. You know the rules." He glanced at the smaller apprentice. "Why don't you go to the medicine den, Deerpaw? Yellowfang can put something on that scratch." Deerpaw nodded and hurried off, looking relieved to get away from the conflict.

"The rules are stupid," Brokenpaw muttered. "We have to make ourselves strong. Only cowards aren't willing to get hurt." His orange eyes flashed meaningfully at Ashheart. Then he turned and sauntered toward the apprentices' den, switching his bent tail.

Ashheart hissed, looking ready to lunge after the apprentice.

"Come on." Blackfoot stepped in front of her to block her path and said the first thing he thought of. "You don't want to strike our deputy's son. You know how protective Raggedpelt is of him."

"I wasn't going to hit Brokenpaw," Ashheart meowed. "I

just wanted to scare him into behaving better."

Blackfoot wasn't sure she wouldn't have hit Brokenpaw. She'd looked awfully angry. And there had been something chillingly defiant in Brokenpaw's cold gaze. Blackfoot wouldn't have been surprised if either of them had attacked the other, and it was his duty not to let things escalate to violence. ShadowClan warriors shouldn't be attacking one another.

"Apprentices are always getting into trouble," he told her uncomfortably. "We can't take it too seriously."

Ashheart scoffed. "You don't really think Brokenpaw is a *normal* apprentice, do you?"

"What do you mean?" Blackfoot asked.

Ashheart's tail twitched. "There's just something . . . *off* about that 'paw."

"You're being silly," Blackfoot told her. The memory of the cold fury in Brokenpaw's eyes flashed through his mind, but he dismissed it. *He was just angry at being scolded.* "He's a bit of a loner, but there's nothing wrong with that. And the other 'paws look up to him since he's the biggest and the best fighter."

"That's one of the things that worries me," Ashheart replied flatly. "The last thing ShadowClan needs is for other cats to start following Brokenpaw's lead." With a shake of her head, she backed away. "I'm going to find Nightpelt and tell him what his apprentice has been up to."

Brokenpaw won't listen to Nightpelt. Guilt stirred in Blackfoot's belly at how sure of this he was, and how little he blamed Brokenpaw for the disdain he openly showed to his mentor.

But *why* had Cedarstar given the most promising apprentice to such a sickly, soft-tempered warrior? As Blackfoot and his littermates had grown out of their own apprentice moons, Nightpelt's cough and shortness of breath had gotten worse and worse. *I could have been a better mentor to him.* But Cedarstar had chosen Nightpelt.

Brokenpaw was crouched by the apprentices' den, observing the rest of camp. Blackfoot went over and sat down beside him. For a heartbeat, he thought of giving the younger cat a friendly nudge, but changed his mind. Brokenpaw didn't like to be touched, except during battle training. "Are you okay?" he asked instead. "Ashheart was pretty hard on you."

Brokenpaw's ear twitched as his cool orange gaze ranged over the other cats. "I don't care what she thinks."

Even when he was training or part of a patrol, Brokenpaw still kept his distance from the other apprentices. "Do you want to talk about what happened with Deerpaw?" Blackfoot asked.

"Nothing happened," Brokenpaw meowed. "He needs to train harder."

"He was bleeding a lot, though." A scratch that deep hadn't been a simple accident. "Were you angry with him? Isn't he one of your friends?" The young cats who had teased Brokenpaw when they'd been kits all looked up to him now.

Brokenpaw snorted, his lip curling. "I don't have friends. I have Clanmates."

"Clanmates are better than friends," Blackfoot answered automatically. He'd never had friends who *weren't* Clanmates, although he knew some cats did. Blackfoot didn't see the point. Why waste time with cats you couldn't count on to have your back in battle?

Brokenpaw shrugged. "A friend is a cat you hang around because they make you *happy*." His voice was scornful. "A Clanmate fights beside you to protect your territory, and hunts so that you all have food. If your Clanmate can't hunt or can't fight, then they're useless."

Blackfoot felt himself gasp, and tried to cover it by taking in a deep breath. *That's against the warrior code!* But even so, Blackfoot's heart ached for the younger cat. He was so *angry*. He'd seemed like such a lonely kit, and now it was like he hated every cat, but that couldn't be true. It must be hard for Brokenpaw to trust his Clanmates, after his foster mother and littermates rejected him when he was so young. He just needed some cat to understand him. Blackfoot brushed his tail across Brokenpaw's back. The younger cat stiffened but said nothing, and Blackfoot pulled his tail back.

"Once you're a full warrior, you'll see that there's nothing better than working beside your Clanmates," Blackfoot told him. "In a Clan, we all take care of one another." Brokenpaw didn't answer. But Blackfoot hoped that he could see that what Blackfoot said was true. The truest thing there was.

Did I say the right thing? Blackfoot was still musing over the moment with Brokenpaw later that day, as he was heading back into camp from the dirtplace. Suddenly he heard Raggedpelt's voice behind him. "Hey, Blackfoot, can I talk to you?"

Blackfoot turned to blink at the brown tabby tom. "Of course."

Raggedpelt gestured with his tail to a spot beneath a nearby pine tree, and Blackfoot followed him. "What's going on?" He tried to think of a reason that ShadowClan's deputy would need to talk to him alone. *Am I in trouble?*

"I heard that you stood up for Brokenpaw," Raggedpelt meowed, his amber gaze warm.

"Oh, right." Embarrassed, Blackfoot gave his chest a quick lick. "I didn't do anything much. Ashheart was just overreacting to the 'paws getting carried away in training."

"Brokenpaw is going to be a great warrior," Raggedpelt told him. "He's strong and brave and smart. But not every cat likes him. It's been difficult for him." The deputy's meow took on a tinge of bitterness. "We both know how hard it is for a young cat not to be accepted by both his parents. I think when he was younger, that was what separated him from the other kits. I hoped that he would never feel unwanted."

Exactly. With a small thrill, Blackfoot remembered that no cat knew who Raggedpelt's father had been, either, although some suspected that he must have been a kittypet from the Twolegplace. *He's just like me. And he's become deputy.* Blackfoot and Raggedpelt had both been rejected by their fathers. Brokenpaw's mother, whoever she was, hadn't wanted him either. *All three of us are the same.*

"I understand that," he told the deputy, his meow coming out rougher than he'd meant it to.

"I'm just glad that there are cats like you around, who will give Brokenpaw the chance to prove himself." Raggedpelt meowed.

"I'll look out for him," Blackfoot meowed. "I trust Brokenpaw. He's going to be a great ShadowClan warrior."

The warm breeze of StarClan's Fourtrees blew through Blackfoot's whiskers again. As his vision ended, Blackfoot's shoulders drooped. The trust they'd shared in Brokenpaw hadn't been wise. Raggedstar's death had been a bloody, terrible one, and Brokentail had been the only witness. At the time, he'd blamed it on WindClan, but much later, cats said Brokenstar had confessed to murdering his father. Blackfoot hadn't heard him say it with his own ears, so he'd pretended that it was a lie spread by Brokenstar's enemies. He hadn't wanted to know. But now, seeing that sullen, angry apprentice through fresh eyes, it felt like an undeniable truth. *Brokenstar killed Raggedstar so that he could become leader.*

Blackfoot swallowed, cold despite the StarClan greenleaf all around him. He had followed Brokenstar wholeheartedly. If the cat he'd believed in had been so snake-hearted, what did that mean about Blackfoot's other choices?

"I can imagine what you've seen," Raggedstar mewed. "Putting our faith in the wrong cat has been a challenge for both of us. Are you sure you want this life?"

Blackfoot looked at his former leader. It was hard to confront the truths of the past, but he still felt ready. "I do," he said.

"Then with this life, I give you trust," Raggedstar meowed.

"Have faith in your Clanmates as you do in yourself."

A jolt ran through Blackfoot, and he crouched as a painful spasm hit him. He could feel the cats of ShadowClan, past and present, around him: cats to watch over the Clan while he slept, to hunt and patrol and stride into battle by his side. He wanted to trust them. He *would* trust them.

His eyes met Raggedstar's as he nodded with a jerk of his chin. He could see a shadow in the other cat's gaze. Trust could be a strength or a weakness.

"We both trusted Brokentail," he told Raggedstar, and the former leader met his gaze wearily. "But it was a mistake, wasn't it? And that was the beginning of ShadowClan falling apart."

Raggedstar bowed his head. "We were wrong to put our faith in him. He killed me in the end. And following him changed you. But what's done is done," he meowed. "If ShadowClan is going to survive, you'll have to trust your warriors. And they'll have to trust you."

Blackfoot swallowed hard. *I want to trust, and I need to. But what if I'm wrong again?*

CHAPTER 4

A much smaller cat—a black-and-white kit—wove his way out of the crowd of StarClan cats.

"Badgerfang," Blackfoot breathed, his chest tight. *My kin. Fernshade's only kit.*

"Blackfoot!" Badgerfang squeaked happily, hurrying toward him, his starry tail lashing with excitement. As he reached him, he craned up, and Blackfoot crouched so that the kit could touch his nose to Blackfoot's face. Badgerfang's scent had changed, he realized with a pang—the sweet kit scent was gone, replaced with a cool tinge of night, like the smell of stars.

At the touch of his nose, Blackfoot felt himself falling into the past.

Blackfoot yawned and wrapped his tail more tightly around himself, puffing up his fur against the cold wind. He'd watched over the camp last night, and he was sleepy despite the chill.

"Let all cats old enough to catch their own prey join here beneath the Clanrock for a meeting!" Brokenstar's yowl cut through the camp, and Blackfoot pricked up his ears, his tiredness falling away. Brokenstar was standing on the Clanrock, his head high and his eyes bright with pleasure.

Pride warmed Blackfoot as he got to his paws and hurried over to stand beneath the Clanrock. Since Raggedstar's death at the paws of WindClan, Brokenstar and his Clan had focused on taking revenge on the cats who had murdered the leader. Brokenstar had led ShadowClan from one victory in battle to another, and he'd chosen Blackfoot to be his deputy. Strong and fierce, he was a leader any cat would admire.

Dawnpaw, Blackfoot's apprentice, brushed against him, and he looked down at her. "Do you know what's going on?" she whispered.

"Shh," he told her. "Listen to Brokenstar and you'll find out."

As the cats gathered beneath him, Brokenstar gazed around at them approvingly. "Cats of ShadowClan," he meowed, "you are fierce and courageous warriors. With every battle, we take vengeance on WindClan, and show that ShadowClan cannot be threatened. Every cat in the forest fears us. The other Clans know better than to challenge us, or even to lay one paw on our territory, and that is because of your bravery and skill in battle."

"ShadowClan! ShadowClan!" Blackfoot threw his head back and yowled enthusiastically along with the rest of the Clan. The cats around him were thin and battle-scarred—Brokenstar had decreed that fighting and training for battle were their top priorities, and that cats must hunt for themselves when they could find time—but their eyes were shining with excitement. Raggedstar's murder had put a claw in the heart of every cat in the Clan, and every strike they made against WindClan made that pain just a little less sharp.

"The youngest members of ShadowClan have shown themselves to be among our most honorable," Brokenstar announced, and Dawnpaw's ears pricked up with excitement. "We've started training our apprentices younger, and they've shown the other Clans how strong the future of ShadowClan is!"

"ShadowClan!" Young Wetpaw, one of the apprentices, piped up suddenly, and a *mrrow* of laughter swept through the clearing. Brokenstar nodded at him in approval.

Yellowfang and Runningnose, the ShadowClan medicine cats, were standing nearby, and Blackfoot saw them exchange a concerned look. He felt a flash of annoyance, then pushed it away. It was natural for them to worry, Blackfoot thought. *Medicine cats don't see all the angles.* The new ShadowClan apprentices might be younger than the other Clans' apprentices, but that only meant they would be fully trained warriors sooner. There was no reason to keep cats who wanted to learn to fight stuck waiting in the nursery.

It was true, though, that Dawnpaw's littermates had died. Medicine cats fought against their Clanmates' deaths, and he knew the deaths were even harder to accept when the cat was young. *But warriors grieve for their Clanmates, too.* Blackfoot felt sick whenever he thought about Mosspaw, his neck broken in a training accident, or Volepaw, who had been killed by an infection from a rat bite. But those deaths hadn't happened because of the apprentices' youth; they could have happened to any cat.

"And now another of our kits is ready to become an apprentice," Brokenstar told the Clan. "Badgerkit, step forward."

Badgerkit squeaked in delight and hurried toward the Clanrock before suddenly slowing down to a more dignified walk, his head held self-consciously high.

There was a strange ache in Blackfoot's chest as he watched Badgerkit stop before the Clanrock. The kit seemed so *small*. Despite himself, Blackfoot glanced at his sister and her mate. Fernshade looked stricken, her eyes wide, and Wolfstep was pressed tightly against her side.

They don't really understand. It could be hard for parents, seeing their kits become apprentices, but it was an honor to start training so young.

"Badgerkit, it is time for you to be apprenticed," Brokenstar meowed. "From this day on, until you receive your warrior name, you will be known as Badgerpaw. Your mentor will be Flintfang, who I hope will pass down all that he knows." Brokenstar looked to Flintfang, nodding at him to come forward. The powerful gray tom approached slowly, his face unreadable, and brushed his tail across Badgerkit's back.

"Flintfang, you are ready to take on an apprentice. You have shown yourself to be fierce and bold, and I know you will train Badgerpaw to be the same."

As his brother dipped his head to touch his muzzle to

Badgerpaw's, Blackfoot let go of the breath he'd been holding. He could trust Flintfang to look out for their sister's kit. *Everything's going to be fine.*

"Are you both crazy?" While Badgerpaw was making the rounds of the other warriors, accepting congratulations, Fernshade pulled Flintfang aside and confronted her littermates. Her fur was bristling with anger, but she kept her voice low, herding them both to the edge of camp where they wouldn't be overheard.

Flintfang shifted his paws nervously and glanced to Blackfoot for help. "I'll look after him, I promise."

"That's not the point!" Fernshade meowed. "He's barely three moons old; he's too young for this! I don't know what Brokenstar's thinking, but he's putting the kits in danger by apprenticing them so young."

Blackfoot straightened up, lifting his head proudly. "He's thinking about the good of the Clan," he told her. "Brokenstar says that our warriors will be stronger if they begin their training earlier. You should be *proud*. Badgerpaw isn't scared. He's thrilled to start training."

"Of course he's thrilled," Fernshade hissed. "He's a *kit*. All he can imagine is being the greatest warrior ever born and taking down the other Clans with just one paw. He's not old enough to realize he should be afraid."

Flintfang stared down at his thick-furred paws. "We can't do anything to change this. Brokenstar is our leader. We do what he says."

Fernshade glared at them both, her yellow eyes blazing. "At least tell me you don't agree with him. Even if you won't do anything, admit you know that this is wrong. You're my brothers. I know you care about Badgerkit."

Flintfang shook his head silently. Blackfoot felt a little sick at the look of fear on his sister's face, but he stared back at her unblinkingly. "Brokenstar was given nine lives by StarClan," he meowed. "Whatever he decides is what's right for Shadow-Clan. StarClan *wants* Badgerpaw to be an apprentice."

Fernshade did not answer for several heartbeats, her ears pressed back angrily. Then she sighed, her tail drooping. Her voice was a low growl. "I am so proud of him. He's a brave kit. But all I can do is hope every cat won't come to regret Bro-kenstar's choices."

Snarls of fury and screeches of pain filled the air as battle raged through the WindClan camp. Blackfoot barreled into Tornear, joy surging in his chest as the wiry gray tabby fell heavily to the ground. "Fox-hearts!" he growled to himself, and ripped his claws through the fur and flesh of the other tom's side. Tornear screeched in pain.

WindClan had murdered Raggedstar in leaf-fall, and ShadowClan had battled WindClan over and over through leaf-bare and into newleaf, sometimes raiding their camp and sometimes merely chasing patrols. Blackfoot and his Clan-mates wouldn't stop attacking until WindClan was destroyed.

Brokenstar had told them that ShadowClan needed to strike fear into the hearts of the other Clans, and now that they thought of nothing but battle, it was easy to do so. *We'll drive them out of the forest,* Blackfoot thought triumphantly. *We're going to destroy WindClan forever. It's what they deserve for trying to hurt ShadowClan.*

The scent of blood was thick in the clearing, and the leader of the WindClan patrol was yowling a retreat. Blackfoot let Tornear slip from under his claws and watched as the tom scrambled away, then turned to run his gaze over his own patrol. Brokenstar was driving off the last of the WindClan cats, his tail high and fur fluffed with excitement. Littlepaw was leaning against his mentor, Clawface, and holding one front paw up high, blood dripping from one of its toes where a claw had been ripped off. Scorchwind was licking at a wounded shoulder, and Boulder's ear was torn. Otherwise, the patrol seemed uninjured.

But where were Flintfang and Badgerpaw? Blackfoot looked around hopefully. Badgerpaw had been so excited for his first battle. He'd wanted to use the new two-pawed attack Flintfang had just taught him. He'd be ecstatic if he'd managed to perform it properly.

Then Blackfoot spotted Flintfang's gray pelt. He began running toward him, when suddenly he noticed the gray warrior's posture. He was huddled over something, and he looked . . . *Oh no.* When Blackfoot saw the look on Flintfang's face, his stomach dropped sickeningly.

Then he saw something small lying on the ground beneath the horrified tom. *Badgerpaw.* The kit's black-and-white fur was matted with blood.

Blackfoot took a few slow steps toward them, his heart beating hard. *He was so excited. Fernshade told him she was proud.*

He could hear them now, as he got closer. Badgerpaw's meow was weak. "I'd like to be called Badgerfang. Like you, because you were such a great mentor."

Flintfang gently rested his muzzle on Badgerpaw's head. His voice was rough with pain. "That is a great honor. Badgerfang is a very good name for a warrior." There was a long pause, and Blackfoot moved closer. He could hear Badgerpaw struggling for breath. "You will watch over us from StarClan for all the moons to come."

Everything was still. The wind had stopped whipping across the clearing, and the leaves on the trees nearby seemed to halt in place. The silence was deafening. Blackfoot couldn't hear Badgerpaw's breathing anymore. *Please,* he thought, a silent yowl to StarClan. But he knew it was too late.

Flintfang was whispering, his voice too low for Blackfoot to hear. As Blackfoot came slowly closer, Flintfang raised his head and stared into his brother's eyes, his face full of grief and horror. Blackfoot knew then for sure that Badgerpaw was dead. The kit's body was limp at Flintfang's paws.

Blackfoot felt as if a strong hind paw had kicked him in the stomach. He gasped for air, his head spinning.

Fernshade was right. He wasn't ready. The thought of his sister made everything worse. How would they tell her that her only kit was dead?

Should I have argued with Brokenstar? Maybe he is wrong to train the kits so young. The thought was terrifying, and Blackfoot shook his head, driving it away. Brokenstar was their leader. His word *was* the warrior code. StarClan had chosen him. Somehow, Badgerpaw's death must be StarClan's will.

I don't understand it. I hate it. But this must be the way things have to be.

CHAPTER 5

A *warm breeze ran through Blackfoot's* pelt and he opened his eyes to find himself once again surrounded by StarClan. Blackfoot tried to catch his breath. Seeing Badgerfang and remembering his death made his grief for the kit feel as sharp as it had that day on the battlefield. His chest ached with sorrow.

"Should I have tried to convince Brokenstar not to train such young kits?" he asked in a low voice. Badgerpaw hadn't been the first kit to suffer because of early apprenticeship. Maybe Blackfoot should have known as soon as Mosspaw died that the kits were too young to train. Maybe he should have known as soon as Brokenstar named the first three-moon-old kit an apprentice. They had belonged in the nursery. But Brokenstar had been so *sure* that a Clan cat's only purpose was battle. "I had to listen to my leader," Blackfoot told the gathered StarClan cats. "That's what makes us different from rogues."

Badgerfang watched Blackfoot solemnly. "You can stop anytime, you know," he reminded him. "I don't have to give you this life."

Blackfoot took in a breath. *It hurts more and more. But I can keep*

285

going. "I don't want to stop," he said. "Please, Badgerfang, give me the life you intended."

Badgerfang nodded and stepped forward. "With this life, I give you perspective," he meowed. "Always seek as many points of view as you can, while knowing that a leader must in the end think for himself."

Blackfoot's muscles tensed painfully as the new life took hold. Memories that weren't his own flashed before him— *Oakfur watched approvingly as Tawnypaw leaped for a vole; Russetfur and Boulder murmured quietly to each other as they patrolled the border; Runningnose inspected Tallpoppy's healing wound, his paw gentle on her side*—and he knew he was seeing through the eyes of his Clanmates. He was dizzy for a heartbeat as the different viewpoints shifted, and then his eyes cleared.

Badgerfang brushed his tail affectionately against Blackfoot's side as he turned and headed back toward the gathered StarClan cats. A pang shot through Blackfoot as his sister's kit got farther away. *Don't go.*

Could I have stopped Badgerfang from dying? Should I have tried to save him?

Blackfoot shook his pelt, trying to drive away the thoughts. *I didn't have a choice.*

The starry warriors all around him were silent. Blackfoot imagined that they were all wrestling with his past actions, just as he was. Some of them seemed accusing in their silence, others sympathetic.

StarClan had chosen Brokenstar. StarClan was choosing Blackfoot. *Can StarClan ever be wrong?*

A sleek, dark gray tom stepped forward.

"I don't know you," Blackfoot meowed warily.

The tom's golden eyes were warm with compassion as he came closer. Something unknotted in Blackfoot's chest. This cat believed that Blackfoot could lead ShadowClan. "I am Gray Wing," the gray tom told him. "I was one of the first Clan cats in the forest. We created the Clans to be separate, but we also understood that the Clans must work together to stay safe and strong."

Blackfoot closed his eyes, steeling himself as he felt the past returning. . . .

"He's late," Blackfoot grumbled, glancing up and down the sides of the Thunderpath that marked the border between WindClan and ShadowClan.

"Tallstar will come," Brokenstar meowed confidently. "He doesn't have a choice."

All through newleaf, ShadowClan had increased their attacks on WindClan's territory. It was rare for a WindClan hunting or border patrol to not find themselves driven to retreat toward their camp by furious ShadowClan cats. The ShadowClan warriors were stronger and fiercer than any cat in WindClan, and Blackfoot knew that the WindClan cats were scared.

He felt a mean, satisfied thrill as Tallstar and Deadfoot, slunk out of the tall grass on the other side of the Thunderpath, their steps hesitant and their gazes wary. Despite his twisted paw, Deadfoot kept pace with his leader. They stopped at the edge of the Thunderpath and glanced at each other before looking at Blackfoot and Brokenstar suspiciously. The WindClan leader and deputy were clearly feeling threatened.

They deserve to be afraid, Blackfoot thought. *They killed our leader.*

Despite everything, though, he felt a touch of respect as Tallstar raised his head proudly, without any sign of fear, and said in a cool, insolent voice, "You wanted to meet, Brokenstar. What do you have to tell us?"

Brokenstar regarded the WindClan cats for a long moment. With a rush of wind, a monster dashed by on the Thunderpath between them, blowing back their ears and whiskers, but neither leader flinched.

At last, Brokenstar meowed evenly, "I want peace between our Clans."

Blackfoot barely managed to keep himself from turning to Brokenstar in disbelief. *That's not why we're here!*

Tallstar looked even more wary as he answered, "We would like peace as well." Beside him, Deadfoot was quivering, his eyes flitting between his own leader and Brokenstar. *They're waiting for the bone in the prey,* Blackfoot thought. The WindClan leader and deputy weren't complete fools, whatever else they were.

"Peace cannot come without sacrifice," Brokenstar meowed solemnly.

"Sacrifice?" Tallstar asked, exchanging a worried glance with Deadfoot. "All we want is to live on our own territory without ShadowClan attacking us. Why should we sacrifice? We've done nothing to you."

Nothing? Blackfoot's grudging respect vanished. Sliding out his claws, he dug them savagely into the ground. Another monster dashed by, the wind of its passing momentarily deafening, and Blackfoot took a breath to keep from snarling at the WindClan cats.

He expected Brokenstar to confront Tallstar and Deadfoot about the way their Clan had murdered Raggedstar—they deserved to suffer *any* kind of revenge ShadowClan could think of after that. Instead, the flat-faced tom just blinked calmly. "Whatever you've done or not done," he meowed, "it's been a hard leaf-bare. Kits have died in WindClan, but ShadowClan's nursery has flourished."

Tallstar flinched a little at the reminder but did not answer.

"ShadowClan is growing," Brokenstar went on. "And our territory is not enough to support us all. We don't want war, but if there's going to be peace between us, you will have to allow ShadowClan hunting rights on WindClan's territory."

Another monster thundered past, its wind beating against them, its roar drowning out Tallstar and Deadfoot's yowls of protest.

As soon as the monster's roars had quieted in the distance, Tallstar spoke. "Absolutely not." His long tail flicked quickly, but that was the only visible sign of his anger. "The borders between the Clans have been there for longer than any cat can remember. We need all of our territory and we aren't willing to give it up. No cat can change Clan boundaries."

"Not without a fight." Brokenstar's voice was cold enough that even Blackfoot felt a chill go down his spine.

Deadfoot's ears twitched anxiously, but Tallstar only narrowed his amber eyes. He looked as if he wanted to charge across the Thunderpath and leap at Brokenstar's throat. "This conversation is over," he spat. "Stay off our territory."

"Wait," Blackfoot yowled as Tallstar began to turn away. "We should discuss the—" But the two WindClan cats were already disappearing into the tall grass behind them. Neither one looked back.

Once they were out of earshot, Blackfoot looked at Brokenstar. "Do you think we stalled them for long enough?"

Brokenstar's gaze was thoughtful. "We'll find out, won't we?"

Excitement stirred in Blackfoot's chest and he felt his tail curl with pleasure. *This could be the end,* he thought. *Revenge for Raggedstar's death at last.*

Life will be good again, when WindClan has been destroyed.

Would ShadowClan be able to become less warlike, be able to hunt for their Clanmates and welcome back their elders—whom Brokenstar had exiled to another part of the territory—once they'd taken vengeance on WindClan?

Checking to make sure the Thunderpath was clear of monsters, he followed Brokenstar quickly across. They looped around to keep out of sight and scent of Tallstar and Deadfoot, but they could see the two WindClan cats ahead, deep in conversation. Tallstar's long tail was twitching angrily, and he and Deadfoot seemed to be arguing in low voices.

No matter how often Blackfoot crossed the border, Wind-Clan's territory made him uncomfortable. His pelt prickled at the feeling of the open sky above him, so different from the comforting protection of ShadowClan's pine trees. His nose twitched at the dry, earthy scent, nothing like the warm peaty smell of ShadowClan; and the rocky soil, not comfortably soft and damp like on ShadowClan's territory, felt wrong beneath his paws. He felt vulnerable here. A bird swooped overhead, and he flinched instinctively, wishing there were something between him and the sky.

Tallstar half turned, his ears pricked, and Blackfoot and Brokenstar crouched, letting the long grass hide them. But Tallstar wasn't looking their way. He had heard something. With a quick word to Deadfoot, he began to run toward WindClan's camp, his deputy hurrying after him.

"Now!" Brokenstar hissed, and he and Blackfoot dashed after the WindClan cats. In just a few strides they could hear what Tallstar had heard: the snarls and yowls of battle. Already, Blackfoot could smell blood. His whiskers twitched eagerly.

They caught up to the WindClan leader and deputy at the edge of WindClan's camp. Tallstar had hesitated just for a heartbeat, taking in the battle before him. Barkface, the WindClan medicine cat, was trying to defend the medicine den, but Cinderfur and Stumpytail were harrying him on each side.

Ashfoot and Morningflower, two WindClan queens, were

blocking the entrance to the nursery, but blood was already running down Morningflower's chest as Clawface hissed at her to move aside. Blackfoot could hear kits wailing. Even though he *knew* WindClan deserved this, his fur rose anxiously at the sound. Everywhere, warriors were locked in combat, and ShadowClan clearly had the upper paw over their enemies.

As Tallstar and Deadfoot gazed at the scene in frozen dismay, Brokenstar took his chance. With a powerful leap, he pounced on Tallstar from behind, knocking the WindClan leader to the ground. Deadfoot whipped around, startled, but Blackfoot was already barreling toward him, and quickly pinned the smaller cat beneath him.

"Snake-heart!" Deadfoot growled, struggling beneath him. "Why won't you leave us alone?"

Fury rose up in Blackfoot's throat, almost choking him. Deadfoot was the WindClan deputy. He *must* know exactly why ShadowClan wouldn't stop until WindClan was gone. How dare he pretend that he knew nothing of Raggedstar's murder? Blackfoot drove his hind paws against Deadfoot's stomach, fiercely pleased when Deadfoot winced and gasped in pain.

"You know we won't stop as long as there's a single Wind-Clan cat left in the forest," Blackfoot snarled.

He could hear Tallstar breathing in short, harsh gasps as he struggled beneath Brokenstar. In the WindClan camp, a cat cried out, a pained yowl. Brokenstar raised his paw just above Tallstar's eyes, his sharp claws unsheathed.

"I could blind you now," Brokenstar hissed. "Try to lead your Clan without sight, Tallstar."

The WindClan leader stilled. "Call off your warriors," he meowed. "We can talk about our borders." His voice didn't shake, but his scent was sour with panic.

"ShadowClan needs your territory," Brokenstar told him, glaring down into Tallstar's eyes. "We gave you the chance to share your hunting grounds, but it's too late now. This is your one warning. If even a single WindClan cat is here tomorrow, we'll kill you all. You know you aren't strong enough to defend your Clan against us."

Tallstar stared up at him, frightened and furious. "Leave the forest?" he asked. "But this is our home. Where would we go?"

Brokenstar blinked calmly at him. "That's not my problem," he meowed, his voice level. "This is your one warning, the only chance that WindClan has to live. Take it."

The two leaders' gazes locked for a heartbeat. Brokenstar's eyes were cold with hatred. Then Brokenstar stepped back, releasing Tallstar, and called, "ShadowClan, to me!"

At Brokenstar's call, Blackfoot leaped off Deadfoot, letting his hind claws scratch the WindClan deputy's soft belly, and followed his leader. Behind him, he could hear the Shadow-Clan warriors streaming out of WindClan's camp, yowling in triumph. The scent of blood hung heavily in the air.

He caught up to Brokenstar. His leader's tail was high and his fur was fluffed with pleasure.

"Do you really think they'll leave the forest?" Blackfoot asked him. ShadowClan had made an impression on WindClan, he was sure of that. Those cats would be seeing ShadowClan warriors in their nightmares for many moons to come. But would the attack, and Brokenstar's threats, be enough to make them flee their home on the moor? WindClan had lived there for many generations, longer than any cat could remember.

Brokenstar's whiskers twitched with amusement as he glanced at Blackfoot. "They'll leave all right," he meowed. "ShadowClan's territory is ours."

CHAPTER 6
❧

As the memory faded, Blackfoot shifted his paws uneasily, afraid to look up at the StarClan warriors surrounding him. If Wind-Clan *hadn't* killed Raggedstar—and they hadn't; it had been Brokenstar who had, as Blackfoot now knew—then the attack that had driven WindClan away was clearly less than justifiable. Worse than unjustifiable, really. Cowardly. Fox-hearted. Villainous. It made Blackfoot look like the snake-heart that Deadfoot had called him.

"We did need the territory," he meowed weakly, staring down at his own large black paws. "There were more of us than there were of the WindClan cats, and we didn't have enough prey." He could sense the StarClan cats all around him, the soft sounds of their breath, their cool, nightlike scent. But none of them said anything in reply. "You don't understand," he went on, suddenly angry. "We had to *survive*."

It was true, but he felt the claw of guilt tugging at his belly fur. Had they really needed to destroy WindClan to survive? *Does StarClan think I've done wrong?*

For a heartbeat, he wanted to deny what he had done: *These were all Brokenstar's decisions. I was only following orders.* But he'd been right beside Brokenstar all the time, hadn't he? He'd been more than happy to carry out his plans. StarClan knew that.

Gray Wing regarded Blackfoot through wide golden eyes. "I know it can be hard to relive the past," he said. "As we've said all along, this is your choice. Do you want the life I offer?"

Blackfoot looked down at the ground. *I was a good deputy. I can be a good leader. I can!* But more and more, he was wondering if the two talents were the same.

"I want the life," he said. But the words came out as a croak.

Bowing his head, Gray Wing touched his nose to Blackfoot's. His breath was cool, but the gentle nudge sent another spike of pain shooting through Blackfoot. It was as if he felt the agony of a hundred cats wounded in battle. "With this life, I give you unity," Gray Wing meowed. "Do all that you can to make sure every Clan is strong. Because if one Clan falls, all the Clans will be lost."

Blackfoot closed his eyes, trying to take the gray tom's advice into his heart. When he opened them, he chanced a glance up at the other StarClan cats, and froze, feeling as if that claw of guilt had slashed his belly open. "Rosetail," he whispered.

The gray tabby she-cat just stared back at him silently, her bushy pinkish-orange tail swishing slowly. After a horrified heartbeat, Blackfoot looked away, unable to meet her eyes.

"Another cat who's not from ShadowClan," he growled, sounding accusing even to his own ears. "Why are these cats giving me lives?"

Sagewhisker spoke from among the gathered cats. "In

StarClan, we are all one Clan." The former medicine cat was watching calmly, no judgment visible in her gaze.

Blackfoot swallowed and glanced back at Rosetail out of the corner of his eye. Her face was blank and cold, and her ears were flattened. She didn't look like she wanted to give him a life, or as if she thought he should be ShadowClan's leader.

He didn't blame her.

He closed his eyes and allowed the past to take him.

"You understand the plan?" Blackfoot asked quietly. "You all know what you need to do?" He doubted the ThunderClan cats would be able to hear his voice from within their camp on the other side of the wall of brambles, but it was important not to take chances. They needed the element of surprise for this attack.

"We're ready," Ratscar answered, flexing his claws. Beside him, Stumpytail and Clawface nodded, their tails twitching eagerly.

"Okay, you three are with me. We're going to go straight through the wall of the camp. There are brambles and gorse, but we've all got thick pelts, and they won't be expecting an invasion from this direction. We should be close to the nursery here."

Blackfoot took a moment to look over his patrol. Lizardstripe, Deerfoot, Russetfur, and Boulder pricked their ears alertly, waiting for his commands. More warriors gathered behind them. This was the largest patrol he had ever led. "The rest of you can go in through the tunnel. There'll probably be a guard, but there shouldn't be many warriors in camp. Take them down as quickly as you can."

It was a little after sunhigh, and Blackfoot wasn't expecting to meet much opposition in camp—Bluestar, the Thunder-Clan leader, had been spotted yesterday, heading for the Moonstone with several of her warriors, and it was unlikely that she would be back before dusk. Most of the other ThunderClan warriors would be hunting or patrolling at this time of day, just after sunhigh. It was a good time to raid their camp. It would mostly be full of elders and nursing queens.

Blackfoot's pelt itched uneasily. He would follow orders, of course he would, but something about this raid seemed . . . *wrong*.

"We must do everything we can to keep ShadowClan strong," he meowed, as much to himself as to the warriors he was leading. "Our enemies are always working against us."

"Do you think that Yellowfang might be with Thunder-Clan?" Lizardstripe asked, her yellow eyes slitting suspiciously.

"I doubt it," Blackfoot answered, disgust curling in his belly. "Why would ThunderClan take *her* in?"

"I never would have imagined Yellowfang could hurt a kit," Russetfur meowed sadly, shaking her head.

Blackfoot twitched his ears in agreement. The medicine cat had always been cranky, and over time she'd gotten less and less supportive of their Clan, challenging Brokenstar's every decision. But it was a long way from traitorous grumbling to murdering kits. She'd been their *medicine cat*, for StarClan's sake. Brokenstar had found her with the bodies of the kits she had killed, her own half-siblings, and she'd been driven away, ordered to leave the forest forever. She'd claimed that she'd only found them, already dead, but her scent had been all over them. "No Clan would shelter her," Blackfoot told the others. "Not after Brokenstar told every cat at the Gathering what she did."

"She must be long gone," Boulder agreed.

The memory of Brightflower's poor, murdered kits gave Blackfoot a new sense of righteousness. ShadowClan had lost too many kits. They would do whatever they needed to do to keep their Clan strong. ThunderClan's weakness would be ShadowClan's strength.

"Wait a little outside the gorse tunnel," he meowed, nodding to Lizardstripe to lead the others. "Be ready to attack when we do."

She dipped her head, then led the others away with a decisive flick of her tail.

"All right." Blackfoot gestured to Ratscar, Stumpytail, and Clawface to come to the camp wall beside him. "Quietly, at first. Once we're past the brambles, we can charge through the rest of the underbrush and into camp." He raised a paw and clawed at the brambles, hurriedly making a hole big enough for his body to fit through. *We have to be quick.* The Thunder-Clan warriors would fight to the death if they realized what ShadowClan was after. His patrol would have to get in and out before they caught on.

With four ShadowClan warriors working together, they'd

soon cleared a path through the brambles. Blackfoot flicked his tail at the other three, gesturing for silence, and listened to hear what he could from the camp on the other side of the underbrush.

Two queens were murmuring to each other, but he couldn't make out exactly what they were saying. The high, bright voice of an apprentice or an older kit broke in on their conversation, followed by *mrrows* of laughter. Guilt churned in Blackfoot's belly, but he swallowed it back. *ShadowClan must survive,* he told himself.

"Now!" he told the others, and charged through the underbrush, Clawface, Ratscar, and Stumpytail right behind him. Sticks and thorns clawed his pelt, but in a heartbeat they had burst through the wall of the camp, at the same time as the other ShadowClan warriors began to swarm through the entrance tunnel. Lizardstripe tackled the warrior guarding the tunnel, bringing her to the ground with a snarl.

The ThunderClan cats jumped to their paws with startled yowls, caught completely by surprise. "Defend the camp!" a thick-furred golden tabby howled. Blackfoot recognized the ThunderClan deputy, Lionheart, with a pang of dismay—he'd hoped the formidable warrior would be away from camp. Clawface dashed to attack Lionheart at the same time as Scorchwind charged him from the other side.

The other ShadowClan warriors spread out across the camp to battle the ThunderClan cats, drawing them away from Blackfoot, who turned toward the nursery.

There were two queens between Blackfoot and the entrance: Lionheart's white-furred mate, Frostfur, and a heavily pregnant gray tabby he didn't know. At a glance from Blackfoot, Russetfur and Boulder attacked, drawing the queens farther away.

Just for a heartbeat, Blackfoot hesitated.

I'm doing this for ShadowClan, he reminded himself, and moved toward the momentarily unguarded nursery. The Thunder-Clan cats were putting up a good fight—there'd been more of them in camp than he'd expected—and he'd have to hurry. Crouching, he peered beneath the thick brambles of the bush that concealed its entrance. Several small faces stared back at him. The ThunderClan kits squealed in fright when they saw him; he could hear them even over the sounds of battle raging all over the camp.

I'm not going to hurt them, he reminded himself. *Any kit should be proud to become a ShadowClan warrior.* These kits were young enough that they'd soon forget their loyalty to ThunderClan. Brokenstar had been clear when he gave the order: The kits would become full members of ShadowClan, no matter what their birth Clan had been. *It'll be an honor for them in the end.*

There was a commotion behind him, and Blackfoot glanced back to see ThunderClan reinforcements charging through the gorse tunnel into camp. Bluestar, the big senior warrior Tigerclaw, and several nearly grown apprentices threw themselves into battle. Blackfoot snarled to himself; he'd hoped they would be gone for much longer. The ShadowClan patrol was outnumbered now. He'd have to hurry.

Crouching, he thrust a paw through the nursery entrance. The kits squirmed away, mewling, and he reached further, ignoring the brambles that scratched at his too-broad shoulders.

Suddenly some cat slammed hard into his side, tumbling him over and exposing his underbelly. Startled, Blackfoot kicked sharply with his back legs, throwing off his attacker. Scrambling to his paws, he saw a gray tabby elder with an orangish tail. *Rosetail,* he remembered, dredging her name up from some corner of his memory.

She hissed at him. "Get away from the kits."

Blackfoot swiped at her with his paw, leaving a long scratch across her throat. She must have been a strong warrior once, but her reflexes had been slowed by age and by seasons spent sitting in the sun outside the elders' den. She was no match for him now. "Get out of my way," he hissed.

Rosetail squared her shoulders and glared, blocking the nursery entrance. Blood was dripping slowly from her wound. "Never."

"You've got no chance against me," Blackfoot told her. He shifted closer, looking for a way past her. "Run, old cat. I'll take the kits, but I won't hurt them."

"They're part of ThunderClan," she spat, her fur bristling. "As long as I can fight, I won't let you have them."

I have to do this. ShadowClan needed him. And they needed kits if their Clan was going to survive. With a snarl of frustration and fury, Blackfoot lunged at the older cat, clawing and biting her viciously. She fought back, refusing to give ground. Behind him, he could hear the yowls of battle. From the screeches of pain and rage, it sounded as if ShadowClan was losing. His time was running out.

With a desperate swipe, Blackfoot drew his claws roughly across the elder's throat. She gave a choking gasp and fell to her knees, red blood spreading quickly across her chest. Behind her, the kits in the nursery shrieked in terror.

ShadowClan needs this. Feeling sick but determined, Blackfoot dragged the elder away from the nursery entrance. She was still breathing, short, labored breaths, but her eyes were glazed. She was dying. "StarClan take you," Blackfoot muttered and drew his claws across her throat once more, ending her suffering rather than letting it draw out.

Turning back to the nursery, he thrust one bloody front paw through, reaching for the kits, who cowered back against the bramble wall, whimpering. Their eyes were huge with terror.

"I won't hurt you," he murmured. "I swear." He caught hold of the first one, a dark gray she-kit, and guided her out. She was too small to do more than try to squirm away, and he reached in again to pull out another kit, a golden brown tabby tom.

He was stretching his paw toward a third, a white she-kit with ginger patches, when stinging claws raked across his side. A familiar voice snarled, "Get away from them."

Blackfoot whirled around, the kits temporarily forgotten. "Yellowfang!" he gasped. He couldn't believe that Thunder-Clan had taken her in. Were they complete fools?

ShadowClan's former medicine cat glowered at him. Her broad, battle-scarred face had meant comfort for a long time, during the many seasons when she'd healed his wounds and given him herbs for his illnesses. But now there was nothing but hostility in her orange eyes. "Take your paws off those kits," she growled.

Blackfoot stiffened in outrage. "I'm not going to hurt them," he hissed. "If ThunderClan lets you roam this camp, then I'm probably *saving* them. I know what you did—murderer."

With a howl of rage, Yellowfang charged toward him. Blackfoot was aware of the kits crawling back toward the nursery entrance, but there was no time for him to go after them. He fell backward, grappling with the angry medicine cat. She had been a warrior once, and she was still strong and fierce. Her claws raked his belly, and he twisted to sink his teeth into her shoulder. She snarled and pulled away, and he slashed his claws across her face, one claw catching on the corner of her eye.

She yowled and backed away a few paw steps, her eye already beginning to swell, and they circled each other, both looking for an opening.

"You're a mouse-brain, Blackfoot," Yellowfang growled. "You always have been."

Blackfoot hissed. "I don't listen to traitors, you murderer."

"I never killed those kits." Yellowfang's voice was tight with pain. "And I never would have left ShadowClan if I hadn't been driven out."

"Liar." Blackfoot didn't know why Yellowfang had turned on her Clan, but he'd seen the tiny bodies that she'd left behind.

With a screech of rage, Yellowfang leaped at him, fiercer than before. Blackfoot met her paw to paw, but she was unstoppable, forcing him backward. A yowl of pain came from behind him—*Lizardstripe,* he realized, recognizing her voice— and he slashed his claws at Yellowfang, then darted a glance back at the rest of the camp as she flinched away.

He saw Lizardstripe's hindquarters disappear into the gorse tunnel as she raced out of camp. Almost all the Shadow-Clan warriors, he realized, were already gone.

He felt a sick sense of dread at the realization that they had failed. He could still hear Rosetail's labored breathing, and the hush of silence when he'd clawed her throat. *All for nothing.* His paws began to shake.

With a last snarl at Yellowfang, he turned and ran. There was no point in staying to be captured, not once he was this outnumbered.

Underbrush crackled under his paws as he raced back toward ShadowClan territory, wondering what Brokenstar would say—what he would do—when Blackfoot reported back to him. Blackfoot remembered Rosetail's eyes glazing over in death. He remembered the kits wailing in terror.

All for nothing, he thought. *What have we done?*

* * *

As the vision melted away, Blackfoot bowed his head. Shame gnawed his insides like tiny sharp teeth. Why hadn't he ever stopped and *thought*? Their attempt to steal the kits of ThunderClan. The too-young apprentices of ShadowClan whose deaths had thinned their numbers, had made them desperate enough to consider it. It wouldn't have been an honor for the stolen kits to join his Clan; it would have been a death sentence.

And maybe it was Brokenstar who had ordered it, but Blackfoot had never spoken against his commands, never even thought about it. He was also to blame.

"Yellowfang didn't kill those kits, did she?" he asked in a low voice, but no cat answered.

When he lifted his head to glance around at the starry circle of cats surrounding him, Rosetail was still staring at him, her expression stony. "Do you want to continue?" she asked. Unlike the previous cats, her voice held no hint of sympathy.

Blackfoot stared at her. Time seemed to widen out, and he wondered for the first time whether this night would ever end. He could make it end, he supposed. *But I can't. I've come this far. I might as well see it through.* "I do," he rasped.

She came toward him slowly and barely brushed her muzzle against his jaw, pulling back immediately.

"With this life, I give you compassion," she meowed flatly. "Do your best to understand the hopes and dreams of other cats in the forest, even if they're not in your Clan."

Pain shot through Blackfoot's body as another rush of memories and feelings flooded his mind. He felt Rosetail's fear as she fell beneath his paws. He felt the terror of a kit separated from its mother. Rage, love, hunger, sorrow—he bit back a howl as other cats' emotions ran through him, and then were gone, leaving him drained and panting.

Chapter 7

❧

What kind of leader ceremony is this? Blackfoot thought dully as he watched Rosetail walk away. *This feels like a punishment, not a reward. If I'm this terrible, why are they giving me the chance to be leader?*

But what other cat was there? After the battles of Brokenstar and Tigerstar's reigns, and the illness that had ravaged the Clan between them, ShadowClan was only an echo of its former self. Some cat would have to hold the Clan together while it healed. If he gave up, would StarClan even allow another cat to lead? Nightstar had taken over after Brokenstar was driven out, but StarClan had never given him nine lives, not while Brokenstar still lived. The sickly, gentle cat had died once and not returned.

As Blackfoot brooded over Nightstar's death and what cat, if any, StarClan might find worthy to lead ShadowClan, another cat stepped forward from the crowd. A she-cat with long gray-blue fur and ice-blue eyes. "Hello, Blackfoot," she meowed calmly.

"Hello, Bluestar." After so vividly reliving the raid he'd led on the ThunderClan camp, it was a relief to not see hostility in the former ThunderClan leader's gaze. Brokenstar had hated WindClan, and Tigerstar had loathed Firestar with every hair on his pelt. The conflict between ShadowClan and ThunderClan had gotten . . . personal. But maybe Bluestar had no real reason to hate Blackfoot. *Except for the time I tried to steal her Clan's kits. And the demands to hunt on ThunderClan's territory. And the times I attacked her camp. And the many other battles between our Clans. And when I helped Tigerclaw try to kill her.*

He winced as she got closer, but she merely touched her nose to his. As the cats around him faded again, Blackfoot remembered the choice that both he and Bluestar had made at different times—and how much it had cost all the Clans.

Tigerstar. He'd been Bluestar's deputy. And then he'd been Blackfoot's leader.

"We almost had him back," Blackfoot growled. They'd been so close to rescuing Brokenstar from the ThunderClan camp. *Then everything could have gone back to normal.*

ShadowClan had driven Brokenstar out because of the lie ThunderClan had made them believe—that Brokenstar had killed his own father. Blackfoot didn't understand how any ShadowClan cat could believe that, after having followed Brokenstar through so many battles, but they had. And then ThunderClan had taken Brokenstar prisoner.

Blackfoot was sure that once Brokenstar was free, he would be able to explain everything. ShadowClan would take Brokenstar back—take them all back. During the moons that he and the rest of ShadowClan's most loyal warriors had been in exile—forced to be *rogues*, even though they had been the only cats to stand by their leader—the thought of ShadowClan had made Blackfoot's chest ache with longing. He just wanted to go home.

"If only those RiverClan warriors hadn't shown up," Tangleburr meowed mournfully. She was lapping at her brown-and-gray fur, trying to soothe a nasty bite on her flank. "We were beating those snake-hearts in ThunderClan easily."

She was right. Yesterday's battle had been going so well, before the RiverClan warriors had charged into camp. But now they were here, huddled in a thornbush on the edge of the Twolegplace, driven out of Clan territory entirely. There were only a few of them left—almost all the rogues that Tigerclaw had helped them to recruit had fled during the battle. *Cowards.* Only Clan cats were worth trusting. Blackfoot took a deep breath. "It doesn't matter. We'll just have to try again."

"Why?" Snag, the only rogue still with them, shook his thick ginger pelt irritably. "He's blind now. He can't lead your Clan."

"He can!" The fur on Blackfoot's spine rose. Out of the corner of his eye, he saw Tangleburr and Stumpytail exchange doubtful looks. "He's still strong. He fought well yesterday, even without being able to see."

"Maybe if we go back to ShadowClan ourselves . . . ," Stumpytail began, but his voice trailed off as Blackfoot fixed him with a glare.

"We're not going to abandon Brokenstar," he told them. "Maybe Tigerclaw will help us again, if his Clan hasn't realized that he led us into camp. . . ." After Brokenstar's capture, the ThunderClan deputy had found Blackfoot and proposed that they join forces. Tigerclaw would bring the ShadowClan exiles and a few carefully recruited rogues into ThunderClan's camp and use their fight to rescue Brokenstar as cover for his own attack on the ThunderClan leader, Bluestar.

Blackfoot's pelt had prickled uncomfortably at the idea of a deputy attacking his leader, but Tigerclaw had explained: Bluestar had been influenced too much by a kittypet she'd allowed to join them. Fireheart would harm ThunderClan if a strong Clan cat didn't take control. He didn't want to drive Bluestar away, but he had to save his Clan.

Besides, what did Blackfoot care what happened to other Clans? His loyalty was to ShadowClan, and it always would be.

His loyalty was to a ShadowClan led by a strong leader like Brokenstar.

Tangleburr twitched her ears. "If Tigerclaw had killed Bluestar, wouldn't he have given us Brokenstar by now? I think he's probably dead."

"Maybe." Blackfoot dropped his head onto his paws. ThunderClan would have had every reason to kill Tigerclaw, if his plan to get rid of Bluestar hadn't succeeded. Tangleburr was no doubt right. He ached all over from yesterday's battle. *What are we going to do now?*

Suddenly there was a sound of brambles being ripped apart nearby, of some cat forcing themselves through the protection of the bushes around them.

"Keep still. Someone's coming." Blackfoot warned, getting

to his paws. They were in bad shape, but they'd fight if they had to. He scented the air. A ThunderClan scent, he realized.

Tangleburr had caught it, too. Her eyes stretched wide with panic. There were too few of them, and they were too injured for a battle. "We can't stay here and be trapped like rabbits," she hissed.

There was no time. They got to their paws and unsheathed their claws, tensing themselves for one more battle. Then, with a snap of branches, a huge, broad-shouldered dark brown tabby charged into their shelter. He was alone and bleeding.

"Tigerclaw. You survived." It had taken Blackfoot a moment to recognize the ThunderClan deputy, who was battered and staggering unsteadily on his paws. A deep gash ran across his belly, his fur was matted with mud and blood, and there were innumerable bloody scratches on his face.

Tigerclaw bared his teeth in a snarl. "No thanks to you."

"We were going to come back for you once our wounds had healed," Blackfoot assured him. *We'll still go back for Brokenstar. However many attacks it takes.*

After the other cats greeted him, Tangleburr and Snag slipped out of their hideout to hunt for them all. Blackfoot nosed tentatively at Tigerclaw's wound, which was filthy and barely scabbed over. As he watched, a spurt of fresh blood trickled through the paler fur on Tigerclaw's belly. "You're bleeding," he told the other cat.

"It's nothing," Tigerclaw snapped. "It'll heal over in a few days." He carefully lay down on his side, wincing slightly.

"Those ThunderClan cats fought more fiercely than I expected," Blackfoot meowed. Tigerclaw had told them it would be easy to defeat ThunderClan, and that hadn't been true. "Especially that so-called kittypet, Fireheart. He may have been born in Twolegplace, but he's learned to fight like a warrior." The orange-pelted cat was stronger and faster than Blackfoot had ever expected.

Tigerclaw tensed and scrambled back to his paws despite his wounds, his face outraged. "He *is* a kittypet! Don't ever speak of him as a warrior. He has no right to be in the forest, no right to speak to Bluestar as if the blood of the Clans runs in his veins." He turned away and paced in a tight circle, flicking his tail. "I will find more cats, and teach you how to fight properly, and then we will take on ThunderClan again and Fireheart will *die*!"

Blackfoot blinked. For a moment, Tigerclaw's amber eyes had blazed and he'd looked half-mad with anger. It was true, though, that a kittypet had no business pretending to be a Clanborn cat. "We'll be ready," he meowed. "Once we rescue Brokenstar, you'll have all of ShadowClan behind you. And we *know* how to fight."

Tigerclaw stared at him for several silent heartbeats, only the tip of his tail twitching. "Blackfoot," he meowed at last, "Brokenstar is dead. ThunderClan murdered him for trying to escape."

Blackfoot couldn't breathe. He felt hollow suddenly, as if he were nothing but fur and bones stretched over emptiness.

What will I do now? Without Brokenstar to lead him, how would he ever find his way back to ShadowClan? Who was he, if he wasn't a ShadowClan cat? "I'll really be a rogue now," he finally croaked, despair washing over him.

Tigerclaw's eyes narrowed as he watched Blackfoot closely. "We can get ShadowClan on our side," he meowed at last.

"We can?" A faint spark of hope lit in Blackfoot's chest. Tigerclaw always seemed so sure of what he wanted, of what was going to happen.

"Once we have ShadowClan, we can take our revenge on ThunderClan," Tigerclaw went on. "They killed Brokenstar. Fireheart stole my place at Bluestar's side. And now they've stolen my kits. They've driven me off and kept them there."

Fox-hearts. Outrage started to burn in Blackfoot, warming him. A Clan like that, a Clan that stole kits and murdered other Clans' leaders, didn't deserve to survive. "Do you have a plan?" he asked.

"I do. I can give you back ShadowClan." Tigerclaw unsheathed his long claws and dug them into the earth. "But I need to know that you'll be loyal. Can you follow me like you did Brokenstar?"

There was a heartbeat of silence between them. *I did everything Brokenstar ever asked of me,* Blackfoot thought. What was he without his leader?

Tigerclaw was strong and determined. There was a familiar gleam in those amber eyes: the look of a cat with a clear goal, who could get other cats to follow him through harsh leaf-bares and into bloody battles. Blackfoot trembled, suddenly overwhelmed with gratitude. Brokenstar was gone, but here was a leader worth following. He wasn't alone after all.

"I won't let you down," he promised. Tigerclaw's whiskers twitched in approval.

CHAPTER 8

❧

I didn't learn anything. Blackfoot hung his head as the vision faded, sick with shame. Of course the gleam in Tigerclaw's eyes had been familiar. He and Brokenstar had been the same: willing to tear apart their Clans to get the power they wanted. Brokenstar had killed his own father and put kits in harm's way, leading to their deaths. Tigerstar had tried to kill his own leader, and when he'd failed, he'd taken over ShadowClan to further his plans for vengeance. They'd cared about nothing but themselves. *And I happily followed them both.*

Bluestar watched him carefully. "Do you want this life?" she asked.

Blackfoot felt exhausted, but he couldn't stop now. He nodded his head.

"I need you to say it," Bluestar mewed.

"I want this life," Blackfoot whispered.

Bluestar stepped forward and touched her nose to his. "With this life, I give you judgment. Use it when making difficult decisions. Consider all the possibilities, and consequences, of the choices you make."

As fresh pain shot through his body, Blackfoot felt a terrible despair, thinking about the judgment he'd shown in the past. He'd been convinced so easily that Tigerstar was the solution to all his worries. But the ThunderClan cat hadn't cared about the cats of ShadowClan—he'd just wanted to use them to get his revenge on Fireheart and ThunderClan. Blackfoot could see that now, watching the past unfold again in front of his eyes.

And it was in following Tigerstar that Blackfoot had done the thing that made him most ashamed now, standing before StarClan.

As Bluestar stepped away, he knew, all the way down to his bones, which cat would step out next from the crowd of StarClan warriors. So when he finally looked up, bracing his paws against the ground as if expecting a blow, he wasn't surprised to see Stonefur watching him.

The RiverClan tom looked much better than the last time they'd seen each other. Then, he'd been ragged and half-starved. Now his pale blue-gray pelt was sleek and shone with faint stars. He looked at Blackfoot for several long moments before stepping forward slowly, as if his paws were almost too heavy to lift. Each step seemed so reluctant, like he didn't want to come closer to Blackfoot, but knew he had to.

Blackfoot couldn't blame him. Of course it would be hard for Stonefur to grant a life to the cat who had taken his.

Stonefur lashed his tail at Blackfoot's shoulder, and Blackfoot felt the present fading. . . .

* * *

Blackfoot crouched on one side of Tigerstar's hill of bones, Leopardstar on the other. From the top of the pile, Tigerstar gazed down on the camp he commanded. Around them, the gathered warriors of TigerClan—once separate as Shadow-Clan and RiverClan, now united under Tigerstar—quivered with excitement.

At the foot of the Bonehill, in the center of the ring of cats, TigerClan warriors—Darkstripe, who had been Thunder-Clan once, and Jaggedtooth, who had once been called Snag—guarded the former RiverClan deputy, Stonefur, and two terrified RiverClan apprentices. All three cats were thin, their ribs showing through their matted fur. Stonefur stood protectively in front of the apprentices, as if trying to shield them from their guards.

From his perch on top of the pile of prey bones, Tigerstar began to speak. "Cats of TigerClan, you all know the hardships that we have to face. The cold of leaf-bare threatens us. Twolegs threaten us. The other two Clans in the forest, who have not yet realized the wisdom of joining with TigerClan, are a threat to us. Surrounded as we are by enemies, we must be sure of the loyalty of our own warriors. There is no room in TigerClan for the halfhearted. No room for cats who might waver in battle or, worse still, turn on their own Clanmates." All around the clearing, TigerClan yowled in agreement.

Blackfoot's lip curled as he looked at Darkstripe. This cat had waited to follow Tigerstar until their leader was safely part of ShadowClan. Darkstripe glared back at Blackfoot. *I don't trust him,* Blackfoot mused.

But that wasn't what Tigerstar was talking about now. There would be time to deal with Darkstripe. Right now, there was another problem TigerClan needed to solve.

Blackfoot could feel a low thrum of excitement building inside him. Their Clan was stronger than any Clan had ever been, united all because of Tigerstar. Every cat in this clearing was focused and ready to fight any enemy of TigerClan. They were unstoppable. *This is where I belong,* Blackfoot thought.

Tigerstar went on. "Especially we will not tolerate the abomination of half-Clan cats. No loyal warrior would ever take a mate from another Clan, diluting the pure blood that our warrior ancestors decreed for us. Bluestar and Graystripe of ThunderClan both flouted the warrior code when they took mates from RiverClan. The kits of such a union, like the ones you see in front of you now, can never be trusted."

Blackfoot saw Tigerstar's glance, and began the cry. "Filth! Filth!" The other cats picked it up, glaring at Stonefur and the two apprentices, who cowered on the ground, their ears flattening in terror. Stonefur stood in front of them and snarled back at his former Clanmates.

Even as he yowled, Blackfoot felt a stab of satisfaction. Cats had muttered behind his back, accused him and his siblings of being half-Clan when they were young. But it wasn't true, and every cat now knew it wasn't true, even if they didn't know who his father was. Tigerstar would never have accepted him as deputy if he hadn't believed that Blackfoot was Shadow-Clan through and through.

As Tigerstar went on speaking, laying out his reasons for hating and distrusting cats whose loyalty could lie with more than one Clan, Blackfoot watched Stonefur standing protectively over the younger cats, and a sudden touch of unease disturbed his excitement. He knew Tigerstar would despise him for it, but he and Stonefur had sat side by side beneath the Great Rock at Clan meetings, united in the way that deputies were, knowing that they might one day lead their Clans, and Blackfoot had respected Stonefur. He'd been a good warrior, despite his parentage.

Blackfoot blew out a quick breath of air, dismissing the feeling. He couldn't get sentimental; he had a Clan to protect. And half-Clan cats couldn't be trusted, not even if they had once seemed to be loyal warriors.

Tigerstar was reaching the end of his speech. Every eye was fixed upon him, bright with excitement. "We must get rid of the abominations in our midst!" he announced. "Then our Clan will be clean again and we can be sure of the favor of StarClan."

Stonefur raised his head defiantly and staggered a bit. *He must be weak with hunger.* They hadn't fed the prisoners for a couple of days. Why waste prey on cats who were no longer Clanmates? But the blue-gray tom's meow was steady. "No cat has ever questioned my loyalty. Come down here and tell me to my face that I'm a traitor! Mistyfoot and I never even knew that Bluestar was our mother until a couple of moons ago. We have been loyal RiverClan warriors all our lives. Let any cat who thinks different come out here and prove it!"

There was a faint anxious stir from the cats who had been RiverClan. As Tigerstar scolded Leopardstar for choosing Stonefur as her deputy, Blackfoot looked around at some of the worried faces in the clearing.

He didn't think they'd fight Tigerstar. Leopardstar was dipping her head in silent apology to Tigerstar, her eyes averted from her former deputy, and her cats would follow her lead. But this was their chance to prove their loyalty, to prove that they deserved to be part of TigerClan. They needed to not just let this happen, but revel in it.

Finished with Leopardstar, Tigerstar looked down again on the half-Clan cats. The tip of his tail twitched once, and then he spoke. "Stonefur, I will give you a chance to show your loyalty to TigerClan. Kill these two half-Clan apprentices."

The fur rose along Blackfoot's spine and his heart beat faster. *Will he do it?* It was Stonefur's one chance to become part of TigerClan. But would he kill apprentices, when he was just as half-Clan as they were?

Stonefur blinked, looking lost for a moment, then turned to his former leader. "I take orders from *you*," he growled. "You must know this is wrong. What do you want me to do?" His voice was fierce, but the look he gave her was pleading.

Every eye was on Leopardstar now. *Who is she really loyal to?* Blackfoot didn't trust her yet. This was Leopardstar's chance to prove herself too.

The former RiverClan leader looked at Stonefur for several long heartbeats, her face blank. Finally, she meowed, "These are difficult times. As we fight for survival, we must be able to count on every one of our Clanmates. There is no room for divided loyalties. Do as Tigerstar tells you."

A few cats gasped, but no RiverClan warrior spoke up to defy their leader. *They're learning to be loyal,* Blackfoot thought with satisfaction. *They're learning what it means to be a TigerClan cat.*

Stonefur stared at Leopardstar for a few moments longer, then turned to look down at the apprentices. They huddled together, gazing up at him with new fear, then slowly straightened and got to their paws, ready to fight.

With a small nod of approval at the apprentices' bravery, Stonefur whipped back around to glare defiantly up at Tigerstar. "You'll have to kill me first!" he spat.

Fool. Stonefur had thrown away his only chance.

Tigerstar looked down at Darkstripe, his tail flicking. "Very well. Kill him."

Darkstripe's tail rose with pleasure, and he sprang at Stonefur.

Too slow, Blackfoot thought in disgust. The black-striped tom was bigger than Stonefur, but he moved clumsily. Stonefur had time to drop quickly backward, extending his claws to rip at the attacking cat. Darkstripe yowled as Stonefur's claws pierced his skin, then aimed a heavy blow at Stonefur's face, which the smaller cat dodged.

They screeched and clawed at each other, rolling across the ground. Blackfoot let his own claws slip out and tore at the earth beneath his paws. Even with Stonefur half-starved, Darkstripe was slower. Stonefur was fighting for his life, and Darkstripe was just fighting. He lacked Stonefur's passion.

The cats around them were silent, following the struggling figures with intense gazes, some apprehensive, some excited.

With a twist of his body, Stonefur sank his teeth into the back of Darkstripe's neck. Darkstripe writhed and shoved him away, and the two cats sprang apart, both panting for breath. Blood was trickling down Darkstripe's face.

Blackfoot hissed in frustration. "Get a move on, Darkstripe! You're fighting like a kittypet!"

Darkstripe hissed, then charged at Stonefur again, and the blue-gray tom dodged neatly away, raking his claws along Darkstripe's flank. Darkstripe staggered, and Stonefur used the other tom's own momentum to tumble him to the ground.

Clumsy. Blackfoot snarled. With the way he was fighting, Darkstripe was embarrassing them all. *He'll need more battle training before we take on the other Clans. He spends more time thinking about the fresh-kill pile than the battleground.*

Stonefur had Darkstripe pinned and struggling beneath him, his tail slashing wildly as he held Darkstripe down. Tigerstar growled and turned to Blackfoot. "Finish it."

Blackfoot's claws had been itching to show how a real ShadowClan—*TigerClan*—cat fought. Without hesitating, he threw himself into the battle, dragging Stonefur off Darkstripe and raising his claws high above the RiverClan deputy's throat.

CHAPTER 9

I don't want to remember any more.

The vision faded, and Blackfoot shuddered, closing his eyes for a heartbeat. *I never even questioned what I was told to do. Stonefur would have been a better Clanmate than Darkstripe; I knew it even then. He was loyal and brave. It didn't matter that he was half-Clan.*

He dragged his gaze up from his paws to meet Stonefur's eyes once again. Part of him ached to beg for the StarClan cat's forgiveness: *I shouldn't have done it. It was all because of Tigerstar.* But the words faded before he could say them. Anything he could say to Stonefur now would only sound hollow. He had killed him without hesitation.

Stonefur approached slowly, his eyes cool. "Do you want this life?"

Blackfoot could barely rouse the energy to answer. He felt empty. "I do," he croaked. *I can't stop now.*

Stonefur's muzzle brushed against Blackfoot's without affection. "With this life, I give you integrity," he meowed, sounding as reluctant as he looked. "Use it with your judgment, to make sure you take yourself and your Clan down the right paths in the future." He jerked back, then turned away without another glance and disappeared into the glimmering crowd.

As the now-familiar pain shot through his muscles, Blackfoot flinched, but at the same time he felt as if his vision were growing sharper. He could see more of his own past. He had done terrible things. He had sought out strong leaders to attach himself to, and he had never considered whether what they did, what they ordered him to do, was right—if it was for the good of the Clans they led, the *cats* they led, or only to quench their own thirst for power and vengeance. The faces of the dead swam before him again, and he was sorry for how much suffering he had caused.

Can I be better than Brokenstar and Tigerstar were? He wanted to be. But with a pain that cut deep into his bones, he knew that he couldn't be sure. *I never even wondered until now if their decisions were right. What does that say about me?*

As the pain of receiving his new life lifted, he looked up at the StarClan cats. They had given him seven lives. No doubt another cat was about to step forward. Once he had been given nine lives, he would be the leader of ShadowClan.

"Can it go on like this?" he blurted out. "You say it's my choice to continue, but I feel like this is wrong. Each memory leaves me more shaken than the last. Am I really fit to lead ShadowClan?" *There must be some cat who would be better.* He couldn't let ShadowClan suffer because of his leadership.

Nightstar padded forward from the crowd, his tail lifted in greeting. They'd been kits together, and Blackfoot couldn't help finding comfort in his old friend's presence. There was no trace of hostility in Nightstar's green eyes. His fur was sleek, and the once-sickly cat looked healthier than he ever had in life.

"You're honest," he meowed, and Blackfoot looked down at his paws. The least he could do was be honest. ShadowClan needed the best leader they could find.

When Blackfoot didn't answer, Nightstar purred warmly in amusement. "Every leader has made choices they regret. It isn't necessary for a leader to be perfect. But it is important that you can learn from the past, and change." He came closer to Blackfoot and brushed his tail reassuringly across his back. "Don't lose the ability to question yourself. A leader needs to be the one who makes sure he's doing the right thing. No other cat will do it for him."

The present faded, and Blackfoot plunged once more into the past, to the time before TigerClan, when he had been a rogue looking for a place to belong.

I'll get to see my home again.

Blackfoot knew that ShadowClan was only permitting him and the other rogues to cross their borders because there was sickness in the Clan and Tigerclaw had offered to hunt for the ShadowClan cats who couldn't catch their own prey. But his paws still felt lighter than they had in moons as he entered ShadowClan's territory, a vole dangling from his jaws. It felt so good to be breathing in the familiar scents of home, to be sheltered under pine trees instead of the oaks and ash trees of their temporary territory out in the wild part of the forest.

And ahead of him walked some of his Clanmates. It didn't matter if they said he wasn't part of ShadowClan anymore. Dawncloud, Boulder, and Flintfang would *always* be his true Clanmates. Dawncloud, who had once been his apprentice! Loyal, steady Boulder! Flintfang, his own littermate!

He crossed behind Tangleburr and came closer to the ShadowClan cats so that he could brush his tail across his brother's back. Flintfang blinked warmly at him. "It's good to see you," he purred quietly. "I've missed you."

"You too." Blackfoot was worried, though. Flintfang looked terrible, moons older than his actual age, his ribs showing, his fur dry and patchy. "How are you? Are you sure you're well enough to patrol?"

Flintfang shook his head grimly. "Every cat in ShadowClan has been sick. I'm better off than most."

As they got closer to the ShadowClan camp, Blackfoot's breathless joy at being back on his home territory began to dim. The stench was terrible: rotting fresh-kill and disease and cats too sick to clean themselves properly.

Just outside camp, Boulder put down the sparrow he'd been carrying and turned to face Tigerclaw's rogues. "None of us have escaped the sickness," he meowed solemnly. "If you don't want to risk getting infected, you should turn back now."

Blackfoot looked at Tigerclaw. They'd promised to follow him, but if the former ThunderClan deputy wanted to leave, Blackfoot didn't know whether he would choose to follow him or to stay. He couldn't leave without seeing his former

Clanmates. Not when they were suffering. But Tigerclaw was his leader now.

Tigerclaw raised his head proudly and spoke around the squirrel he carried. "We are not afraid to deliver help." Blackfoot nodded, feeling a surge of gratitude toward Tigerclaw. A cat who could care for cats of another Clan would never have attacked his own leader without a good reason. Surely, this was a cat worth following.

Boulder led them through the brambles into the clearing at the center of the ShadowClan camp. With Tigerclaw in the lead, the rogues carried their prey to the nearly empty fresh-kill pile. Blackfoot looked in satisfaction at how much prey they'd brought: At least today, the cats of ShadowClan wouldn't go hungry.

Turning away from the fresh-kill pile, he saw the cats watching them from the edges of the camp and barely suppressed a gasp. Flintfang hadn't been lying when he had said that he was in better shape than most of the others. The eyes that shone at Blackfoot from the shadows were bright with fever, and many of the cats looked too weak to stand, as if they'd simply fallen where they now lay and had been left there by their equally ill Clanmates.

Rowanberry, whom they had met patrolling earlier, came out of the warriors' den. She was thin and ragged, but able to walk. Like Flintfang, she was one of the healthiest-looking of the ShadowClan cats, and even she tottered as if a gust of wind might knock her down. "Dawncloud told us you were going to hunt for us," she meowed. "We didn't expect you to deliver it yourselves."

Tangleburr ran forward, touching her muzzle to the brown-and-cream cheek of her former Clanmate. "We had to know how you are. Please don't send us away."

Blackfoot's heart ached at the affectionate greeting between the two she-cats. *Please,* he echoed in his mind. *Please let us stay.* It had been so long.

There was a rustle of branches and Runningnose, the ShadowClan medicine cat, and Nightstar, who had taken over as leader when Brokenstar was driven out, stumbled out of the medicine den. At the sight of Nightstar, Blackfoot lost all his anger toward his old friend for the other cat's involvement in Brokenstar's exile. Nightstar was fur and bones, each of his ribs clearly visible beneath his dull pelt. And he could barely walk, judging by how he wobbled slowly toward them, leaning heavily on Runningnose. "You did a brave thing, coming here," he told Tigerclaw.

Tigerclaw bowed his head. "Your former Clanmates would not stand by and let you starve, and my loyalty is to them now. This is not courage; it is merely following the warrior code."

Blackfoot was warm with gratitude. Tigerclaw, for all his rough edges and sometime harshness with the cats who followed him, understood that in times of trouble, a Clan would always come back together. He wouldn't stop his followers from taking care of their former Clanmates. He'd help instead.

As Dawncloud urged Nightstar toward the fresh-kill pile, Deerfoot staggered forward, his eyes bright with fever. "We can still hunt for ourselves," he growled. "These cats left our Clan for a reason. Maybe we should think twice before welcoming them back."

Don't listen to him, Blackfoot begged silently. All he wanted was to be welcome here again. He'd feed every cat in camp himself if he had to.

Runningnose's ears flattened in annoyance. "'These cats,' as you call them, may have saved us all from starving to death," he meowed. "Show them some gratitude, Deerfoot."

No other cat spoke against them, and, after a few heartbeats, Blackfoot let out his breath. Apparently, they were welcome to stay.

As Tigerclaw, Runningnose, and Nightstar continued to talk about what had happened to ShadowClan, Blackfoot spotted his sister and her mate, curled together in the shadows outside the warriors' den. They were so still that his throat clenched. Were they dead? But as he walked toward them, Fernshade lifted her head. "Blackfoot," she meowed weakly. "Are you okay?"

"I should be asking you that," he told her. She was so painfully thin. Quickly, he walked over to the fresh-kill pile and took a fat frog, then came back to Fernshade and Wolfstep. With his claws and teeth, he carefully divided the frog between them, making sure each got some of the soft belly.

Wolfstep blinked at him appreciatively. "I haven't had frog for a while," he meowed. "Before the sickness got so bad, when

I could still sort of hunt but wasn't quite myself, they got too fast for me."

"Eat," Blackfoot meowed. "You need your strength to get well. Rowanberry said the sickness came from the rats at the carrionplace?"

Fernshade nodded. "That was the first sign that something was wrong, when all the rats started dying." She shuddered. "Cats have died, too."

"I know." Blackfoot looked around the camp. He could see that there were empty spaces among the cats, and that every ShadowClan cat's gaze was tired and full of pain. Cinderfur, Nightstar's deputy, would have been by his side if she could have been. "Is Cinderfur dead?" he asked.

Wolfstep sighed and nodded. "And Nightstar's been too ill to appoint a new deputy. Thank StarClan he has nine lives."

Blackfoot's belly stirred uneasily. *Did* Nightstar have nine lives? It was hard to be sure. He'd been appointed leader when Brokenstar was still alive. Could StarClan change which cat had nine lives? Would they? Blackfoot didn't like the nervous way Runningnose hovered around his leader. It didn't seem like the medicine cat was sure how many lives Nightstar had either. "I'm sure he'll get better with plenty of fresh-kill," he meowed, feeling doubtful.

As Fernshade and Wolfstep ate their frog, Blackfoot wandered among his old Clanmates, bringing them fresh-kill and trying to make them comfortable. The moss in the warriors' den was foul-smelling and dry, so he and Stumpytail pulled it out and replaced it with fresh bedding.

He brought moss soaked in water to Russetfur, who was hot with fever. "Are you all back?" she asked hopefully, in a raspy meow. "Are you staying?"

"I hope so," he told her quietly, and licked at the fur on her side, smoothing it down.

Moving from one ill ShadowClan cat to another, Blackfoot's heart ached with affection for all of them. They'd exiled him, driven him out with all of Brokenstar's closest supporters. But that didn't matter now. He didn't care that they'd made him a rogue, if only they'd let him come back and be one of them again.

He'd never felt more like a ShadowClan cat than he did right now.

CHAPTER 10

♣

Blackfoot sighed and looked up at Nightstar as the images of the past faded. The sharper vision that Stonefur had given him was not a favor from StarClan, but a curse. "Tigerstar didn't care about the sick ShadowClan cats, did he? He just wanted you to make him the next deputy, so that they would accept him as their leader when you died."

Nightstar blinked affectionately at him. "He fooled me, too," he meowed. "But what matters now is that *you* cared about the ShadowClan cats. You weren't looking for revenge or some advantage over ShadowClan; you only wanted to help your Clanmates."

"I guess that's true," Blackfoot meowed, a little hesitantly. He still felt hot beneath his pelt with fury and shame. Why had he ever believed in such a treacherous cat? *Two* such treacherous cats: Brokenstar and Tigerstar had both cared only for their own power, their own hatred, not for the cats they led. They'd been vicious and manipulative, and he'd believed in them both. Between them, they'd left ShadowClan in tatters.

When I lead ShadowClan, I'll be better than either of them, he promised himself. Then, realizing the truth of his thought, he took a deep, relieved breath. Whatever he did, he wouldn't make Tigerstar's or Brokenstar's mistakes. A purr began to rumble deep in his chest.

He knew now what he was supposed to do. It was simple. He'd always cared about his Clan more than anything. He'd protect the cats of ShadowClan.

I don't know if I'll be a good leader, but I'll do my best for the cats I lead, he thought.

"Do you want this life, Blackfoot?" Nightstar asked.

This time, Blackfoot replied with certainty. "I do."

Nightstar pressed his cheek against Blackfoot's, still purring. "With this life, I grant you loyalty. To the warrior code, to all the cats of the forest, and especially to ShadowClan."

Pain flowed through Blackfoot once more, but now he felt like it was making him stronger.

As he looked around at the starry warriors of StarClan, he wondered if they'd planned it this way. Perhaps they knew he had to be brought low to see how he needed to change. That was why they had given him these lives, from these cats. They understood that, although he'd followed vicious cats and done terrible things, he could still be a good leader.

Nightstar brushed his tail across Blackfoot's back as he padded away. Blackfoot was sorry to see him go.

When he had disappeared into the crowd of starry cats, one more cat stepped forward. Her fur was just as black as Nightstar's and her eyes were a vivid green. She looked at Blackfoot as if she knew everything about him, even though he'd never seen her before.

He dipped his head, instinctively wanting to show this stranger respect.

"Do you know who I am?" she asked, watching him closely.

Blackfoot's mouth dropped open. He *almost* knew, he was sure of it. There was a name he was on the verge of speaking. He couldn't say it.

After a few heartbeats, the black she-cat purred in amusement. "I'm Tall Shadow. You know me as Shadowstar. I was the first leader of ShadowClan."

Blackfoot gasped, his heart beating faster. "You're going to give me a life?" he asked. "*You* want me to lead ShadowClan?"

Shadowstar padded closer. Her green eyes were sharp. "I hope you're up to the job."

Blackfoot shifted from one paw to another. "I hope so, too," he told her. "I'll try. Surely, we're due for a few peaceful seasons."

"Try not to be too naive," Shadowstar meowed drily, flicking her tail as she paced past him, then came back to stare into his eyes. "It won't be easy. Don't think everything will be fine from now on. The Clans might have won the battle against Scourge, and the territories might be safe for a little while, but the Clans' troubles are like the seasons. They always come around again."

What's going to happen? Blackfoot opened his mouth, but before he could ask, visions began to flash before his eyes, rushing faster and faster past him. Unlike the memories he'd seen with each previous life, these were things that had never happened.

Monsters were ripping up the earth, their great teeth tearing it apart. Blackfoot cringed in horror, sick with terror, as the Great Oaks fell, shaking the ground beneath his paws.

Cats raced past him, unseeing. Twolegs came after them, and Blackfoot looked at their faces, spotting Mistyfoot, Stonefur's sister in RiverClan, but unable to recognize any of the others, they ran so quickly.

In the next, his Clanmates—he saw Russetfur's face clearly for a heartbeat—padded around the edges of a lake he didn't know, somewhere far from their territory. He thought he saw his own white pelt among them, but the image was gone before he could be sure.

Now cats were sick, dying, yowling for water. He caught the scent of illness, and then it was gone, washed away by the fresh scents of Fourtrees in greenleaf.

He saw himself again for one jarring heartbeat, older and looking defeated, an unknown tom whispering in his ear, pale yellow eyes narrowed. *What am I doing?*

Cats he didn't know, in a place he didn't know, turned their backs on a dark ginger tom and walked away.

The visions faded, leaving him back in the warm night of Fourtrees, and he gasped for breath, nauseous and dizzy with the speed of everything he'd seen. "Is that the future?" he demanded of Shadowstar. "Are those things that are going to happen? Is this a warning?"

Shadowstar's tail slashed the air. "There are many paths to the future. Even StarClan doesn't see everything that's going to happen," she told him. "They're only dreams of what *might* happen. The choices you make will matter."

Blackfoot was still panting, trying to catch his breath. He didn't want to see Fourtrees fall. He didn't want to listen to that pale-eyed tom or wear that awful look on his own face. "I'll do my best to make the right choices," he promised.

"That's all we can ask of you." She came closer and brushed her muzzle against his. She smelled of a cool night just before dawn. "With this life, I give you the quality that your Clan will need above all others in the long days to come. Leadership."

She waited. As the sharp pains of his new life made his muscles spasm and contract and he bared his teeth in pain, she watched quietly. He thought there was a touch of sympathy in her gaze, but it didn't help the pain.

When the spasms ceased, he felt calm for the first time since he had entered Mothermouth. He had to be careful from now on, had to weigh his words and actions. ShadowClan was depending on him. He met Shadowstar's bright green eyes and nodded.

She dipped her head, then drew herself up, looking even taller than before. "I hail you by your new name, Blackstar," she told him. Blackstar raised his head, his chest filling with pride.

"Your old life is no more," Shadowstar went on. "You have now received the nine lives of a leader, and StarClan grants to you the guardianship of ShadowClan. Defend it well; care for young and old; honor your ancestors and the traditions of the warrior code. Live each of your nine lives with pride and dignity."

"I will," Blackstar told her, his mouth dry.

She wheeled to face the cats of StarClan, and together they chanted the name of the new leader of ShadowClan.

"Blackstar! Blackstar!"

BRAVELANDS

Heed the call of the wild in this action-packed series from **Erin Hunter.**

Have you read them all?

○ #1: Broken Pride

○ #2: Code of Honor

○ #3: Blood and Bone

○ #4: Shifting Shadows

○ #5: The Spirit-Eaters

○ #6: Oathkeeper

Also available as downloadable audios!

HARPER
An Imprint of HarperCollins Publishers

www.warriorcats.com/bravelands • www.shelfstuff.com

WARRIORS:

THE BROKEN CODE

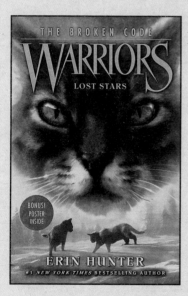

Have you read them all?

○ #1: Lost Stars

○ #2: The Silent Thaw

○ #3: Veil of Shadows

○ #4: Darkness Within

○ #5: The Place of No Stars

WARRIORS

How many have you read?

Dawn of the Clans
- O #1: The Sun Trail
- O #2: Thunder Rising
- O #3: The First Battle
- O #4: The Blazing Star
- O #5: A Forest Divided
- O #6: Path of Stars

Power of Three
- O #1: The Sight
- O #2: Dark River
- O #3: Outcast
- O #4: Eclipse
- O #5: Long Shadows
- O #6: Sunrise

The Prophecies Begin
- O #1: Into the Wild
- O #2: Fire and Ice
- O #3: Forest of Secrets
- O #4: Rising Storm
- O #5: A Dangerous Path
- O #6: The Darkest Hour

Omen of the Stars
- O #1: The Fourth Apprentice
- O #2: Fading Echoes
- O #3: Night Whispers
- O #4: Sign of the Moon
- O #5: The Forgotten Warrior
- O #6: The Last Hope

The New Prophecy
- O #1: Midnight
- O #2: Moonrise
- O #3: Dawn
- O #4: Starlight
- O #5: Twilight
- O #6: Sunset

A Vision of Shadows
- O #1: The Apprentice's Quest
- O #2: Thunder and Shadow
- O #3: Shattered Sky
- O #4: Darkest Night
- O #5: River of Fire
- O #6: The Raging Storm

Select titles also available as audiobooks!

HARPER
An Imprint of HarperCollinsPublishers

www.warriorcats.com • www.shelfstuff.com

SUPER EDITIONS

- ○ Firestar's Quest
- ○ Bluestar's Prophecy
- ○ SkyClan's Destiny
- ○ Crookedstar's Promise
- ○ Yellowfang's Secret
- ○ Tallstar's Revenge
- ○ Bramblestar's Storm

- ○ Moth Flight's Vision
- ○ Hawkwing's Journey
- ○ Tigerheart's Shadow
- ○ Crowfeather's Trial
- ○ Squirrelflight's Hope
- ○ Graystripe's Vow

GUIDES   FULL-COLOR GRAPHIC NOVELS

- ○ Secrets of the Clans
- ○ Cats of the Clans
- ○ Code of the Clans
- ○ Battles of the Clans
- ○ Enter the Clans
- ○ The Ultimate Guide

- ○ Graystripe's Adventure
- ○ Ravenpaw's Path
- ○ SkyClan and the Stranger
- ○ A Shadow in RiverClan

EBOOKS AND NOVELLAS

The Untold Stories
- ○ Hollyleaf's Story
- ○ Mistystar's Omen
- ○ Cloudstar's Journey

Shadows of the Clans
- ○ Mapleshade's Vengeance
- ○ Goosefeather's Curse
- ○ Ravenpaw's Farewell

Path of a Warrior
- ○ Redtail's Debt
- ○ Tawnypelt's Clan
- ○ Shadowstar's Life

A Warrior's Choice
- ○ Blackfoot's Reckoning
- ○ Daisy's Kin
- ○ Spotfur's Rebellion

Tales from the Clans
- ○ Tigerclaw's Fury
- ○ Leafpool's Wish
- ○ Dovewing's Silence

Legends of the Clans
- ○ Spottedleaf's Heart
- ○ Pinestar's Choice
- ○ Thunderstar's Echo

A Warrior's Spirit
- ○ Pebbleshine's Kits
- ○ Tree's Roots
- ○ Mothwing's Secret

HARPER
An Imprint of HarperCollins Publishers

Don't miss these other Erin Hunter series!

SURVIVORS

Survivors
- ◯ #1: The Empty City
- ◯ #2: A Hidden Enemy
- ◯ #3: Darkness Falls
- ◯ #4: The Broken Path
- ◯ #5: The Endless Lake
- ◯ #6: Storm of Dogs

Survivors:
The Gathering Darkness
- ◯ #1: A Pack Divided
- ◯ #2: Dead of Night
- ◯ #3: Into the Shadows
- ◯ #4: Red Moon Rising
- ◯ #5: The Exile's Journey
- ◯ #6: The Final Battle

SEEKERS

Seekers
- ◯ #1: The Quest Begins
- ◯ #2: Great Bear Lake
- ◯ #3: Smoke Mountain
- ◯ #4: The Last Wilderness
- ◯ #5: Fire in the Sky
- ◯ #6: Spirits in the Stars

Seekers: Return to the Wild
- ◯ #1: Island of Shadows
- ◯ #2: The Melting Sea
- ◯ #3: River of Lost Bears
- ◯ #4: Forest of Wolves
- ◯ #5: The Burning Horizon
- ◯ #6: The Longest Day

HARPER
An Imprint of HarperCollinsPublishers

www.shelfstuff.com

www.warriorcats.com/survivors • www.warriorcats.com/seekers